THE PACT

Dawn Goodwin

An Aria Book

First published in the the United Kingdom in 2020 by Aria,
an imprint of Head of Zeus Ltd

This paperback edition first published in 2021 by Aria

9 7 5 3 1 2 4 6 8

A CIP catalogue record for this book is available from the
British Library.

ISBN (E): 9781788549356
ISBN (PB): 9781800245921

Typeset by Siliconchips Services Ltd UK

Cover design: Leah Jacobs Gordon

Printed and bound in Great Britain by
CPI Group (UK) Ltd, Croydon CRO 4YY

Aria
c/o Head of Zeus
First Floor East
5–8 Hardwick Street
London EC1R 4RG

www.ariafiction.com

For my parents, who bought me my first typewriter.
Little did they know...
or maybe they did....

I

The box was heavy in her arms as Maddie Lowe slid the key into the front door and pushed it open. The door swung back hard against the wall, leaving a dirty mark on the crisp white paint that she would only notice later. A bruise on the wall marking the day she moved in. She could hear Greg huffing and puffing behind her as he struggled into the main entrance hall of the small block of flats with more boxes.

Maddie hesitated in front of the open door, despite the weighty box in her arms.

'Are you waiting for me to carry you over the threshold or something?' Greg said behind her with a chuckle.

She flinched at the inappropriate joke.

Maddie stepped into the flat and dropped the box at her feet, her back aching as she straightened up.

'Thank God it's not on the next floor up. Looks like the lift is broken.' Sweat had broken out on Greg's forehead. 'Where do you want this?'

'Um...' Maddie looked around the empty open-plan living space. It looked deceptively spacious with very little furniture in it. Everything clean and sparse, a blank canvas on which to start anew.

'Anywhere, I guess,' she replied around the stone lodged in her throat.

Greg headed towards the kitchen area and thumped the box down in the corner. 'Look, Maddie, I...' He rubbed at his hair and she wanted to reach out and still his hand, tell him not to do that, that it was thinning there and he would only make it worse.

Instead, she said nothing. His thinning hair was Gemma's problem now.

An awkwardness filled the space between them, hanging off the end of his unfinished sentence as he pained over what to say next. In the end, she bailed him out again, saying, 'It'll be lovely with some plants and bright curtains. Some furniture is being delivered on Monday. A few nice cushions...' She looked around at her new home. The first place she would have lived in entirely on her own.

'I hate bloody cushions, but you can have as many as you like now.' This time he didn't laugh at his own joke.

'Right. Well, the next time you come, it will be much more homely, I'm sure.'

He chewed at the inside of his lip. 'That little garden out there is nice,' he said, nodding towards the sliding doors on the far side of the room. 'Could be a bit of a sun trap. You could grow herbs or vegetables maybe.'

Maddie remained rooted to the spot.

'Right, well, let me get the rest of these boxes in.' He scurried out and she sighed, looking at the postage stamp of grass outside, so different to the large, landscaped garden she had left behind.

She followed Greg back into the corridor.

A few more trips to the van Greg had hired and Maddie's

meagre belongings and bags of clothes were stashed in the flat, taking up a depressingly small amount of space.

Greg looked around, hands on hips and his legs firmly planted. 'There we go, all done. Do you need a hand moving these boxes around?' His eyes darted to the door.

'No, thanks. I've got it from here.'

'Right, well, I'd better— oh, I nearly forgot!' He disappeared out to the van again and returned with a glittery gold gift bag, which he held out to Maddie awkwardly. 'Um, Gemma sent you a housewarming gift, something for your first night in your new home.' His eyes didn't quite meet hers as he handed it over.

'That's… very kind of her, thank you. I'll, er, open it later, I think.' His phone chirped a text alert in his pocket and he looked at it briefly before putting it away again.

'You should get going. Gemma will be wondering where you've got to.'

'Yes, right, that's her now. Well, enjoy your evening and call me if you need anything. Anything at all.' He leant forward as if to kiss her, then hesitated awkwardly, before retreating backwards towards the door while waving at Maddie with both hands, like a politician on a meet and greet.

She watched him go, suddenly not wanting him to leave her there alone. Despite everything, she'd rather he stayed.

She closed the door and turned to survey the room. The air smelled like fresh paint and new carpets. Greg had dragged some mud in on his shoes and it sat on the new beige carpet, taunting her in its filth. He had never been any good at wiping his feet.

The silence was imperfect, peppered with the noise of

cars from outside and the hum of the fridge in the small kitchen. But her pulse beating in her ears drowned much of it out. She swallowed around the stone still wedged in her throat, hoping to dislodge it before it brought the inevitable flood of tears. She didn't want to cry today.

Maddie looked down at the gift bag dangling from her hand. She realised she was holding it away from herself, like it was malodorous, tainted in some way. She sank to her knees on the soft carpet and slowly opened the bag. Buried in layers of absurdly pink tissue paper was a small bottle of champagne, a box of expensive-looking chocolates, a rose-scented candle and a white hand towel monogrammed in gold with the initial 'M'. She gripped the towel to her face and breathed deeply, then shoved it back into the gift bag.

For a moment, her chest felt tight, like a held breath just before you break the surface of the water, lungs aching as your brain shouts at you to inhale. She pushed to her feet and stashed the champagne and chocolates into the almost empty fridge next to the bottle of milk she had bought on their way here. The rest of the groceries – cereal, bread, biscuits, grapefruit – stood on the countertop, still in bags.

Maddie felt rooted to the spot, unsure what to do or where to start.

A cup of tea would help. A cup of tea could fix anything.

Tea and a chocolate digestive later and Maddie felt moderately more stable, albeit still with a tight band around her chest. The boxes were littered around the room haphazardly and she knew that if she stared at them for any longer, she would give up before she had even started, so she forced herself to her feet and opened the nearest box, marked 'Kitchen' in scrawled green Sharpie. New plates and cutlery, still with the labels stuck to them; cheap and cheerful mugs from the supermarket; her baking trays and cake tins, because apparently Gemma wasn't much of a baker, so wouldn't need them. Maddie had left her slow cooker behind after Greg suggested Gemma would use it to cook family meals. Maddie used to love cooking for him. But it was hard to make a dinner for one in it, so it made sense that Gemma should keep it.

Once the kitchen was arranged, Maddie moved into the bedroom, hanging the new curtains, putting the fresh sheets on the bed that was delivered yesterday. The sheets were bright and floral, completely at odds with the masculine, navy blue patterns that Greg had always favoured in their old bedroom.

Once done, she stepped back and looked around her again. God, it was all so pathetic. From her bedroom window, she could see the parking spaces for the flats, her white Fiat 500 sitting in its designated space next to a motorbike, and beyond that the busy road, cars flying past, people going about their weekend chores, runners sweating into the pavement and dogs pissing on lampposts. All so normal and yet so alien, like she was seeing it all for the first time. This being on her own would take some getting used to. For now, she closed the curtains, blocking everything out.

*

Hours later, Maddie had showered the move off her skin, donned clean pyjamas and was propped up in her new bed with the box of chocolates and bottle of champagne. She had no champagne glasses, so would make do with a mug.

She started making a list in her head of everything she still needed to get. Lists always made her feel better, more in control. Kitchen scissors; doormat; bedside lamp; champagne glasses... Then she laughed out loud, the noise obscene and intrusive. How many parties was she planning to throw that she thought she needed champagne glasses any time soon?

The cork shot from the bottle without much persuasion. Maddie stared into the bubbles, then set the mug down on her new bedside table without tasting it.

She used to like a drink now and again, but she'd stopped when advised to and hadn't had much since. Surprising, considering everything she had been through. You would've thought she'd have been driven back to it.

She had no television yet or broadband, so she stared at the blank wall in front of her.

Wall art. Another thing for the list.

It was too quiet. The air sat heavy around her, expectant, like it was waiting for her to do something. Then a siren wailed in the distance, building in crescendo before fading. She sipped unenthusiastically at the champagne and took a bite from one of the chocolates. Turkish Delight. It tasted like soap in her mouth. She spat the half-eaten chocolate back into the box, washed the taste down with the champagne and picked the next chocolate along.

Before long, she had taken just one bite from every chocolate in the box.

Maddie snatched up the box and threw it hard across the room where it hit the bare white wall with a slap.

She stared at the spilled chocolates, willing herself to leave them, let them squish into the carpet. She didn't care. But in the end, she got up, cleaned up the mess and climbed back into bed.

Her phone chirruped next to her, making her jump. A text from Greg.

Hope you settled in ok. Enjoy your first evening in your new home. Let me know if you need anything. Greg x

If his girlfriend thought it strange that he was still so much a part of Maddie's life, she had never let on to Maddie in so many words, but Maddie could imagine the conversations that went on behind closed doors. It wasn't that Gemma resented Maddie or felt threatened as such. After all, what was there to feel threatened by exactly? No, it was pity Maddie saw in Gemma's face when she looked at her. And annoyance – like she was the stubborn five pounds in weight you couldn't shake after the summer holidays. There for now, but you were hopeful it would eventually disappear without too much of a struggle.

Maddie couldn't blame Gemma really. She'd be annoyed too. For her part, Maddie was well aware that a lot of the attention from Greg was firmly rooted in guilt.

Maddie sighed into the quiet, drained what little was left in the mug, then reached over and turned out the light, even though it was only eight-thirty.

She tossed and turned but must've eventually fallen asleep because she woke with a start and sat bolt upright in bed. She started to say to Greg in the dark, 'Did you hear that?', then remembered she was alone, the other side of the bed still neat and cold.

A door slammed. Voices were raised. A woman, shrill and piercing, shouting at a man, who replied in low rumbles like thunder.

Maddie's heart hammered in her chest. Did she lock the front door? Put the chain on?

The woman was swearing loud, crass words. Maddie crept out of bed and along the hallway towards the front door. The light from the entrance hall outside shone through the gap below her front door and she could see shadows cutting into the light as someone danced around. She approached timidly, could feel the draft of cold air blowing under the door onto her bare toes as she peered through the peephole. She could make out bodies, hands waving, a man's broad shoulders. She reached over to check the chain was on, then put her eye back to the peephole.

A woman was standing with her back to Maddie's door, her peroxide-blonde ponytail swinging as she accused the man mountain of being a 'lying, dickless lowlife'. His response was muffled before he stormed from the building, the walls reverberating as the door to the outside slammed behind him. The woman stood still, her back stiff.

The woman then moved over to the door opposite Maddie's, almost out of sight of the peephole, and began to hammer on it with closed fists. 'Did you hear all that, Peggy? You nosy bitch! Did you get every word?' She kicked at the door with heavy black boots, leaving dark scuff marks on the paintwork. 'You can go back to bed now, Peggy!' Her voice was noxious.

Maddie felt like she had stopped breathing as she watched. The kicking stopped and the woman looked like she was going to leave. Then, quick as a flash, she spun around and launched at Maddie's door. A glassy blue eye filled the peephole as she peered in from the outside.

Maddie gasped and ducked, keeping perfectly still and silent. After a moment, she felt foolish. Surely no one could see in from the other side. Maddie took a breath and peeked again, but the corridor was now empty.

She double-checked the lock and chain, then padded quietly into the kitchen, her hand trembling as she filled a mug with water and gulped it down.

She headed back to bed, then retraced her steps and turned the hallway light on. She crept back into her still warm bed and pulled the covers up to her chin, feeling small and childish as she sank down into the warmth and watched the shadows in the bedroom dancing in the light from the hallway.

Her heart was still hammering and she didn't expect to fall back asleep. A check of her phone showed that it was 3.30 a.m. She lay on her back so that she could see the whole room in front of her, her eyes flitting around with every creak and groan of the unfamiliar building.

Was this what it was going to be like every night?

Surprisingly, before long, her eyes felt heavy again and began to droop.

Then music started upstairs, thumping and insistent through the ceiling, the bass thick and weighted, and Maddie was fully awake once more.

2

Despite the lack of sleep, Maddie's body clock had her up and in the shower by 7 a.m. She turned on the radio in the kitchen, made tea and sat on a box containing unpacked recipe books to eat half a grapefruit with a sprinkling of sweetener. The politely interested voice of the newsreader on the radio was telling her that a woman who had fallen in front of a train at Clapham Junction last week had been identified as Vicky Dean and that the police were still unsure whether it was an accident or something more sinister. Maddie sipped at her tea, thinking about how desperately unhappy you must have to feel in order to reach the point of standing on the edge of a platform, the fog of trains and dullness of commuters around you, contemplating ending it all by throwing yourself in front of a train.

The idea made her feel inexplicably sad.

She got up and turned the radio off before she could acknowledge that she might know what that sort of despair actually felt like. Then she grabbed a couple of chocolate biscuits to make herself feel better.

So, Maddie, how are you going to entertain yourself today? What will you do with all this newfound independence?

The voice in her head sounded like Davina McCall for some reason.

She had to tackle the list of things she still needed for the flat, so by 9 a.m. she was throwing on her coat and heading out the door.

The shared entrance foyer for the four flats in the building was quiet. A door numbered 1 faced directly opposite hers and the black scuff marks on the bottom of the grey paint were evidence that last night's disruption had been real and not a weird dream. *I should introduce myself to my neighbours sometime*, Maddie thought, while wondering who Peggy was and what she had done to annoy the peroxide woman.

She peered up the stairs to the first floor, but it all looked the same as the ground floor. Clearly, whoever had been arguing and playing music into the early hours lived upstairs, probably directly above Maddie in Flat 4. There was a small lift tucked away in the corner, which was indeed out of order according to the handwritten note taped to it.

As she turned to leave, something tiny and furry on the stairs caught Maddie's eye. Her breath hitched, initially thinking it was a mouse. It was too big surely. Please God, not a rat. A little kitten maybe? Crouching, frightened, in the corner? She approached it gingerly with her hand outstretched, but it didn't move. She gently stroked its dark grey fur. It felt synthetic under her fingers. It still wasn't moving and Maddie had the sickening thought that she had just stroked a dead cat before she realised with an embarrassed chuckle that it was a soft toy. She picked it up and glanced up the stairwell again, then rested the toy on the side of the stairs so that anyone coming down would see it. Her heart leapt absurdly at the thought that a small child lived somewhere in the building.

Maybe this place wouldn't be so bad after all.

It seemed odd that the car park for the supermarket was so empty. Maddie parked in a space right outside the entrance and climbed out. It was cold. Only September and yet autumn seemed to be setting in pretty quickly.

Then she realised her mistake. It was Sunday and the store wouldn't be open for some time yet. She returned to her car and sat in the still warm interior, mulling over what to do next. Maddie had lived in this area of Teddington for years now and knew that not much would be open apart from coffee shops and newsagents. Why had she forgotten what day it was?

She immediately had an urge to call Greg and tell him about her silly mistake. He'd tease her and they'd laugh about it. In fact, she could pop in on him. Any excuse if she could go and see little Jemima. The house they'd lived in for most of their marriage was only a few streets away. Maddie's new flat was almost in his back garden. That was one of the reasons she had agreed to this new arrangement. She picked up her phone to call him, then hesitated.

A text would be better. She sent him a quick message saying she was at a loose end and could she come and say hello to Jemima. The response came back quickly.

We're just having breakfast. Maybe another time? G x

She put her phone back in her bag, immediately regretting sending the message. She needed to start being independent, to forge her own path. Yet here she was on day one and sending him messages. He had picked his side and she had to live with that.

Annoyed at herself, she got back out of her car, locked it and walked towards the High Street in search of a cup of tea.

Cardboard cup in hand, she walked past the closed gift shops and restaurants to the playground. It was already buoyant with lively toddlers and exhausted dads, their hair on end and nerves jangling as they helped small bodies onto the climbing frame and pushed swings on autopilot, their partners left at home to enjoy the luxury of a lie-in while Dad was on duty. Maddie sat on the bench and took it all in. The excited whoops from a boy dressed like Batman as he flew down the slide; the gentle smile on the face of a little girl as she sat in the swing seat with her doll in her lap, legs dangling, her father yawning and stretching in between pushes.

Maddie knew nothing about the level of exhaustion reached by a parent of a small child, but she'd spent a lot of time on this bench over the last few years, observing, living vicariously, wishing she could be that worn out, itching to reach out and touch the wriggling, warm bodies playing around her.

A woman was struggling to get her pushchair through the gate to the playground. Maddie set her tea down on the ground at her feet and jumped up to help, holding the gate for the woman while the pushchair reversed in. The woman was shorter than Maddie, no more than five foot, and her peroxide-blonde hair was scraped back into a scalp-pulling high ponytail that highlighted her dark roots. Maddie caught a whiff of cigarette smoke as she passed, mumbling her thanks.

Maddie looked down into the pushchair to see a little boy of about three years old clutching a Matchbox car in each fist, his eyes wide and tears standing out on his ruddy cheeks. He had a knitted hat pulled down low over his eyes.

Maddie returned to her seat and retrieved her tea while she watched the woman lift the boy from the pushchair and give him a shove towards the climbing frame. The woman then leant casually against the fence and pulled her phone from her pocket.

Most of the children were oblivious to each other as they clamoured and jumped around. The little boy seemed lost, unsure what to do with himself. Then he climbed up the steps of the slide, perched at the top and let his car slide all the way down to the bottom. He smiled, followed it down on his bottom, collected it up and repeated the process happily for a while.

Maddie watched mesmerised, enjoying the mundane yet satisfying repetition of the boy's activities.

After a while, the boy dressed as Batman wandered over just as the car landed at the bottom of the slide for the umpteenth time. Batman reached down, grabbed it and ran off towards the swings. The boy on the slide looked confused, his eyebrows knotted together, then angry. His cheeks turned puce and he started to scream.

His mother finally looked up from her phone, swore

under her breath and said loudly, 'What is it now, Ben? You're really testing my patience this morning.'

The boy gulped through his tears and pointed a shaking finger at Batman, who was now happily driving the car in the dirt below the climbing frame.

'Use your bloody words and tell me what's wrong, Ben. Otherwise, we'll have to go home. I can't be doing with your tantrums today.' Her words were sharp, exhaustion weighing down the syllables.

Ben cried harder.

'Right, that's it. We're going,' the mother said, her temper flaring. She shoved her phone into her back pocket and stormed over to the slide. 'Come down here right now.'

Maddie's heart broke for Ben, who was now distraught and only cried harder. Everyone had turned to stare, apart from Batman who resolutely played on with the pilfered car.

Maddie got to her feet and approached Ben's mother. 'Um, excuse me?'

She turned towards Maddie, her eyes flaring. 'Look, he's not having a good day, ok? No need to butt in.'

Maddie held her hands up in surrender. 'I know. It's just... um... that boy over there took his car. That's why he's crying.'

The woman looked over at Batman, then back to Ben, before marching straight over to Batman and demanding that he hand over the car. Batman's dad was standing to the side of the playground, scrolling through something on his phone, but upon seeing Batman being told off by a stranger, he weighed in too.

Sensing that the situation was getting uncomfortable,

Maddie threw her now empty cup in the bin and headed back to her car.

The handles of the plastic bags cut into her hands as Maddie struggled into the flat. One of the bags snagged on the handle and the plastic tore open, spilling apples, ginger and shampoo onto the floor.

Muttering under her breath, she put the other bags down, then went to retrieve the produce rolling around. As she stooped to pick everything up, she heard the entrance door open over her shoulder.

Maddie looked up and immediately recognised the woman from the playground, now reversing into the foyer with the pushchair.

'Oh!' Maddie said. The woman turned sharply.

An apple rolled next to her foot and she bent to pick it up before handing it to Maddie.

'Thanks,' Maddie said and smiled. She looked down into the pushchair and saw that Ben had both cars clutched in his tiny fists again. 'So, you managed to get Ben's car back then?'

'What?' The woman narrowed her eyes at Maddie.

'The car? I'm sorry, I was in the playground this morning. I was the one who told you that Batman had stolen his car?' Maddie realised what she must sound like.

The woman stared at her like she was an exhibit in a zoo, then smiled cautiously. 'Oh, right, yeah.'

'Hi, Ben,' Maddie said, crouching down. 'Cars are your favourite, I guess? Say, I don't suppose you've lost a little fluffy kitten, have you? I found one on the stairs this morning. It was…' She looked over at the stairwell, but the soft toy was gone.

The woman followed her eyes, then turned back to her with a frown before slowly backing away with the pushchair.

Maddie got back to her feet and followed her, saying enthusiastically, 'Can I help you up the stairs with the pushchair?' She could hear the desperation in her voice and hated herself for it.

'No, thanks, we'll be fine. I manage all the time on my own. Fucking lift never works.'

Maddie flinched at the expletive. 'I don't mind. In fact, I insist.'

The woman glanced around her, as if hoping for back-up. Before she could object, Maddie put her hand on the bottom of the pushchair between Ben's tiny feet and lifted it from the floor. The woman had no choice but to lift the handles before Ben was tipped out of his seat.

Maddie could hear herself jabbering away as they climbed the stairs to the first floor. 'My name is Maddie Lowe. I moved in yesterday. Just me… on my own… long story. Anyway, if you ever need help or a babysitter for Ben, just knock. I'm in Flat 2. Happy to help. I love kids. Of course, I know you don't know me, but I'm very reliable.'

They'd reached the top of the stairs, but the woman made no move to head towards either of the doors in front of them. Maddie realised with embarrassment that she probably didn't want to let on which flat she lived in, considering the rambling mad woman standing in front of her.

'Anyway, nice to meet you. Bye,' Maddie said and quickly headed back down the stairs.

Just before she reached the bottom, she heard the woman say above her head, 'Maddie, was it?' Maddie looked up the stairwell to see her leaning over.

'Yes, it is,' she replied, pathetically pleased.

'Nice to meet you. I'm Jade Tingly.' She smiled briefly, then disappeared.

Jade sat on the floor, tidying away the toys that Ben had flung around the room earlier during his tantrum. So someone had moved in downstairs. Not a total surprise. She'd seen the decorators coming and going for the last few weeks.

Jade thought about the woman she'd met. Maddie Lowe. She seemed a bit highly strung, nervous maybe, and desperate to make a good first impression. Actually, when she had spoken to Jade in the playground, Jade had thought her a bit of a nosy cow. The kind of woman who would feel nothing about telling you exactly where you were going wrong with your child.

But thinking about it now, perhaps this was fortuitous.

Time would tell, though.

Her phone buzzed on the coffee table. She reached over and grabbed it. The message was brief. She didn't reply straight away. She needed to think up an appropriate response, come up with a viable excuse. Enough to put him off but also keep him keen.

She got to her feet and headed towards the kitchen. She could do with a cigarette. Ben had been annoying all day and she was glad of the peace and quiet now. She had a bottle of cold wine in the fridge that had her name on it for tonight. She planned to sit on the couch, find something to watch on Netflix and finish the bottle. Maybe see if Deon wanted to come over. He'd have forgiven her for last night by now.

The middle of her foot landed on something sharp and she screeched. A Matchbox car lay on its back like a stuck turtle, the wheels spinning. Ben and his bloody cars!

She grabbed the car and launched it at the wall. It fell short and bounced under the television stand. Jade limped to the couch and sat, rubbing the sole of her foot where the car had left a hot red mark on her pale skin.

Now she really did need that drink.

Greg Lowe sat in the rocking chair, cradling his daughter in his lap. She was buttoned snugly into fleecy pyjamas covered in frolicking unicorns, a dummy in her mouth. Occasionally she would suck half-heartedly on the dummy as she nodded off, but as the minutes ticked past, the sucking slowed and the dummy began to dangle from her ridiculously red lips.

Greg gazed at her in awe. The smoothness of her skin and the tufts of white-blonde curls that refused to be tamed, the tiny nub of a nose and impossibly small fingernails.

The story he was reading her had long since finished, but still he sat, gently rocking back and forward in the chair, not wanting to break the bond by putting her in her bed.

Maddie would love this. He could imagine them fighting over who would read her a story, both of them desperate for one last cuddle. He felt bad about not letting her come over that morning, but as soon as he'd mentioned the text to Gemma, she had made her feelings clear, saying in an arctic hiss, 'You spent all of yesterday with her. You don't need to see her today as well.'

'Greg!'

He shifted his gaze over to where Gemma now stood in the doorway, her arms crossed over her artificially modified chest.

'You're spoiling her! I've told you not to let her fall asleep in your arms. She'll expect it all the time. Come on, enough now. And take that dummy out of her mouth.'

Greg sighed. 'I'm coming.'

Gemma tutted and stalked off, leaving a puff of disappointment behind her.

Greg sneaked one last kiss onto his baby girl's forehead and gently tucked her into her bed with a smile, leaving the dummy within easy reach of her fingers in case she needed it.

3

When the rest of Maddie's new furniture was delivered on Monday, she was still in her pyjamas and dressing gown, her shoulder-length brown hair pulled into a messy ponytail and her teeth furry and unbrushed, despite it being 11.30 a.m. The delivery men made no comment, merely came in, unpacked the furniture and left with a signature to say that all of Greg's purchases were now safely installed in Maddie's new home.

Sitting on the stiff new couch made her feel pathetic. She gathered up all of the leftover packaging and shoved it into black bin liners. Leaving her front door open, she carried the bags out of the main door to the communal bins at the side of the building. As she returned, she was met by a thin, pale man standing with his foot propped in her door. She pulled up short.

'Hi.'

'Oh, hi, I figured you were outside,' he said in a quiet voice.

'What are you doing?'

'Um...' He ran his fingers through dark, scruffy hair, looking awkward. 'I saw your door open and that door open—' he pointed to the outside '—and then your door started to swing shut and…' He shrugged.

'Oh, thanks. I would've been locked out.'

'Yeah, I figured,' he said. He still had his foot in the door.

Maddie shuffled past him back into her flat. 'Thanks,' she said with an embarrassed smile.

He shrugged again and wandered away. With a backward glance, he said, 'I'm Luke. Flat number 3,' and nodded at the stairs.

'Maddie,' she said in reply. 'Flat number 2 obviously.'

He smiled and disappeared.

That brief interaction seemed to sap the strength out of her and since she had nothing to do and nowhere to go, she took herself back to bed.

On Tuesday, an engineer arrived to install her broadband and phone line. He avoided eye contact when she answered the door, still in her pyjamas and dressing gown at 12.15 p.m. Another signature and he was on his way.

She sat on her stiff, new couch and logged into the Wi-Fi with her laptop, immediately looking up Greg's Facebook page. The smiling, happy faces and jaunty status updates made her feel bilious, so she returned to bed, pulling the covers over her head.

She had no reason to even get up on Wednesday. No deliveries. No calls. So she didn't. She ate a stale doughnut and immediately regretted it. She opened her laptop while propped up in bed, logged into her Netflix account and scrolled through her list, but it was mostly Greg's choices and some others she didn't remember adding. Then she realised this was now Greg and Gemma's account. She deleted all the programmes that were clearly Gemma's choices in a sudden fit of childish rebellion and burrowed back under the covers.

By Thursday she couldn't avoid how hungry she was, but the milk in the fridge had turned and the vegetables were limp. She considered getting dressed and going to buy more, but ordered Uber Eats instead and ate Thai food in bed, marvelling at how you didn't need to ever leave the house these days and trying not to drop noodles on her new duvet cover. Greg would be horrified and Gemma probably hadn't eaten a noodle since 2003, which made the food taste even better.

She received a text from Greg that evening asking if she still had access to their old Netflix account and knew she'd been busted for deleting Gemma's romantic comedies.

On Friday afternoon she managed to get herself out of bed and onto the couch, although still with her duvet on top of her. She created a new Netflix account for herself and was midway through a binge session of *Gilmore Girls*, wishing she had a Luke Danes in her life to bring her food and coffee, when there was an insistent knock on her door. She wasn't expecting any more deliveries and certainly not any visitors. She felt a sudden burst of joy at the thought that Greg had come to visit, then horror at what he would think when he saw her. She hauled herself over to the door and said, 'Hello?', patting at her greasy hair before putting her eye to the peephole.

'Maddie Lowe? I have a delivery for you.'

Her heart fell as she unchained the door. Pulling her gown tight around her neck, she opened the front door to see a delivery man obscured by a large bunch of flowers.

'Here you go,' he said, handing over the arrangement. He looked her up and down briefly, then said, 'Hope you feel better soon,' before heading back out of the door to the street.

Maddie realised she must look like an invalid. Shame washed over her. What if it had been Greg? Was this what she wanted him to see? He'd seen her in worse states though. She went to close the door just as a pair of blindingly white trainers and skin-tight white jeans descended the stairs.

It was Jade, shrugging into a denim jacket and chewing on a Twix, her hair once more pulled into an eye-watering ponytail. She looked up and said, 'Nice flowers. They look expensive. Secret admirer?' She looked brighter today, less haggard than the last time Maddie had seen her.

'No, er—'

'Oh, are you ill? That's a shame. Hope you feel better soon.'

'I'm not. I'm...' What was she? Depressed? Lonely? Struggling to cope? She couldn't explain any of it to this stranger. How the last few years had nearly finished her off more than once. How she had had everything she cared about and yearned for ripped away and now felt like an empty husk, fragile and crumbling. Petrified of being alone, but not wanting to be with people, not knowing what to do with herself or where to start with putting her life back together. How some days she couldn't be bothered to get dressed, talk or even breathe.

Instead, she said, 'I'm better now, really. Just taking an extra day, you know. A duvet day. How is Ben? Where is he?'

Jade fussed with the collar of her jacket. 'With his dad.' Her voice was terse.

'Sorry, none of my business.'

Jade turned to go, then looked Maddie over again. 'You sure you're ok?'

'Yes, thanks. I'd better get these in water.'

'I didn't thank you,' Jade said quickly as Maddie turned away. 'For the other day with Ben, I mean.'

'Oh, it's nothing. I just didn't like seeing him upset.'

'He's a sensitive kid. It doesn't take much to upset him.' She was peering at Maddie with intensity. 'Listen, do you fancy coming up and having a drink later tonight? We are neighbours after all. If you're up to it, that is?'

'Um, well, I'm not much of a drinker...' Her mind latched on the opportunity to see Ben again, maybe play with him, make him laugh, and she suddenly didn't want to be alone again tonight. 'Sure, why not? What time?'

'Say 7 p.m.?'

'Ok, great.'

'I'm in number 4. Directly above you. Great, see ya later.'

Maddie smiled and headed back indoors. She could feel Jade's eyes on her back, watching her go, but when she looked over her shoulder, Jade was heading out of the building.

Maddie put the flowers down on the kitchen counter and pulled the card from the leaves.

Happy housewarming! Much love, Greg x

Sunflowers.

Her favourite, as he knew only too well.

By six o'clock that evening Maddie was showered, teeth finally brushed and hair washed. She had eaten a large chicken salad and was feeling more human and wholesome than she had in days. A trip to the shops earlier that afternoon meant that she had a bottle of wine and a box of chocolates ready to take upstairs. She had also picked out a new Matchbox car for Ben and was far more excited to see him than she was at sharing the evening with Jade. Maddie hadn't quite made up her mind about Jade yet, with her tight hair and cursing mouth. Her comment about Ben being with his dad implied that she was likely divorced, so the evening would probably involve discussing exes and having a moan about the state of their love lives.

Moaning about Greg was not something Maddie liked doing. He had been good to her since they split up and she wanted to think he was a good person who hadn't intended to hurt her like he did. What they had been through over the last few years... well, it didn't bear thinking about now, but it wasn't entirely Greg's fault. He had suffered too. And he had had Maddie to look after on top of everything else. She guessed he had found comfort somewhere else. It happened, especially for men. They liked to be looked after, didn't they? And they liked to fix a problem, but she had turned out to be one he couldn't fix.

No one's fault.

The clock ticked towards six-thirty. Maddie sat on the couch and waited.

Would it be so bad if she went early? If she didn't go now, she would talk herself out of it altogether. Besides, she might catch Ben before he went to bed, could maybe offer to bath him or read him a story.

Fuck it, I'm going, she thought, then felt scandalous at hearing the curse word in her head and giggled into the empty room.

The entrance hall outside her front door was cavernous, her footsteps echoing off the walls. She climbed the stairs to the first floor and looked around at the bare walls painted the same magnolia as downstairs. In the far corner it looked like another corridor led off from the landing. The door directly opposite her was number 4.

Maddie knocked, then stepped back and waited, pulling on the sleeve of her cardigan with her free hand. She suddenly felt silly. Why was she even here? She turned to flee, excuses bouncing around her head, just as the door was flung open.

Jade stood in front of her in loose tracksuit bottoms, her hair still pulled tight. Her black T-shirt was emblazoned with the Def Leppard band logo. Maddie wasn't sure if that indicated her musical taste or if she just wanted people to think she was a metalhead. Maddie felt overdressed in her jeans, blouse and cardigan.

'Hey,' Jade said with a wide smile and stepped back with bare feet. Her toenails were naked but her fingernails were shaped into long talons and painted bright orange. The talons were tapping the side of a glass of wine and she said, 'I've already started. You need to catch up.'

Maddie stepped over a takeaway menu on the carpet. The same one had been shoved under her own door a few days ago. She bent down and picked it up, then closed the door behind her.

The room was identical in shape to Maddie's downstairs, but decorated very differently. The walls were covered in a beige, swirly wallpaper that was peeling in places. In one corner, the wallpaper had been torn away completely and crayon was scribbled on the lining paper underneath. There was stuff everywhere. A small dining room table in the corner of the room was covered in magazines, plastic bags, clothes and empty mugs. The floor was a cheap-looking, wood-effect linoleum, with a large blue rug covering most of the centre of the room. It looked like it could do with a vacuum cleaner run over it. Instead of a garden beyond the sliding doors, there was a balcony with a drying rack strewn with women's underwear that swayed in the breeze.

Jade clearly wasn't one of those who cleaned frantically before anyone came over. There was very much a sense of 'this is who I am, like it or not' about the place.

A dark brown leather corner couch dominated the room, facing a large flat-screen TV that was attached to the wall, on display like a piece of art. *The evening news* was on mute. Jade pointed at the screen and said, 'Can't stand that Mary Nightingale. Too much of a stuck-up cow for me.'

'Um, yeah,' Maddie said, although she didn't have strong feelings about Mary Nightingale or any other newsreaders either way.

She followed Jade into the kitchen, still holding the menu in her hand. The countertops were strewn with empty dishes and unopened letters that looked suspiciously like bills, all addressed to Miss J Tingly. Maddie added the takeaway menu to the pile.

Jade was rummaging in a cupboard, her back to Maddie, so Maddie took the opportunity to look her over again. The seat of her tracksuit bottoms was baggy and her T-shirt had a tear at the back, as though it had caught on a door handle. A long thread dangled down from the hem like a tail and Maddie had to fight the urge to reach out and snap it off. Jade was definitely younger than Maddie, maybe in her mid-twenties, but her make-up-free face looked sallow, her skin the colour of paste.

Jade finally found a glass and sloshed some wine into it.

Maddie reached into the bag on her arm and handed Jade the bottle of red wine and chocolates she had brought along. 'Here you go, thanks for having me over.'

'Oooh, posh chocolates! Thanks, we'll crack into these later.' They weren't particularly posh, but Maddie was pleased Jade thought she'd made a special effort. Jade handed her the wineglass and Maddie noticed an old line of lipstick still painting the rim. She rubbed at it subtly with her thumb, then rotated the glass so that the lipstick stain pointed away from her.

'Cheers,' she said. The white wine was cold but sharp and acidic, setting her teeth on edge.

Maddie looked around for Ben, surprised he hadn't come running to meet her. 'Is Ben here or is he in bed already?'

'No, I told you he's at his dad's,' Jade said sharply.

'Oh, that's a shame. I brought him a present.'

Jade looked at the toy car Maddie held out, then took it and tossed the box onto the kitchen counter, saying, 'I'll give it to him when I see him next, thanks. Truth is, I'm shattered, so I'm pleased the little shit isn't here.' Maddie's eyebrows shot up, but Jade didn't seem to notice as she walked past her and flopped onto the couch. 'Sit, sit,' she said, gesticulating with her wineglass again.

Maddie sat primly on the couch, adjusting the cushion behind her, and set her bag at her feet.

'So...' Jade said, staring at her. 'What's your story then?'

'My story?'

'Yeah. You're married, but you live alone?' She was looking at the thin wedding band and shiny, square-cut diamond Maddie still wore on her left hand.

'Oh! We're separated.' Maddie tucked her hand beneath her.

Jade raised her almost non-existent eyebrows. 'But still wearing the ring, so newly separated. Interesting. Who cheated? You or him? I can't imagine it was you. You look too... nice.'

'It wasn't like that—'

'And kids?' she continued before Maddie could clarify.

'No, I—'

'Smart woman. Little buggers suck the life out of you.' Maddie realised that Jade was already a little drunk. She slurped her wine, then noticed the look on Maddie's face and said quickly, 'Sorry, Ben is a sweetie when he wants to be. It's just hard work sometimes, you know?'

Maddie didn't know.

'Do you work?' Jade continued.

'Not anymore. I used to work for my husband – bookkeeper and admin for his company.'

'Oh, shit, so you lost a husband and a boss? That sucks.'

'Yes and no. I still have the job if I want it. I don't know if I do though.' Maddie sipped on the wine for something to do. 'What about you? Do you work?'

'Ben is my work, ha!' Her attention was diverted by the television. 'Don't judge me, but I love this show!' Jade turned the volume up as *The One Show* started.

They sat in silence for a while, Jade occasionally laughing out loud, while Maddie looked around some more, curious at how different the flat felt to her own. It was certainly more chaotic and messy, but also more *lived in*, like things happened here, stories were told, dramas unfolded. Her own flat still felt sterile and cold in comparison, with no memories to warm up the walls just yet. There was a basket of toys in one corner near to the wall art scribbles. Down the corridor she could just make out an open bedroom door with a glimpse of an unmade king-size bed. The door to the second bedroom, which she assumed was Ben's, was closed. Maddie's small second bedroom in the flat downstairs was filled with the boxes she hadn't unpacked yet. A dumping ground of old memories, shared mostly with Greg.

In one of those boxes was a shoebox. She thought of that shoebox now, what it contained, then pushed it from her mind.

Jade jumped to her feet and returned with an open bag of cheese-flavoured nacho chips that she flung onto the couch between them. The leather made a farting noise as she sat down again. Jade was jabbering on about the celebrity guest on the television, telling Maddie that she looked like a pool inflatable from all the plastic surgery she'd had. Maddie looked at the screen and could see what Jade meant. The woman was stretched and plumped, her face pulled tight like an inflated balloon, but Maddie would never say that out loud. Well, maybe to Greg, who would laugh conspiratorially and tell her she was being bitchy.

Jade's hand was diving in and out of the chip bag as she munched loudly. 'Actually, I should tweet that. It'd be a laugh!' She leapt up, licked the orange dust from her fingers enthusiastically and grabbed her phone from the coffee table. Her fingers flew across the touchscreen, typing furiously. When she was finished, she threw the phone back down. 'Are you on Twitter? You should follow me.'

'Don't you worry about posting stuff and people getting upset?'

'Oh please, celebrities deserve it! They get paid enough and if they didn't like it, they wouldn't put themselves in front of the cameras all the time. Besides, it's just a bit of a laugh.' Jade's T-shirt had ridden up and her rounded belly was on show, like a rubber ring over the waistband of her tracksuit pants. Maddie wondered what Jade would think if she posted about that. She probably wouldn't find it that funny. She had what looked like a tattoo of a dolphin jumping over her belly button and Maddie was fascinated by it, had to force herself to look away.

Maddie was starting to wish she hadn't come. Maybe she could say she wasn't feeling well again and leave. If the truth be told, Maddie realised as soon as Jade had said that Ben wasn't there that she had only been coming to see him. To hear the giddy laugh of a small person, smell his clean, apple-scented hair and stroke his smooth, rosy cheeks, feel his tiny hand fit into hers...

Her pulse started to race uncomfortably. She drank some more wine, still not enjoying the taste of it and feeling an uncomfortable fuzziness settle into her head.

'Been watching anything good on Netflix lately?' Jade said as the programme on the television ended.

'Not really. I've been watching old stuff – *The Crown*, *Gilmore Girls*, that kind of thing.'

'Oh right, yeah, I like all of that.' Her face told a different story. 'I'm also into newer stuff – *American Horror Story*, *Stranger Things*, *Sex Education*. You should watch them. You'd enjoy them. Drink up.'

Jade talked like a machine gun, firing the words with velocity and aggression, as though daring Maddie to disagree. She was staring at Maddie again, challenging her with sharp blue eyes, and Maddie felt withered. She took a healthy drink of the wine, then another to finish the glass before handing it back to Jade. Maddie tried not to grimace as she swallowed.

'Good girl.' Jade got up, the couch bouncing and farting as she did.

'I should probably... um... get going actually,' Maddie said, getting to her feet.

'What? Why? You've only just got here. Come on, we'll watch something together. Your choice.' She pushed Maddie none too gently back down onto the couch. She looked panicked and Maddie realised that she was possibly hanging on just as much as Maddie was, but showing it in a different way.

Maybe she also didn't want to be alone. Otherwise why would she beg Maddie to stay? Why would anyone beg Maddie, of all people, to spend time with them? She found herself dull, uninteresting, sad and pathetic, so what did that say about Jade? Perhaps they were just as lost as each other but showed it in different ways. Maybe Jade's desperation for attention and affirmation came across as aggression as she hid behind her internet profile. Maybe she just needed someone to show her how to be kind rather than cruel. Sometimes it only took one person to make a difference. Maddie had read all the posts to that effect on Instagram. Suddenly all Maddie wanted to do was take care of Jade.

'Ok, I'll stay,' she said. She sat back down and drank some more of the cheap wine, noting the relief on Jade's face.

Jade stood in the kitchen and watched Maddie as she perched neatly on the couch, her legs crossed at the knee and one ballet slipper of a shoe dangling from a thin, pale foot.

Although Jade had done a lot of the talking, Maddie was still very much a closed book. She asked a lot of questions about Ben, which was unnerving and a bit weird, but otherwise she hadn't said very much.

Maddie had an air of sadness about her. It oozed from her like a vapour you couldn't see but could sense tainting the air. There was definitely a story here and Jade was curious. A few more glasses of wine and maybe Maddie would loosen up a bit.

Jade had turned down a well-deserved night out with girlfriends at a club in Clapham for this, so she hoped it was worth it. She'd give it another hour and if Maddie still hadn't loosened up, she would send her packing and see if she could still meet up with the girls.

By 10 p.m. Maddie's fingers were stained orange from the nacho chips and her head was filled with cotton wool from the wine. The second bottle had tasted nicer, probably because it was the red wine she had brought with her. A pizza box from Dominos sat on the table, containing one lonely crust and an empty pot of dip. They had settled on watching old episodes of *Friends*, laughing together as Ross struggled with his leather trousers and Rachel made Thanksgiving trifle with custard and minced beef.

Maddie remembered watching the series in the 1990s when she and Greg were newlyweds. They would lie together on one couch, curving into each other. She could remember the feeling of his chest bouncing against her back as he laughed. Maybe that was why she loved this programme so much.

While they watched, Jade encouraged Maddie to sign up to Twitter and Snapchat. They giggled as they took photo after photo with silly filters, each one funnier than the last.

It had been ages since Maddie had had such a good time.

Jade commented on Maddie's iWatch when it pinged to remind Maddie to stand up. 'Those are expensive,' she said and Maddie explained it was a birthday gift from Greg last year.

'I swim sometimes and he got it for me so that I could measure my distance better. But sometimes I think it's the only thing that believes in me,' she said. 'It'll say things like, *'Come on, you can do it!'* and *'You've got this!'*, and I believe it. How ridiculous is that! It's just a bloody watch, but I actually find myself talking to it.'

'It's a fucking generous birthday present. I bet that handbag was from him too?'

She had clearly clocked Maddie's Gucci handbag and, yes, it was another gift from a work trip Greg had taken to Milan a few years ago. Maddie explained that Greg had always been generous and that by the end of their marriage, he had resorted to elaborate gifts rather than quality time with her.

Maddie showed Jade photos of Greg on her phone, but Jade seemed more taken with the fact that Maddie had a new iPhone 11 – an upgrade secured by Greg, of course. In return, she showed Maddie her iPhone XS with its cracked screen and complained at how poor the camera quality was on it. Maddie noticed her screen wallpaper was a photo of Ben eating ice cream and her heart clenched like a muscle spasm. Maddie's wallpaper was a generic photo of sunflowers.

Maddie asked Jade to show her photos of Ben and she took her time scrolling through – Ben playing with the toys Maddie had noticed earlier; his face covered in tomato ketchup with a McDonalds Happy Meal in front of him; another of him splashing in a puddle wearing bright green wellies. Looking around the lounge, there was only one photo on show in a frame – Jade and Ben smiling into the camera behind a birthday cake marked with three candles.

One photo popped up on Jade's phone of a tiny baby Ben held in the arms of a tall, dark-haired man. 'Is that Ben's dad?' Maddie asked.

Jade hesitated and looked away.

'Don't worry, you don't have to tell me,' Maddie added hastily.

'No, it's fine. It's just... Yes, that's Mark. We're not together now.' She picked at a small hole in her T-shirt. 'We split up before I was pregnant, but then one drunken night a couple of months later and bam!' Jade explained conception like it was nothing. Like it was the easiest thing in the world. Maddie supposed for most people it was.

'Mark got a really good job on the oil rigs and moved up north. He was making proper good money. I texted him to tell him I was pregnant and sent him photos and stuff. He sees Ben as much as he can and he's always been good with paying child maintenance, which is great.'

Maddie couldn't imagine having that kind of removed relationship with her own child. 'Doesn't he mind not being more involved? Missing so much of Ben growing up?'

'No, not really. He has a new girlfriend and she's pregnant now, so...' Jade shrugged. 'Actually, he's talking about moving closer to here now. I'm not sure if I want that though. It works like it is now. He gets time with Ben and I get time away on my own. It would be too... complicated if he lived closer.' Jade's face looked tight and pinched as she spoke.

'It can't be easy for you raising Ben on your own,' Maddie said gently.

Jade ignored her and they watched TV in silence, the atmosphere dampened.

After a while, Jade lurched to her feet and headed into the kitchen, returning with the chocolates and more wine. Maddie's head was starting to thud, a sign of what tomorrow would be like, but she wanted to resurrect the atmosphere of earlier, didn't want to leave on a flat note.

Until they had mentioned Ben's dad, she had been enjoying herself. Men always knew how to ruin things. Jade had a brittle sense of humour that had had Maddie in fits of giggles all night. Her tongue was so sharp it could clip a hedge and she was quick to share her strong opinions on most things, like she had a childish need to show off for her new friend. Maddie decided one more glass wouldn't hurt. The damage was probably already done anyway and it wasn't like she had anything to do tomorrow.

'Tell me about Greg,' Jade said. 'A bit of a sugar daddy, is he? He certainly buys you lots of nice stuff.' Her eyes were greedy with delight.

Maddie shuffled uncomfortably. 'It's complicated, but he is still very much a part of my life.'

'Really? So it's a friendly divorce. Are you just being nice to keep the maintenance cheques coming?' She grinned and winked.

'No! We're... friends. He's been my best friend for so long – and we're not actually divorced yet.'

'Riiiight...'

'It's complicated.'

'So you said. So are you going to divorce him? Holding out for a good settlement, I hope?'

'I haven't really thought about it. I guess I need to get a lawyer at some point, but for now we are just ticking along. He still lives in our house. It's not far from here.' Jade's mouth gaped open and Maddie felt the need to defend herself. 'But he bought the flat for me and he pays me my salary like before, even though I'm not working right now. He's held my job for me if I want it, says I can work from home instead of the office, because it would be awkward.'

'For you or him?'

'For both of us. And his girlfriend, who was his PA before everything, so...'

'Oh my God! This just gets better.'

Why was Maddie telling her all this?

'They have a baby together, little Jemima.'

'So basically, you're stringing him along, milking him for money while he plays happy families in your house?' Jade sounded almost envious.

'I've said I'll get a new job and I think the arrangement will change when we finally get divorced and they get married, if they get married... It's funny, but if he died now, I would get everything because I'm still married to him and I'm a partner in the business. He's actually worth more dead than alive.' The thought had come from nowhere and she suddenly found it amusing. She wondered if Gemma knew that. In her inebriation, it was quite a delicious concept. She smiled into her glass. Then just as quickly, a wave of hurt nipped at her, demanding to be let in.

'Well, I say string him along for as long as you can. Divorces are expensive,' Jade said.

'I think she is pushing to get married, so I'm sure he'll ask for a divorce soon enough and things will change.'

'Yeah, I think I might have similar problems.' Jade slurped at her wine and fidgeted. 'God, I need a cigarette, but I'm trying to stop smoking. Do you vape?'

Maddie was feeling very drunk, but Jade now looked sober and alert, her eyes darting around and her words crisp, unlike Maddie's rounded, slurred diction. Jade suddenly sat forward, causing Maddie to slop some of the wine over the rim of her glass.

'You know, we should work together, make a pact,' Jade said excitedly.

'Oh?' Maddie's attention was diverted by one of her favourite episodes of *Friends* starting on the TV. She was glad of the distraction, didn't want to talk about Greg and

Gemma and money anymore. 'Oh, this is my favourite episode – Monica's hair!' She giggled.

'If our respective fellas try to change our agreements, we should team up. Do something to help each other out. I don't want to be out of pocket over their mistakes with their dicks.'

'Sure,' Maddie said, her eyes on the TV. 'Like what? Kidnap them and rough them up until they agree to carry on paying up?' Maddie laughed giddily at the absurd thought of her trying to rough anyone up. Jade, on the other hand, could probably hold her own.

Jade was watching Maddie earnestly. 'Maybe... have you ever thought about the perfect murder? How to get away with it?'

'Can't say I think about murdering people very often. Well, apart from Greg...' She giggled again.

Jade stared into her glass. 'Ben is in Mark's will. Mark told me that once. He earned a lot on the rigs and if he died, it would go to me for Ben until he is old enough. Especially if his other kid hasn't been born yet.'

Maddie watched Jade as she chewed on her lip, thinking it over, and chuckled. 'Look at you, the devious criminal mastermind! Well then, you've got it all sorted. Now we just have to figure out how to kill them and get away with it.' Maddie wrung her hands together like a Bond villain, playing along with Jade. 'Maybe a sharp shove off a cliff? A poisoned vindaloo? I tell you what, if you kill mine, I'll kill yours.'

'Deal.'

'I'll drink to that!' Maddie held her glass up and chinked it against Jade's, then drained it.

Jade grinned at her, showing teeth stained red from the wine, and Maddie shivered, suddenly feeling cold. She felt the smile slide from her own stained lips.

Maddie had forgotten what it was like to be drunk. It had been years since she'd felt this loose, finding everything either hilarious or infuriating – and nothing in between. Her head was full of noise, like there were one hundred people whispering to her, all trying to get a word in, but she couldn't make out what they were saying. It was just a constant buzz of background noise, both pleasantly entertaining and annoyingly chaotic at the same time, and she had an urge to rest her head for a minute, maybe close her eyes, just to still the buzzing for a moment. Jade's face swam in and out of focus, like someone was manipulating a camera lens in front of her eyes.

She drank some more wine and as the alcohol surged to her head, her stomach lurched. She staggered to the bathroom and threw up, her arms clutching the toilet bowl like a life preserver.

Then

The music is loud in my ears, reverberating through my feet and up my legs as I stand in the corner of the room. Tracey is chatting up some guy, her head tilted to the side as she giggles and flirts. It's a routine I've seen a few times in the last few weeks as she continues her search for a boyfriend before the end of term, just so that she will have someone to invite to the end of year dance. I'm hoping she doesn't hook up with anyone though because then she will have to go with me. I won't go on my own, that's for sure, but I'd rather not go at all than spend the whole evening with a date I don't like.

Looking around at the boys at this party, they all look the same, sound the same. Their jeans are too baggy, hanging loose in the crotch and making them look bigger than they are. Size is apparently important. The two standing next to me have been discussing the same game of football for about twenty minutes, reliving every goal and referee decision. They shove at each other while they talk, sniggering and trying to sneak swigs of alcohol from hipflasks they've swiped from their dads' golf bags. There's no need. There's booze at the party – beer and boxed wine aplenty.

I move off through the mass of people squeezed into

the small, overheated terraced house as I search for the bathroom. I pass couples snogging, like they're trying to swallow each other whole, and I want to gag. I breathe in thick, heady cigarette smoke as girls try to look cool by dangling sticks of nicotine from their lips. Underlying the smoke is the smell of teenage hormones and warm beer.

The hallway is lined with people too; some I know and I greet them with a nod or a smile as I slide past. At the top of the stairs is a number of doorways. The bathroom could be through any one of them. I try the one straight ahead of me, jiggling the door handle.

'Busy!' someone calls through the door and I hear a toilet flush.

I lean against the wall and stare down the stairs at the bobbing heads below me, writhing to music that is so loud I'm wearing it like an extra layer, the lyrics distorted by the volume. Tracey and I were invited to this house party by Connie, a classmate at our school. I've known her and most of these people for years. We all moved from junior to secondary school together and finally we are on the brink of parting ways. I have mixed feelings about the impending split. While I've had some fun in the last few years, I find it all a bit tiresome now. Most of these people wouldn't be able to have a sensible conversation about politics or economics, even if they wanted to. I'm actually looking forward to the exams and getting on with the next stage of my life.

It's Connie's eighteenth birthday party and her parents agreed to give her the house for the night as a last celebration before we all go into study leave hibernation. I'm not sure they knew what they were letting themselves in for though. Connie is very popular with the boys at our school and it looks like most of them are here, along with a fair few plus ones that weren't on the original invitation list. Word of mouth has spread like wildfire and the place is packed.

I hear the bathroom door unlock. The guy who steps out of the bathroom looks familiar, but I can't quite place him. Something about his dark hair that is two weeks too late for a haircut maybe or the utterly uncool Coca-Cola T-shirt he is wearing.

'All yours,' he says with a smile. He steps aside to let me pass.

As I'm about to move, a girl flies past me in floods of tears and slams the bathroom door in my face. I can hear the lock slide into place.

'What the—?' I say, gaping.

'Wow, someone's in a hurry,' he says.

'Yeah, looks like I'll have to wait a bit longer.'

He nods, looks around, then says, 'I'm Greg, by the way.'

'Madeleine, nice to meet you.'

'I think we've met before.' He's scrutinising me like I'm a painting on display. I push my hair behind my ears awkwardly. 'Wait, were you at Stacey's party a couple of weeks ago?'

'Yeah, I was.'

'That's it then! I was getting a drink and I got one for you too? That cocktail thing she had in the big bowl – God, it nearly blew my head off.'

I laugh. 'That's right, I remember now.'

'How about I get you another drink now? There's no punch on offer tonight, but is there anything else you'd like? A beer or something?'

'I don't really drink beer. Maybe a diet coke though?'

'Great.' Then he does a bad *Terminator* impression: 'I'll be back.'

It's a good ten minutes before he returns and I didn't expect him to. I have taken to sitting on the landing with my legs stretched out in front of me, forcing people to step over me as I wait for the girl in the bathroom to unlock the door. My patience is running thin. A fluffy-haired girl called Lola knocked and was let in; I heard muffled sobs and screechy words; then a guy I don't know with long hair the colour of flames also knocked and was admitted. If it is as simple as that, I'm willing to knock myself and see if I can fix the problem. There have since been raised voices, amplified as Lola then opened the door and left the two lovebirds to fight it out, but by the time Greg returns, the bathroom is suspiciously quiet.

'Sorry, the place is heaving,' Greg says as he plops down next to me on the carpet. He hands me a warm can of diet coke. 'You not been in yet?'

'No,' I say with a scowl. 'From what I can gather, this girl Michelle seems to be having a few issues with the guy that's in there with her now. Larry or Lonny or something. I think they might be making up now though.' I pull a face. 'Hope they hurry up. I'm bursting.'

As I say it, the bathroom door opens and Michelle emerges draped over a very flushed Larry/Lonnie, his cheeks now the same colour as his hair. I leap to my feet and dash into the bathroom before anyone else can, leaving Greg sitting on the floor.

When I come back out, he is still sitting there, waiting for me.

'Oh, hi. Still here?'

'Yeah, thought I'd wait for you. This party is kind of lame when you're not hooked up with someone, so I thought I'd... you know, hang out with you.'

'And what makes you think I haven't hooked up myself?'

He shrugs. 'I just don't think you'd be into any of these doughnuts. Not your type.'

'And what is my type? Wait, don't tell me. You are.' He blushes, but I don't give him any sympathy. 'You're right, though. They aren't my type because I don't have one – because I'm not interested. I've got exams coming up and then university and I'm not interested in hook-ups.'

'What universities are you looking at?'

And that's how I met Greg. We talked all night, mostly sitting in a cramped hallway in a terraced house while drunk teenagers stepped over our legs.

We were 18. And by the end of that night, I was drunk on him.

4

Maddie woke up the next morning to a mallet hammering at her skull and only fleeting memories of how she got down the stairs and back into her flat. Jade had helped her of sorts, but there was much ricocheting off the walls and stumbling on the stairs while Jade cackled with laughter. Maddie had a vague recollection of handing Jade her keys to open the front door, but the next thing she knew, the sun was streaming through the open curtains of her bedroom and she was slumped face-down on her bed, still wearing her top and cardigan, her neck twisted at an unnatural angle. She'd managed to shed her jeans somehow. They lay abandoned in the bedroom doorway alongside one shoe, like the aftermath of a nasty road accident.

She felt dreadful.

Dribble had dried on her chin and her tongue was painted to the top of her mouth. How much wine did they drink in the end? Three bottles? Considering that Maddie was a two-glass limit kind of girl these days, no wonder she felt like something had crawled into her mouth and died. She peeled herself from the bed and carried her thumping head in her hands as she staggered into the bathroom and sat on the toilet, feeling ashamed of her overindulgence.

Then a new memory came to her in technicolour. Jade suggesting fresh air and opening the door to her little balcony. Maddie holding onto the drying rack as she leant over and threw up over the railing.

Maddie's garden was directly below Jade's balcony. She had to stop thinking about it. It was hurting her head too much.

She sat longer than was necessary, breathing deeply, swaying a little and considering whether she was going to be sick again or not, before slowly making her way to the kitchen to pour herself a large glass of water. On her way back to bed, she drank in small sips before crawling under the covers and burying her face.

Greg cradled his daughter in his lap while she chatted away to her favourite teddy in a language only she understood. Her blonde curls tickled his chin, but he didn't notice. She pushed up onto her feet unsteadily for a moment, using Greg's shoulders as leverage, then plonked back down again. It wouldn't be long before she was walking. He couldn't wait to be able to hold her hand as she walked next to him. Daddy's little girl.

He pulled her to him and squeezed her tight, thinking about Maddie. She wriggled against him and he released her.

He was worried about Maddie. He still felt terrible that he had ultimately evicted her from her home, but Gemma had insisted it was the right move. It did make sense – this was a big house and Gemma was talking about having more children. Meanwhile, Maddie was now on her own and didn't need very much. The thought made him feel wretched with guilt.

For the last near-on two decades, Maddie's sole focus had been having a family with him, to the point where everything else had come second, including him and the business they'd set up together. It was desperately sad that she had invested so much into what had turned out to be a fruitless endeavour. If it had been a business deal, he would've advised cutting their losses years ago, but she had always been so single-minded about it.

But the guilt was still there and the self-recriminations. He knew she was hurting and much of it was down to him. So making sure she remained a part of his life – and Jemima's – was important to him, not least to alleviate his own guilty conscience.

Besides, she had been his best friend for so long. He still found himself thinking of things he wanted to tell her, sharing jokes he knew she would laugh at, buying her quirky things she would like.

And then there was Gemma, who was proving difficult to navigate. He knew she wanted Maddie as far away as possible. He had told her numerous times that Maddie was not a threat, that his feelings for her were based more on their history than on any possible future, but she still felt threatened. Part of it was because of how brilliant Maddie was with Jemima. She was a natural mother with every child she met. Gemma had to work hard and it *looked* like work most of the time. He would never admit this to anyone, but he sometimes wondered if Gemma actually even *liked* Jemima. She spent more time taking her to classes and crèches than cuddling and playing with her. But then he made up for it with silly games and story-time every day. If he could give up work and be Jemima's full-time parent, he would, but then he wouldn't be able to afford to keep Gemma in the lifestyle to which she was accustomed. That beauty cost money to maintain – and he was happy to spend it because a happy Gemma was a happy house.

Maddie was a lot lower maintenance in the beauty stakes, but much harder to please emotionally. Gemma's tastes may be material, but they were easy needs to meet. Maddie wanted something he couldn't provide – and for a man who liked to fix problems, that became untenable. If only he could combine the best of both women into one, he would be a happy man.

Late last night Maddie had called him. He had been downstairs loading the dishwasher and catching up on *Question Time* when his mobile rang. She hadn't said very much and what she did say he struggled to understand because she was laughing and sounded absolutely hammered. This was unusual in itself. She wasn't much of a drinker. There had been someone else with her – a woman with a throaty cackle of a laugh, who was swearing like a football hooligan in the background.

He had to admit, he had felt a little jealous. He hadn't heard Maddie laugh like that in years.

He'd tried to talk to her, but she'd gabbled at him and hung up. He'd been about to call her back but the baby monitor had burst into life as Jemima started to grizzle and he'd rushed upstairs to settle her before she woke Gemma.

But he thought about it now as he sat in his daughter's impossibly pink bedroom, with the smell of nappy cream in his nostrils, tinged with sour milk from where she had thrown up on him a few minutes ago when she drank too quickly from her bottle. He finally had what Maddie had always yearned for, but it was with someone else. And all he wanted was for Maddie to find a happiness of her own, to move on from the sadness that had engulfed her all these years, but at the first sign of her doing just that, he found he was jealous.

It used to be him that made her laugh like that.

But he also knew Maddie inside and out. The woman he'd heard in the background with the filthy mouth and smoker's cackle didn't seem the kind of person Maddie would befriend for long. She was a bleeding heart for anyone with a sob story, but she was also very practical.

Jemima shoved her teddy in his face, interrupting his thoughts, and he laughed and tickled her. She really was his entire world. Gemma could be as difficult and high-maintenance as she wanted to be if it meant he had a few more of these little creatures running around the house.

At that moment, Greg realised he was happier than he had been in years, but a cloud hovered in the distance all the same. A Maddie-shaped cloud that rumbled with his self-reproach. If he could just find a way of helping Maddie to find some contentment while still keeping her in his life… That's what the flat was about – close enough that she could still enjoy Jemima, but just far enough for Gemma to be comfortable and so that his happy family wasn't thrown in Maddie's face all the time.

He would call Maddie later and check in on her. She

would likely have a huge hangover after the state she was in.

He chuckled to himself. She was terrible with hangovers, always had been. Gemma didn't drink much at all – too many calories apparently.

Jemima was pressing a book into his hands now. He took it and she curled up in his lap again and rested her head against his chest. He kissed her head and began to read about lions and tigers and bears.

'Greg!' Gemma hollered up the stairs. 'I'm going to yoga!'

'Have fun – take your time!' he called back.

'Mummy's gone, yay!' he said in a whisper to Jemima and winked. She popped her thumb in her mouth and gazed at him adoringly.

It felt like hours had passed as Maddie tossed and turned, at times lying as still as possible so that her head wouldn't thud and her stomach wouldn't writhe. Apart from the occasional lurch to the bathroom, she remained buried, every now and then sticking a foot out of the covers for cool relief. By 3 p.m. she was feeling a little more human, so wrapped herself in her duvet and shuffled to the couch, grabbing a banana on the way. She'd read somewhere once that they were good for a hangover. Potassium or something. She turned on the TV and stared at some adverts for Bingo and online betting, before turning over to Netflix to search for some of the shows Jade had mentioned last night.

Some of her recommendations did not appeal to Maddie at all – what the hell was *American Horror Story* all about? – but she gave *Stranger Things* a go and before long had binged three episodes. Getting up to grab her phone and a large bag of salt and vinegar crisps, she sent Jade a message through Snapchat:

Sitting under a duvet binge-watching Stranger Things! It's brilliant! Had a fun night last night. Feel horrible today though.

She didn't expect Jade to read the message straight away, let alone reply, but a message came back immediately.

Good choice! Also feeling rough. Good laugh though! What episode are you on?

They spent the rest of the afternoon messaging back and forth, and it helped Maddie feel better. It struck her as bizarre that Jade was directly above her and yet they were having a conversation online as though they were hanging out in the same room. This was what friendships were like now, weren't they? Maddie could see the appeal. It was easier to be funny, eloquent, charming and confidently opinionated when you weren't looking someone in the eye. Maddie found herself saying bolder things in the Snapchat messages, throwing in a swear word or two, offering opinions that in the past she wouldn't have dared say out loud in case she was judged, criticised or ridiculed. Greg was always telling her to be careful what she said so as not to offend. She could think what she liked but should never say it out of good manners.

Jade was different. Part of it was that she was still quite young, a millennial, while Maddie was supposedly a baby boomer. The irony in that was not lost on her. Jade had said last night that she was 28 – ten years younger than Maddie, but it felt like much more. She was opinionated and still believed the world owed her everything while Maddie had learnt that the world owed you nothing and never played fair.

The idea of female friendship was something that Maddie had effectively missed out on until now. After meeting Greg when she was a teenager, he quickly became Maddie's best friend and they married young, fresh out of university and starry-eyed with hope and ambition. As the years of their marriage unfolded, any girlfriends she may have had all but dissolved away as she invested her entire being in him, their business, their family, to the point where she had few people she could call a friend now.

She thought about the people she had in her life and it painted a depressing picture. Her father had left when she was very young and her mother had died when Maddie was at university. Her old friends were all married, a few divorced, all with families of their own and living spread out across the globe. It had been just her and Greg for so long. He had been her entire existence.

For Maddie, this was a chance at a new start. She realised that she had never truly been independent before. As she sat, still in her pyjamas, eating custard creams out of the packet at 5 p.m., she felt suddenly liberated. She had gone from living with her mother to flat sharing at university to living with Greg. There had been no time for discovering who she actually was herself, in her own space. She had always shared space with Greg, had him to look after her, manage her life for her, make her decisions. Her mother had taught her to have an independent spirit, but the luxury of having someone shoulder the responsibility for you was addictive.

And now that could change. She needed to change her mindset. Her impending divorce was an opportunity rather than a failure. Jade had come along at the right time too, despite their clear differences. She thought about how independent Jade was – a single mum, living alone, making her own decisions – and she wanted a bit of that. And of course, there was Ben.

Of course she wanted Ben.

As if she knew what Maddie was thinking, Jade's next message was a video of Ben laughing into the camera while she spun him around, her ponytail like a propeller, and Maddie's heart expanded like a balloon as she listened to his fits of giggles, saw the sheer, childish joy on his face. Maddie replied:

That is adorable! I could eat him up! Is he home?

She put the phone to her chest and shuffled further down the couch under the duvet, trying not to cry. The phone vibrated again in her hand and she expected another message from Jade, but it was a call.

Greg.

She hesitated, then answered.

'Hi.'

'Hey you. How was the head this morning?'

'My head?'

'Yeah, you sounded pretty toasted last night.'

Maddie had no recollection of calling him last night.

'And who was that laughing in the background?'

A vague memory was teasing her, the two of them calling Greg, but she couldn't remember what they had said to him or even if they had said anything at all.

'I'm sorry, we were just hanging out, drinking wine and then things got a bit silly...'

'Who were you with?' His voice had an interesting edge.

'The woman who lives above me. She's really nice, has a three-year-old son called Ben.'

'Maddie, don't—'

'I'm just making friends, having some fun. That's all.'

'She sounded a bit... you know, not our kind of person, Mads...'

'And what kind of person is that?' Annoyance clipped the edge off her words.

'You know what I mean. You're just being obtuse now.'

'No, actually, I don't know what you mean. Are you referring to immaculately made-up women who shop in Waitrose and think a good night out is two slimline gin and tonics before an early night? Women like Gemma, maybe?'

'Hey, what's got into you? I'm just worried about you.'

She was uncharacteristically annoyed at him now. How dare he imply that Jade was not worthy? So she may be a bit crass, did everything with the volume turned up high and wore clothes that were a little cheap, but she had also been kind, welcoming and fun to hang out with last night. He didn't know her, hadn't even met her.

Maddie wanted to shock him, make him see she didn't need him anymore. What would Jade say to him right now? 'I think the days of you having the right to worry about me, tell me what to do, or have anything at all to do with me were over when you decided to shag your PA behind my back, don't you?'

Then she hung up on him.

Her head was pounding again and she could barely breathe. She had never spoken to Greg like that before. If they had argued in the past, it had always been with voices barely raised above conversational, with Maddie offering an opinion and him telling her she was wrong or dismissing her outright. She felt at once rebellious and brave, then immediately foolish and immature. This was Greg, after all. He knew her better than she knew herself. She could picture his face now, the way he chewed on the inside of his lip when he was perturbed or rubbed at the back of his neck when he was uncomfortable.

She called him straight back and before he could speak, said, 'I'm so sorry, it's the hangover. I don't know what came over me.'

But it was Gemma's icy voice that replied. 'He's not here, Madeleine.' She was the only person to call Maddie by her full name since her mother had died and it set Maddie's teeth on edge every time.

'Oh, I was talking to him two seconds ago.'

'Jemima needed him. She wanted a cuddle from her daddy.'

'Right.' Maddie's throat felt like it was closing up. 'Ok, well, tell him I'm sorry.'

'Sure,' Gemma replied and hung up. Somehow Maddie knew she wouldn't pass the message on.

Maddie sent Jade another Snapchat, telling her what she had said to Greg, but omitting that she had called him back to apologise. Jade replied with a 'You go, girl!' and a punching fist emoji, followed quickly by:

Remember the pact. I'll kill yours if you kill mine.

Maddie giggled and replied with the laughing emoji and a thumbs up.

Then

'I really want to do this, Maddie. I want us to do it together. I think we'd make such a great team.'

My back is cold against the chair. Greg has left the kitchen door open and the draught is blowing through to where I'm sitting at the breakfast bar. This flat might be small and cheap, but it's cold in the winter. But then Bristol winters can be so biting. This is our second winter at Bristol University together, where we share a student flat with two med students, Michael and Bryan. Greg and I share the biggest bedroom, Michael has the box room and Bryan has moved a bed into the lounge, meaning that Greg and I spend a lot of time sitting at the breakfast bar rather than being able to slob out on the couch, especially since Bryan parties hard and sleeps long. I have no idea how he will pass his course, but that's his problem.

I pull my dressing gown tightly around me. 'But a business degree? It sounds so... boring,' I say.

'Our *own* business, Mads! Think about it, how amazing it would be. No bosses; no rules. All our own. You and me together. I need someone with a good business head and you're so smart, especially with figures and money and stuff.

Look how well you keep us three in line with the budget for this place.'

'There's a big difference between running a company and working out whose turn it is to buy toilet rolls.'

All I've ever wanted to be is a political journalist after watching Kate Adie on the television, a bulletproof vest strapped to her chest as bombs went off behind her. Now Greg is trying to convince me to change my degree. He has an idea for a business and he wants us to do it together.

'It's your dream, Greg, not mine.'

'It could be yours too. Come on, Mads, you want to do journalism, but it's so competitive. You don't know how long it'll be before you get a firm job offer. At least with a business degree you'll have something concrete, something real, and with my dad willing to invest in my idea, we can build something for our future together. You can still write in your spare time, like a hobby.'

'And we could break up tomorrow. Then where will my supposed career be? How would that work with our joint business?'

'Maddie, I love you. You're not going anywhere; I'm not going anywhere. We're in this together, you and me. For the long haul.' He drops to his knee on the cold linoleum floor and grasps my hand in his. Despite my annoyance, my pulse bubbles as I realise what he's doing. 'I want us to be a partnership. I want you to be my wife. Will you marry me? After we graduate, I mean, and get the business going and stuff. Not right now.' His words are tripping over themselves, but his eyes are alive and dancing. 'I want us to have the world. The big house, loads of kids, posh cars in the driveway, the lot. What do you say?'

Not the most romantic of proposals, here in our draughty kitchen wearing dressing gowns and thick socks, but I feel like someone has opened a bottle of champagne in my stomach, all fizzing and popping and gurgling.

'Yes, yes, I'll marry you!' I shriek and leap at him, knocking him backwards onto the floor. I kiss him hard, then pull back. 'Wait a minute, loads of kids? How many are we talking? That could be a deal-breaker,' I say.

'Well, at least four surely? Two each,' he says, grinning.

'Hmm, ok then. Two each,' I say and kiss him again, just as Bryan wanders in in his boxer shorts.

'Take it elsewhere, you two. I've got a hangover,' he says with a groan.

We did take it elsewhere and we did get married. I changed my degree and we started the business as equal partners after we graduated. Then, over the years, as my focus on the business waned when our marriage was hit with blow after blow, my shares slowly dwindled along with my independence, spirit and will to live.

5

Sunday. A day of rest. But that's what she did yesterday.

Maddie wandered from room to room, then did another lap since the flat wasn't very big. She opened the curtains to the garden and considered the little puddle of vomit still on the lawn. Grabbing a big bowl from the kitchen, she filled it with water and went outside to slosh the puke away.

It was the first time she'd been in the small, enclosed garden. She peered through the wooden fence, but couldn't see much of her neighbour's garden on the other side, but what she could see looked neat and brightly coloured. She still hadn't met her neighbour. Perhaps she should go over there today.

Maddie's little patch was completely in shade and she wrapped her arms around herself in the chill morning air. There was a square of grass, muddy and worn in places, and something that was trying to be a flowerbed along the fence on one side. A washing line ran from the back fence to the door, with a few broken pegs swinging forlornly from it. Spiderwebs glistened in the weak autumn sun, like tiny insect trampolines, and broken pots were stashed in one corner. Growing anything here would be a challenge. It was not, as Greg had put it, a 'sun trap'.

Maybe she could grow a few simple vegetables and herbs, although she didn't know where to start. Greg had employed a gardener when they had moved into the house down the road. Peter, with his quiet smile and baggy, grass-stained trousers, would arrive every Thursday, let himself into the garden, weed, prune and mow, then let himself out again. Sometimes when she was lying in bed when things got really bad, she would hear the lawnmower, smell the cut grass and imagine she could hear children laughing and playing football outside. It reminded her that there was a world going on outside. Even now, the smell of cut grass made her feel inexplicably sad. Every Christmas she would leave out a hamper of homemade mince pies and shortbread for Peter with a fifty-pound note tucked into a Christmas card. She had no idea if Peter was married or had children, if he liked shortbread or loathed mince pies, but she liked to think he was pleased to receive it.

The polite ignorance of the middle classes.

The same could be said of the cleaner they had employed for years. Maddie would communicate with her by text message and leave money on the kitchen counter for her. She would let herself in once a week, so that when Maddie came home from work, the house would be immaculately tidy and smelling of citrus and bleach. Maddie knew her first name was Aneta, but knew nothing about her family or where she lived, but when everything felt like it was spiralling out of control, Aneta knew to leave the main bedroom untouched, to let Maddie sleep, not to intrude on her grief. It was never discussed though. She just knew. Maddie realised with embarrassment that she had seen her in person only a handful of times and yet this woman had cleaned up many of Maddie's most intimate messes.

A train rumbled past in the distance and tyres squealed on the road outside. The cardigan she was wearing was doing a poor job of keeping the morning chill out. She looked around one more time, then picked up the bowl and turned to head back indoors.

Ben's tiny face was peeking through the railings on Jade's balcony above her. She wiggled her fingers at him and he watched her, his face serious. Maddie could hear Jade calling his name, but he didn't move, just carried on staring at her, like an animal trapped in a cage at the zoo.

'What are you staring at?' Jade appeared behind him, her face impatient, then it visibly softened as she looked down and saw Maddie below, like a mask had slipped into place.

Maddie waved up at her. 'Hi, neighbour!'

'Hey! Getting rid of evidence?' She smirked and Maddie blushed.

'Yeah, something like that. Typical that it hasn't rained when I want it to.'

'You're a badass, you are!'

No one had ever called her that before and she grinned. Ben was still staring down at her, his little fists clamped around the railings. Jade looked at him, then Maddie. Jade reached out and stroked his hair. 'We're going out to the park in a bit, maybe feed the ducks if you want to join us?' she said.

'I'd love to!'

'I'll knock when we're ready then, maybe half an hour?'

Maddie skipped back inside and started rummaging through her cupboards for kid-friendly snacks to take with her. She pulled a tub of hummus from the fridge and started cutting carrots and cucumber into neat little batons, humming while she chopped.

With plenty of time to spare, she was ready, coat on, snack bag packed and waiting, her fingers tapping against the countertop. It was closer to forty-five minutes later when she finally heard the knock.

Maddie opened the door and immediately crouched down to say hello to Ben, who was strapped into his pushchair, the straps pulled tight so that it looked like his yellow raincoat was swallowing him whole.

'Hi, do you remember me? I'm Maddie, but you can call me Mads if you like?'

He blinked at her and said nothing, but she noticed he was clutching the new car she had bought him and her chest puffed out.

'Right, let's go,' Jade said, then noticed the bag. 'What's in there?'

'Snacks, you know, in case we decide to sit for a bit.'

'Well, I have to have him back by twelve.'

Maddie tried to disguise her disappointment. 'Oh, why?'

Jade looked away. 'You know, his nap and stuff…'

'Ok, well, let's see. You never know, he might nap in his pushchair if we're out longer?'

'He's a creature of habit, our Ben. He likes his own bed and can be a right little shit if he doesn't get enough sleep,' she said quickly. 'Aren't you, Benny Boy?' She reached down to rub his cheek.

'Ok, no problem,' Maddie replied, but she was

disappointed. She had had the whole morning planned in her head, could imagine them feeding the ducks, having a picnic, chasing a ball around.

Jade was already heading towards the door to the street. Maddie slammed her front door behind her and rushed over to hold the outside door open for Jade.

'Oh, and don't be too surprised if he doesn't say much to you. He's not much of a talker. I'm trying to get him to use his words, but… you know… they do what they want when they want,' Jade said.

'What does his nursery school say?' They were out in the noise of the street now, with cars driving past and people wandering around with cups of coffee in one hand and phones in the other.

'Oh, you know …' she replied vaguely. They passed a coffee shop and Jade said, 'Fancy a coffee?'

'Why not? I'll get it.'

'No, you stay here with him. Whatcha want?'

'Americano, please – no sugar. Here, take this. My treat.' Maddie rummaged in her purse for some money.

Jade took the proffered twenty-pound note without argument and disappeared into the coffee shop. Maddie crouched down to Ben again and said, 'Do you like your car?'

He looked at her with wide eyes, then at the car in his hand and gave an almost imperceptible nod of his head.

'Good, I'm glad. When we get to the park, maybe you can show me how fast it goes.' He blinked. 'Can you say Maddie? Maddie?' He blinked again. She reached out to push his hair from his eyes and he shrank away from her. She hesitated, then pulled her hand back. Too much, too soon. She didn't want him to be frightened of his Aunty Maddie.

She really needed him to like her.

'So did you have fun with your daddy?'

He whispered something that was carried away in the street noise. She leant closer. 'Sorry?'

'Mumma,' he said.

'No, Daddy yesterday. Did you have fun with Daddy?' she repeated.

'Mumma,' he said again.

Jade's shadow fell over her. 'He doesn't like talking about his dad, it makes him upset.' She looked annoyed.

Maddie shot to her feet. 'Oh! I'm so sorry.'

'Come on, let's go.' Jade shoved the coffee at her. Maddie could see a brown paper bag from the coffee shop poking out from Jade's handbag. She must've bought a cookie for Ben. She waited for Jade to give her back the change from the coffees, which wouldn't have cost twenty pounds, but nothing was forthcoming. Jade gripped the pushchair with her free hand and steered it into the pedestrians, the atmosphere between them suddenly crisp.

Maddie followed Jade like a faithful puppy, chattering about the weather, the shops they passed, the people around them, until they reached the gate to the park. She could hear herself overcompensating for the lack of conversation coming from Jade, but couldn't stop herself from babbling. Maddie held the gate open for Jade, who pushed past her without a word. Maddie had to jump backwards to avoid the wheels of the pushchair running over her foot.

The grass was wet underfoot, with leaves mushed into the ground. A small, black dog ran over to them, sniffing at the pushchair and wagging its tail. Ben smiled and reached out to touch it and Maddie smiled with him.

'Hey there,' Maddie said to the dog while bending down to let it sniff her hand. 'You know, Ben, you should always let a dog sniff your hand first before reaching out to it – like this – so that it doesn't get frightened.'

Ben copied her and giggled as the dog licked his hand. She could feel Jade watching them quietly. The dog's owner whistled from further up the path and it ran off, all flopping ears and lolling tongue. Ben followed it with his eyes, still smiling, and Maddie couldn't help herself. She reached out and touched his cheek lightly, her heart aching.

'You really like kids, don't you?'

Maddie stood up quickly. 'Yes, I do,' she said with a sigh.

'So why don't you have any?'

Maddie hesitated, but if Jade had noticed her reticence, she didn't retract her question. She just carried on staring at Maddie, waiting for an answer. 'It's complicated. We tried… for years,' was all Maddie said.

'Ah, Greg shooting blanks, was he? But wait, isn't the new girlfriend pregnant? Oooh, is it not his?' Her eyes lit up at the whiff of scandal.

'It is his. He wasn't at fault. I was.' Maddie swallowed thickly and set off up the path towards the pond.

Jade followed, more animated now. 'So what happened?'

'What they call "unexplained infertility". I don't want to talk about it though.'

Jade eyed Maddie curiously, like she was a specimen in a jar, as though if she stared hard enough she could see what was wrong with her. It's a look Maddie had seen on Greg's face before.

'Oh, look, Ben! There's a beautiful swan!' Maddie pointed at the water. Ben strained to get out of the pushchair, so she reached down and unclipped him. He darted up with youthful clumsiness in his little welly boots and toddled towards the water.

'Careful! Not too close to the water!' Maddie said and followed him, pleased to leave the conversation behind.

The cup of coffee was still hot in her hand and she sipped at it as she watched him. Jade came to stand next to her. She had the bakery bag in her hand and pulled a millionaire's shortbread from it. Her eyes flicked over to Maddie and she said begrudgingly, 'Want some?'

'Er, no, thanks.' Maddie wasn't sure what to make of her rudeness. Maybe it had slipped Jade's mind to return Maddie's change, but it looked like she had bought herself a treat and nothing for anyone else, which was selfish and bad manners. Maddie certainly wouldn't buy herself something in a bakery without getting another for whoever she was with – or for her son.

Jade saw the look on Maddie's face and said around shortbread crumbs, 'Oh, sorry, I would've got you one, but you don't look like the cake-eating kind.' She gestured at Maddie's body, crumbs falling as she gesticulated at her. 'You're such a skinny arse. I swear I could snap you in half. That's a compliment, by the way. Besides, you have to be really careful these days. Everyone is allergic to something or other.' She carried on chewing.

'I'm not allergic to anything. Greg is – a severe nut allergy. I always had to be careful. I just don't really have much of an appetite – *usually*.'

Jade ignored the inflection. 'Well, there you go, see? So

Greg has an allergy, huh? Me, I think about food all the time. Food and fags – ha! Cigarettes, not gay people,' she added unnecessarily.

Feeling annoyed, Maddie stared at the people around them. The mums with their small children chasing balls; dogs sniffing, digging and playing; runners huffing and puffing past, their breath like clouds. She breathed it all in, remembering why she liked coming here and wishing not for the first time that she could bring her own children.

'Speaking of food, what's in your picnic then?' Jade coughed loudly, a hacking bark that vibrated straight through Maddie, making her teeth clench. Her initial excitement at the possibility of a friend in her building was starting to wear thin. Jade's little habits were grating on Maddie's nerves today – like how she chewed on the inside of her cheek when she wasn't talking, her mouth twisting and gurning as she bit at herself, or the way she walked in small steps on her toes, bouncing along.

Maddie could feel the weight of the bag on her shoulder and was in two minds as to whether she should just head home, maybe take a longer walk through the park so that she could enjoy the fresh air.

Then Ben ran up to her, pointing and giggling at the swans, saying, 'Maddie, Maddie, look!' and her mood lifted instantly. Who cared if Jade was selfish and irritating? Ben had just called her by her name! The truth was if she wanted to spend time with Ben, she would have to be friends with Jade. Did her broodiness outweigh her annoyance?

Without a doubt, yes.

'Shall we find somewhere to sit, Ben? Then you can feed the ducks with some of the bread I brought along,' Maddie said, then turned to Jade. 'I just brought a few snacks in case he got hungry,' she said apologetically. 'It's nothing much. Just crisps, cucumber, you know…' She saw a park bench around the other side of the pond. 'There's a bench over there.'

'Ben, babe, we're going to sit over there. Let's go around that side, yeah?' Jade started walking towards the bench. 'I tell you what, Maddie, you're a natural mother. You can look after Ben anytime.'

Maddie grinned. 'Thanks. I brought wholemeal bread for him to feed the ducks,' she said, digging in the bag. 'You're not supposed to feed them white bread. It's bad for them apparently.'

'Ducks with gluten issues. Who knew? Come on, Benny Boy.'

He trailed after them, his little feet kicking at the fallen leaves. Jade plonked herself down on the bench and sighed. 'I'm shattered.'

Maddie realised then that maybe she was being hard on Jade. She was a single mother, after all, and it couldn't be easy.

'Yeah, you must be,' Maddie said sympathetically, sitting down next to her. She pulled a bag of chocolate buttons from her bag and offer them to Jade. 'Here. A little pick me up.'

'Oooh, yeah. Thanks.' Jade tore open the packet and dove right in.

'Does Ben want anything? I have breadsticks, crisps…'

'Crisps! Lush – what flavour? Don't worry about Ben. If he's hungry, he'll say.'

'Oh, ok.'

The snacks were for Ben, not Jade, but she was now digging in the bag looking for salt and vinegar crisps. She found a bag and Maddie watched her curiously as she held the packet up to her face and breathed in deeply while opening it, inhaling the salt and vinegar with relish. 'God, I bloody love salt and vinegar crisps,' she said. 'Oh Jesus! Look at that annoying cow over there!'

Maddie's eyes followed where Jade was pointing towards a middle-aged woman with a bag over her shoulder that said in gold lettering, *'Oh no! Have I bought prosecco instead of milk again?'* Maddie wondered where she'd bought the bag because she liked it.

'I hate women like that – who think it's *fun* to carry slogan bags. She's probably got loads of jumpers with stars on them and three pairs of white trainers,' Jade scoffed.

Maddie didn't comment, not least because she herself had three pairs of white trainers, with stars on them in various colours, and slogan jumpers galore. Jade had a way of holding a mirror up to Maddie, so that she could see what others saw – and Maddie didn't necessarily like the reflection staring back. And yet Jade was completely unapologetic about herself. Maybe Maddie should be more like her, then she wouldn't feel like the world's biggest doormat sometimes. Lately she was starting to realise that she had spent too much time worrying about what others thought of her and had lost sight of who she was, what she even liked. She had a vague recollection of herself from before she met Greg, but then she'd put on a fancy dress costume of the perfect wife, with the sensible clothes and controlled mannerisms, and eventually found she couldn't take it off again, like the zip had got stuck and there was no one there to help her out of it.

Jade was chewing loudly next to her with her mouth open, sucking the salt from her fingers. It was mildly repulsive to watch.

Maddie hadn't realised that she was still staring at the woman across the pond, but the woman had noticed and was now stalking over to where they were sitting. With a sickening lurch, Maddie recognised her as she drew closer.

The woman was livid. 'You.' The word dripped from her scowling mouth.

Maddie jumped to her feet. She felt cold all over. 'Look, I don't want any trouble…'

'You are supposed to stay away from me.'

'I didn't know you'd… I'm sorry.'

The woman turned to Jade and said in a quivering voice, 'You need to keep an eye on your son when she's around,' then turned on her heel and stormed away towards the park gate.

'What the hell?' Jade said, her forehead crumpled in confusion.

'Just a misunderstanding years ago…' Maddie slumped back onto the bench, her legs shaking. She exhaled slowly and clasped her hands together tightly.

'But what did she mean about keeping—'

Ben ran over then and interrupted them, saying, 'I'm hungry.'

Jade hesitated, then said, 'Here, Ben, pick something from the bag that lovely Maddie brought. She's very kind, isn't she?'

The way she said it made Maddie wonder if she was making a point.

'There's chocolate over there too,' Maddie said to Ben, ignoring the side eye Jade was giving her.

He found the chocolate buttons, grabbed a bag of mini breadsticks and trotted away again.

A phone's text message alert chimed and Maddie retrieved her phone from her bag to check it. It was a text from Greg. Her stomach dropped as she remembered what she had said to him yesterday. She put her phone back in her bag without reading it, her hands still shaking.

The silence stretched and twisted between them.

'You can answer it. I don't mind,' Jade said.

'It's Greg. It can wait,' Maddie replied.

Jade was watching her closely again, unnervingly so.

'Listen, I'm sorry about that woman. It was years ago…'

Jade waved her away. 'Hey, it's fine. We all have a past, a few skeletons in the closet and all that. I'm not one to judge.'

Maddie exhaled and reached into the bag for some cucumber.

'Ben's dad was in touch yesterday. Wants to start making formal plans to get custody and stuff,' Jade said with her eyes on the swans as they glided past.

'Oh, wow!' Maddie said. No wonder Jade was in a strange mood today. 'Is that what you want?'

Jade scrunched up her crisp packet in a tight fist. 'No, but I don't really have a choice… unless me and Ben run away or something…'

'What? You can't run away with him. That won't solve anything and it's not fair to Ben – or his dad.'

Jade turned abruptly in her seat. 'Whose side are you on?' Her tongue was razor sharp.

'Yours, of course. It's just… I know what it's like to not be able to spend time with your kids. It's a cruel punishment for anyone.'

'You don't have any kids, so you don't know what it's like.'

'Yeah, well, I can imagine anyway.' Maddie paused. Could she though? Her pain had been from wanting and not getting rather than having something taken away. 'Ok, maybe I don't know what it's like, but he is Ben's father. He should be involved in his life.'

The truth of it was that *she* wanted to be a part of Ben's life.

'If he's around, but Ben would forget him pretty quickly if he wasn't.' Jade's voice was low. 'Kids are resilient.'

Maddie frowned at her. 'I don't know if it works that way.'

'He's really young. He'd move on.' Jade's voice was cold.

'Jade, you can't honestly believe that! What did Mark do to you that was so bad?' Maddie expected her to say that he had cheated on her or, God forbid, hit her or something.

'He dumped me by text message! What kind of twat does that?'

'While you were pregnant?'

'No, I told you. We were together for a few months, he dumped me by text message, then I got together with him for one night later on – revenge shag, you know – and then I found out I was pregnant.'

'But what was his reason for dumping you in the first place?'

'He just said that since we hadn't been together long and he had the new job on the rigs starting, that it was best to end it before he left rather than have me hanging around, waiting for him.'

That didn't sound too unreasonable, but Maddie was not about to admit that. Jade's eyes were booming and crashing with anger.

'Anyway,' Jade continued, her voice trembling, 'we need to talk about our plan. We said we'd help each other out if things changed. Well, it looks like things might be changing for me, so… you know…'

Maddie had no idea what she was talking about.

'What do you mean?'

Jade's voice dropped to a whisper, as quiet as a breath. 'The plan. You know, you kill mine and I'll kill yours. We mustn't talk about it here though.' Jade looked around anxiously. 'Anyone could hear us. And keep any messages between us to Snapchat, so that they delete straight away.'

Maddie started to giggle. Jade certainly had a weird sense of humour – or maybe had watched too many Tarantino movies. 'Yes, you're right. That woman over there with the Daschund looks like she could be trouble.' Maddie nudged her playfully, pleased the atmosphere had lifted again. 'So tell me more about the others living in our flats.'

'Well, downstairs is Nosy Nora. Her name's actually Peggy and she's about 90, likes to stick her nose in everyone's business. Always poking her head out the door when I'm coming home with someone. Her place smells like cat piss and cabbage. It's nasty. She's proper old.'

Maddie thought about the kicking on the door and screaming the night she arrived.

'Maybe she's just lonely? Do you know if she gets any visitors? Has any family nearby?'

'How would I know? I've not stopped to ask her life story. She's always having a go at me. Stupid stuff like making sure the entrance door closes properly behind me and not playing my music too loud. She's a right pain.'

'And the other flat?'

'That's Luke. You'll never see him. He's in his mid-thirties or something, works in computers I think and obsessed with gaming. He's like a vampire – all skinny and pale, doesn't like sunlight. Nice-looking though if that's your thing. I had a one-nighter with him once last year. Didn't go anywhere with it 'cos he doesn't say much. I don't think he earns much money doing whatever it is he does. He's harmless enough though.' She looked at her watch. 'Shit, I have to go. I need to get Ben home for—' She broke off, flicked her eyes at Maddie, then said, 'You know, nap and stuff...'

'Oh, yes, right. Well, why don't you take the rest of the picnic with you? There's cut-up vegetables, hummus, that kind of thing.'

'Thanks, but that's all a bit healthy for me.'

'Ben can have it later?'

Jade fidgeted. 'Oh, don't worry. I have his lunch planned already, but thanks anyway. Ben! Time to go, come on.'

Maddie couldn't work Jade out. One minute she was biting Maddie's hand off for free crisps and the next she was turning down freebies. Maybe hummus just wasn't her thing.

Ben looked up from where he had been digging in the wet soil and obediently toddled over to them. Jade strapped him into the pushchair. 'You coming?'

Maddie paused, then said, 'I might stay here for a bit, actually. It's nice. Fresh air.'

Jade raised her eyebrows. 'Whatever. Suit yourself. I wouldn't spend any more time than I had to around other people's kids and dogs, but knock yourself out. I'll Snapchat you later, yeah?'

'Ok. Bye, Ben,' Maddie said with a big smile. He smiled back and waved, and she watched them walk away, feeling inexplicably sad for him.

To Maddie, he looked like a child who really needed a hug.

She wanted to give him that hug.

He would be happier with me.

The thought came and went in an instant, but left an indelible mark.

Then

There is a nervous tension in the room as everyone watches the countdown. My dress is tight around my chest, but it's worth it from the admiring glances Greg has been shooting me all night.

I sip at the champagne I'm holding, but it tastes metallic and bitter, so I put it on the table next to me as the room starts to chant: 'Ten, nine, eight…'

I feel Greg slip his arm around my shoulders as he counts down with everyone else and I look over at this man, who I love more than I love myself, and I think how happy I am. I look down at the shiny square-cut diamond on my finger and smile to myself. There is only one thing that could make the next year better than the one that's just passed and that would be for us to start a family.

It was my idea to start trying for a baby straight after we get married in a few months. I hope it won't take too long. I eat well; I run three times a week; I don't drink much. But sometimes these things do take a while, don't they?

The business is still in its initial stages, but growing steadily, thanks to Greg's dad and his generous investment. We are still a small operation and there are months when we teeter between having enough money to pay our small team of staff and paying ourselves as well, but we've decided to give a family a go.

And it's all I can think about now that it's a possibility.

Greg is less keen. He likes having me all to himself, I think, and he's really invested in getting the business profitable as quickly as possible.

I'm surprised at how broody I have become so quickly. Now that I've accepted that I won't be an award-winning journalist after all, it's like I need a new passion and the business is not it. Greg loves it of course, all the wheeling and dealing, networking and negotiations. But I'm not enjoying it as much, so I distract myself with other dreams. I do still write, but mostly journals and poetry, stuff for me and no one else.

Everyone starts cheering and shouting as Big Ben chimes the beginning of a new year on the television. Greg pulls me into his arms and hugs me tight before kissing me full and hard. 'Happy new year, Mads. You and me against the world.'

'Happy new year. I love you.'

'And I love you.' I smile and breathe him in.

Greg's friend, Tim, rushes over, shouting and whooping. 'Happy new year, lovebirds! This one's gonna be a cracking year!'

Greg releases me and laughs at Tim. 'I don't doubt it, Timmy.'

I reach for my champagne, take a sip and weave through the room, wishing the friends and acquaintances around me a happy new year. Suddenly the room tilts and I feel my legs give way.

I come around to the sight of three faces peering down

at me in concern. I feel myself being lifted and propped up on the couch. Someone is waving a magazine in my face like a fan.

'Mads, you ok?'

I blink, disorientated. 'What happened?'

'You passed out,' Greg says, concern paling his face.

'But I've only had one glass of champagne.'

'Have you eaten anything? I'll get Tim to get you some of the nibbles from the table.'

The others start to move away now that the drama has passed, resuming their drinking and dancing.

I sit higher up on the couch, feeling a cold sweat on my forehead. My friend Belinda comes over with a glass of water and asks if I'm ok.

'I think so. Probably just need to eat something,' I say, accepting the water and drinking half the glass in one.

Tim hurries back with a plate loaded with canapés and I thank him before nibbling on a sausage roll. I feel a bit better, less lightheaded already. Greg sits on the couch next to me, still concerned.

'What's going on with you? You've been a bit off for a few days now.'

'I know. Maybe I should go to the doctor when—' Then it hits me. 'Oh God, Greg.'

'What?'

'I haven't had my period. I think I might be pregnant.'

His face lights up like a firework. 'Really?'

'Well, I don't know. I'd have to do a test to make sure, so don't get too excited.'

But he is. We both are. I can't stop grinning.

'Here's to a new year and a decade of children – one a

year for the next ten years. What do you say?' Greg says, scooping me up in his arms and twirling me around.

I laugh. 'Steady there, tiger! One at a time! And we're not even married yet!'

'Scandalous!'

I gaze up at him and can't help but wonder how I got so lucky.

My life is perfect.

6

Returning to her flat an hour or so later, Maddie remembered she hadn't read Greg's text from earlier. She opened it:

Fancy joining Gemma and me for a late lunch today? She's making a roast. Jemima would love to see you. Let me know. G x

Maddie loved Jemima. She was a chubby, delightfully energetic baby, full of smiles and laughter. Quite a different child to Ben, although much younger. Who knew though? Perhaps Ben had been a bubbly, gurgling baby too.

But the familiar ache in her chest was back after seeing Ben this morning, as though she'd held the world in her arms but someone had come along and snatched it away. Again. Self-preservation dictated that having to say goodbye to Jemima later would make things worse rather than help to fill the void. Not to mention watching Greg and Gemma as they lived out their domestic bliss in front of her.

She began to type a reply to say she wouldn't be coming, but instead found herself typing:

I'd love to. What time should I come and what can I bring? Pudding? M x

When it came to Greg, she couldn't say no. Force of habit.

He replied straight away, putting in a request for what Maddie knew was his favourite: sticky toffee pudding.

She had another shower, washed her hair and spent time styling it to look as though it wasn't styled at all. Her outfit was planned so that it looked like she had made just the right amount of effort. Then she started making the sticky toffee pudding, ensuring there was extra toffee sauce and a homemade custard to go with it. Greg had always loved her cooking and she got the feeling that Gemma wasn't quite as accomplished, which secretly filled her with joy. There was still something Maddie could do for him that Gemma couldn't.

She turned on the radio while she worked and sang along to some eighties' classics. She couldn't help looking forward to seeing Greg and Jemima. Gemma not so much, with her perfect smile and tiny waist. She was all creamy, sickly loveliness with her blonde waves and immaculate highlights.

There was no denying that Maddie's life would be so much better if Gemma wasn't around. She could move back in, look after Jemima, look after Greg... maybe she should suggest that Jade get rid of Gemma for her instead of Greg. She giggled at the thought.

The timer on the oven pinged and she pulled out the steaming pudding, breathing in the heady smell of dates and toffee.

She packed everything into Tupperware and foil trays,

ready to transport it over to Greg's. The house wasn't far – easily walkable in fifteen minutes – but she decided to drive instead. As well as the pudding, she had a bottle of prosecco, a bag of chocolate buttons to give to Jemima, along with a little outfit she saw the other day that she had to buy for her. She would never be able to carry all of it.

She bundled everything into her car, then closed the passenger door and went around to the driver's side. As she did, she noticed Jade above her, staring down from her bedroom window. Maddie smiled and waved, and Jade smiled back vaguely, but carried on watching as she drove away.

Jade watched Maddie drive away, her mind still working through what had happened in the park earlier. The woman coming up to them, her pointing finger, the fury in her words making her whole body shake.

What the hell had Maddie done to her? The whole thing had been weird.

There was clearly more to Maddie than Jade had initially realised. A bit of a dark horse.

But the most concerning part was what the woman had said about keeping Ben away from Maddie. What was that all about?

Was Maddie dangerous? She didn't want Ben to get hurt.

Jade could just see Maddie's tiny car sitting at the junction waiting to turn onto the busy road, the indicator ticking away. Jade stared at it, as though it would give her some answers. She couldn't believe cardigan-wearing Maddie was a danger to Ben. She'd seen how Maddie was with him – almost painfully desperate for him to like her and respond to her. Ben rarely responded to anyone though – he was a complex kid – but Maddie was going out of her way to bond with him. That didn't strike Jade as a dangerous person.

Unless she had an ulterior motive?

She must've done something to that woman. In fact, Maddie hadn't denied that something had happened between them. She could've said it was mistaken identity, but instead she'd just clammed up.

Why?

Now Jade was more curious than ever about the woman living downstairs, a woman who on the surface seemed so… vanilla. There had been no hint of a temper or volatility in the few encounters they'd had so far. In fact, she'd been the epitome of good manners and politeness, not even challenging Jade when she had pocketed her change earlier. That had been a little test in itself, to see if she could get a rise out of her, but even then good manners had prevailed.

But they said they quiet ones were the most dangerous, didn't they?

Jade would need to keep an eye on her.

For Ben's sake.

Maddie parked up on the gravel driveway of her old house and sat for a moment. The front looked like it always had. A double-fronted, detached house with lovely bay windows and a dark green front door framed by miniature bay trees. That shade of green had taken ages to choose.

The only difference now was the presence of a large,

silver Range Rover looming in the driveway alongside Greg's Porsche Panamera. He'd traded in Maddie's BMW X5 then. Her tiny Fiat 500 sat in the shadows between the two larger cars, completely dwarfed. She climbed out and began to unpack everything from the passenger seat as she heard the front door open behind her.

'There you are!' Greg said and came to greet her, a wide smile on his face. Maddie tried not to hope he might've been watching for her car.

He looked different, not least because he had grown a beard in the last week that was flecked more with grey than anything else. It made him look like he was trying too hard.

'Hi, how are you?' Maddie said. 'This is new.' She gesticulated at the facial hair.

'Oh, yes, thought I'd try something new,' he said and there was a hint of a blush in what she could see of his cheeks. 'Do you like it?'

'Sure. Very distinguished,' she replied, wondering why he cared what she thought.

He was wearing a light grey sweater over navy chinos that had a crisp pleat down the front of the leg. He looked relaxed and happy, and for a second, she wished she could see something else, a sense of exhaustion, a tightening of the lips maybe or shadows beneath his eyes, something to make her think he was struggling just a little bit.

But there was none of that. He looked happy.

He leant in to kiss her on each cheek while saying, 'You look well.' She breathed him in. He smelled of an unfamiliar sandalwood aftershave. Maddie wondered if he had noticed she was wearing the perfume he had bought her for their last anniversary together.

He took the pudding from her. 'You angel! You made your famous sticky toffee pud!'

'Well, you asked so nicely,' she replied, resting her hand lightly on his arm.

He smiled at her warmly and she could feel her stomach flip. Like an addict, no matter how much he had hurt her, she still couldn't stop herself from reacting to him.

A chillier voice over her shoulder interrupted the moment. 'Maddie, how nice to see you.'

She dropped her hand. 'Hi, Gemma. Thank you so much for having me.'

Gemma's face was pinched, like she could smell something bad in the air. 'A pudding. You shouldn't have. Did Greg not mention our diet? He's on a healthy eating plan to try and get rid of that lovely little muffin top.' Greg blushed again. 'But you weren't to know, of course. I'm sure you've not spoken much this week, have you? Anyway, let's not stand out here in the cold.' She turned with a swish of her long hair and stalked away on thin-heeled boots.

All Maddie could think was that those boots would be making a mess of the parquet floor inside.

I really hope she sprains an ankle. Maddie fought the urge to giggle.

'That's why I asked you bring it,' Greg said with a conspiratorial wink. 'I'm sick of kale smoothies. Come, come. Jemima is having a nap but will be awake soon.'

Maddie followed him inside.

She tried not to notice the changes Gemma had made since she moved in, but her eyes were drawn to each and every one. It was like Gemma had erased Maddie almost completely from the house that she and Greg had bought and renovated together. The antique mirror that used to hang in the hallway, which they'd chosen at an antiques fair in Harrogate, had been replaced by an art deco style mirror that lacked personality in Maddie's opinion. And there were photo frames everywhere. Maddie was sure Gemma added extra ones every time she knew Maddie was coming. It was like there was a frame strategically placed wherever her eye would fall. All those smiling faces leering at her as she walked through the hallway to the open-plan kitchen and dining room at the back of the house.

Eyes following, watching, judging.

Plotting.

The bi-folding doors to the large garden were closed against the chill, but the garden looked as immaculate as ever through the glass. Peter was still doing a good job. A tiny handprint smudged the glass in the bottom corner. Maddie zoned in on it, momentarily fascinated.

'Glass of wine or prosecco for you, Mads?' Greg was saying.

'Um, prosecco, thanks. I brought a bottle with me – and there's something small here for Jemima.'

'Oh, how kind of you. I'll take it,' Gemma said, holding out her hand.

'Well, if you don't mind, I'd like to give it to her myself.'

Gemma's eyes narrowed, but she spun away, saying, 'Of course. But she's sleeping now.'

'I have this card for you… to say thank you for the flat-warming gifts,' Maddie said to her back. She laid the card on the kitchen counter as Gemma flashed a cold smile over her shoulder.

'How are you settling in?'

'Fine, thank you. I've been getting to know the woman who lives upstairs, Jade. She has a son, Ben. He's three.' An ill-disguised look passed between Greg and Gemma. 'The other two in the building I don't really know yet, but there's an elderly lady opposite me and a guy who works in computers upstairs who I met briefly. He seemed nice.'

'And is the flat ok? Do you need anything?' Greg asked.

Gemma still had her back turned, but Maddie noticed it stiffen. 'I'm sure Maddie has everything she needs, babe,' Gemma said.

'Yes, thanks, Greg. You've been a huge help. And thank you for the sunflowers. My favourite – you remembered.'

He froze, his eyes flicking to Gemma.

'Flowers? What flowers?' Gemma spun around, her eyes wide and her mouth forming a thin line that was a far cry from a smile.

'I thought Maddie would like some colour in her flat, you know, to make it more homely as she settles in.'

'Well, you have been spoilt by both of us, haven't you?' This time she showed her teeth, like a dog growling a warning.

'I have indeed – and it means a lot, so thank you.'

Greg exhaled and waved away her gratitude while handing her a glass of prosecco.

Silence landed heavily between them. Greg busied himself with opening a bottle of beer.

'Get a glass, Greg. Don't drink out of the bottle,' Gemma said. She pulled on a pair of oven gloves. She could make even that look sexy. Maddie looked away.

'How is Jemima? She must be getting so mobile now,' Maddie said to Greg.

'Yes, she's crawling, so getting into all sorts of places that she shouldn't.' Pride puffed out Greg's chest. 'She'll be awake soon and you'll see for yourself how she's keeping me on my toes.'

Maddie swigged at the prosecco, feeling the bubbles tickle her nose. 'Can I help with anything, Gemma?' She was clattering pans and stirring things briskly.

'No, no, you sit still. You're a guest in *our home*, after all.'

Maddie's jaw tensed.

'Yes, and it's lovely to have you,' Greg added a little too quickly. 'We should make this a more regular thing. Maybe every weekend. Cheers!' He raised his beer bottle in the air.

Gemma's hand stilled over the gravy, then resumed stirring but with extra vigour. Gravy slopped over the edge of the pan.

Maddie smiled sweetly at Greg and tapped her glass to his bottle. 'Cheers! Here's to families, whatever shape they come in.'

Gemma turned towards them and said pointedly, 'I would join in the toast, but I'm not drinking at the moment. Greg and I are trying for another baby.'

The room swayed in front of Maddie for a split second. 'Oh,' she said.

Greg glared at Gemma before saying, 'Um, yes, I was going to tell you over lunch. It would be lovely to have a brother or sister for Jemima.'

Maddie swallowed more prosecco. 'Yes, it would.'

Gemma threw out a triumphant smile and turned back to her pans, just as a wail erupted from deep in the house.

'Oh, speak of the devil! Jemima is awake,' Greg said in delight and trotted out of the room.

The air filled with a leaden silence in his absence. Gemma was still standing at the oven, stirring her gravy. She was wearing skin-tight white jeans and a loose-fitting beige roll-neck jumper, and Maddie wondered how she wasn't getting brown splatters on her jeans. She found herself fascinated by this – the arrogance in knowing that you wouldn't spill on yourself, that your baby wouldn't wipe a sticky hand on your pristine thigh, that nothing would ruffle your perfect image. Maddie doubted she would ever have that kind of confidence.

Gemma must've felt Maddie staring because she spun around again. Maddie blushed and rearranged the look of distaste on her face.

'You know,' Gemma said, 'I'm so pleased you're finally in your own flat. It's nice that we can all move on from all that... unpleasantness of last year, don't you think? I'm sure you're keen to get on with your life, make a fresh start.'

She made it sound like a wardrobe refresh. Maddie frowned at her. 'Well, I wouldn't say it's as easy as that.'

'Oh, no, of course not. But Greg was just saying last night how pleased he is to see you so independent after all this time. You two were together a long time and it must seem strange to now be on your own, master of your own destiny as they say, but also such fun.'

'I guess it is.' Maddie's teeth were clenching painfully.

'Of course, we are always here to help, but you know what Greg can be like. He's too nice for his own good.' How anyone could be too nice was beyond Maddie. Gemma continued, 'Having him hovering over you and dropping everything to come and help you probably won't be beneficial for either of you in the long term, would it? Just delaying the inevitable really.' She paused. 'You look tired – are you eating ok? Today should help, fill you up. It must be so difficult trying to cook for *one* person.'

Maddie could hear Greg babbling to Jemima down the hallway and she wanted to shout out to him to tell Gemma to stop, to come and rescue her. Gemma's words might seem harmless to anyone else, but to Maddie each one was a tiny poisonous dart piercing her brain.

'Anyway, I'm pleased you're making friends. Makes all of this easier, doesn't it? And with us trying for a new baby, Greg will have less time than ever soon, so a good opportunity for all of us to loosen the ties a bit, don't you think?'

Maddie got to her feet. 'This isn't like ripping off a plaster, you know.' Her voice sounded shrill. 'I can't just forget and move on, no matter how much you might want me to. I not only lost a husband, I lost a best friend and the chance at a family too.'

'There, there, Maddie. Don't go getting yourself upset.'

'You think you have it all figured out, don't you? Well, I promise you this, one day I'll—'

'Here she is!' Greg came back into the kitchen, then paused. 'Everything ok?'

'Yes, fine. Gemma was just telling me that I look tired and thin.' She was still glaring at Gemma.

Greg looked panicked, his eyes flitting from Maddie to Gemma and back again. 'Well, it's been a stressful time for you, for everyone... Say hi to Aunty Mads, Jemima!'

The tiny little girl in Greg's arms was watching Maddie

with big blue eyes, her blonde curls framing her little face like a cloud, and Maddie melted. 'Hey there, baby girl.'

She reached out and took her from Greg, ignoring the annoyance on Gemma's face, and breathed in her warm, vanilla innocent baby smell.

This was what made her feel complete.

Greg looked around the table, feeling a warm glow of contentment. In fact, it wasn't just contentment. He was feeling smug. He felt like he had in fact achieved the impossible. After what seemed like years of getting it completely wrong, he was finally getting something right. He had his girlfriend, his wife and his daughter all sitting at the table, eating together and not stabbing each other with the cutlery. He sat back in his chair, his hands on the table, and surveyed the tableau playing out in front of him.

Gemma sat at the other end of the table from him and God, she was beautiful. Ok, so right now her lips were pursed like a cat's bum and she was clearly very tense, but even on edge, she turned him on. He wouldn't ever admit out loud that that may have been a factor when he had hired her all those years ago, but it was nice to have something pretty to look at when he was at work. Especially back then, when things with Maddie weren't going so well and there were days when his wife wasn't even getting out of bed, when she wore pyjamas or stained tracksuit bottoms day in and day out.

Of course, the affair was never planned. In fact, he would proudly tell anyone if asked that he'd avoided being alone with Gemma for ages. But she could be quite single-minded when she wanted to be and she eventually wore him down. Yes, she was beautiful – not exactly good at her job in the beginning, but then he could forgive her that. Maddie used to wonder why he persevered with her as his PA when he seemed to be clearing up her messes more than anything else, but it was like she had put a dazed spell on him.

Of course, that beauty was expensive to maintain – his bank account was hammered regularly by hairdressers, spa appointments, make-up purchases and God knows what else in order to keep her looking a million pounds, but she was worth it.

He looked to his right where Maddie was sitting gazing at Jemima in her highchair. His heart fell then, but only because he still loved her – or at least the girl she was before everything. The girl that had his back, fought his corner, laughed at his jokes. He remembered the countless evenings drinking red wine and discussing politics and socioeconomics, or curling up on the couch and watching films that made them laugh or cry. All things he didn't do with Gemma. He and Maddie had been inseparable for so long. He looked at her now with the fine lines on her face and the flecks of grey in her hair. The last few years had aged her, but ultimately she was still Maddie – another woman he couldn't say no to. To be perfectly honest, Maddie was a much nicer, warmer and kinder person than Gemma, who had a coldness to her and a selfishness. The Maddie of old had wanted to help people, always saw the best in them, often misplaced, and yet she had never seemed to catch a break herself.

He hoped that the old Maddie was still in there, that the last few years hadn't changed her irreversibly. There'd been some things that she'd done that had worried him; he hoped that was all behind them now.

Maddie was pushing her food around her plate, a look of poorly disguised displeasure on her face. He could almost hear what she was thinking and wanted to laugh out loud. Gemma was a terrible cook and today was no different. She had wanted to do some vegetarian bake of sorts that involved kale and lentils, but he had convinced her to make a traditional roast, blaming it on Maddie being a meat-lover, but in actual fact he couldn't face any more of her plant-based torture. He knew he had to get back into shape if he wanted to keep a woman like Gemma interested – God knew he was punching above his weight – but he couldn't take much more of it. He gagged when he thought about soya milk and the flatulence from all the vegetables and lentils was getting embarrassing at the gym. He'd started sneaking out to buy takeaways at lunchtime and binning the evidence before he got home. If Gemma found out, she'd kill him, but his bloody nut allergy made it really difficult to find anything even vaguely nice to eat that didn't include a deadly ingredient and he was starving all the time.

Then there was Jemima. She sat next to him in her highchair, playing the drums with her spoon and giggling. She was his entire world. For a while he'd thought he would never be a father. In fact, he had resigned himself to that fact. Of course, Maddie never gave up hope and that was what ultimately drove them apart. Maddie would've been enough for him, but he wasn't enough for her.

When Gemma told him she was pregnant, his first thought was shock and fear. In fact, he threw up a little in his mouth. Then very quickly afterwards came the excitement, followed by fear again at having to tell Maddie. He vowed then to make sure she was involved in Jemima's life. Ok, so it was a little weird to involve your ex in your daughter's life, but he knew better than anyone how much Maddie had wanted a child and if this was the closest she would get, then he would make damn sure she was involved.

Of course, Gemma had not been keen, to say the least. But on this he wasn't budging. He knew she was spiteful to Maddie when he wasn't around, but he also knew that Maddie could give as much as she got if cornered. He hoped he would never have to pick sides between them because he didn't honestly think he could.

But this, in front of him right now, was an embodiment of having your cake and eating it too.

He smiled again – the proverbial cat who got the cream – and picked up his cutlery to attack the piece of leather on his plate.

Maddie stared at the plate in front of her. The meat was overcooked, the Yorkshire puddings flat and rubbery, and the gravy lumpy, even after Gemma had run it through a sieve. Regardless, Greg was tucking into his plate of food like he hadn't eaten in weeks. Looking at him now, eating was one thing he had definitely been doing. Gemma was right about the muffin top. It would seem all those lentils and avocados were not good for his waistline.

Jemima was sitting opposite Maddie, banging her spoon against the table of her highchair, little flecks of carrot flying off with every exuberant clank of metal on wood. Maddie noticed Gemma flinch every time the spoon made contact and Maddie wondered how long she could stand it before she took the spoon away.

'Jemima, sweetie, too loud,' Gemma said through gritted teeth and snatched it away.

Not very long at all, it would seem.

'Are you still swimming, Maddie? Exercise is always so good for one's mental health,' Gemma said.

'I haven't been lately, but I must get back in the pool sometime soon.'

'Not my thing, swimming – makes me think of verrucas and communal changing rooms,' Gemma said. 'Give me a clean yoga studio any day.'

'Actually, it's lovely to swim at the outdoor pool. It's like swimming in a warm bath and the people are really friendly.'

Silence fell over the table, the only sound the scrape of cutlery and gurgles from Jemima.

'So, tell us more about this woman who lives upstairs, Maddie,' Greg said around a mouthful of burnt roast potato.

Maddie pushed a bit of leathery beef around in the gravy, hoping for lubrication. 'She's... nice. Not the type of person I would normally meet, really.'

'I can't say I've ever met any of your friends,' Gemma said.

'Well, a lot of our friends are also Maddie's friends, Gem,' Greg said.

Maddie ignored the smirk on Gemma's face. She knew that many of Maddie's so-called friends had backed Greg when they split up. It was too uncomfortable to be friends with Maddie, what with how unstable she had been. The

98

sorrow coming off her in waves was quite the repellent socially. She became something to be whispered about deliciously at dinner parties rather than being invited to them.

'Well, it's a good time for you to branch out and meet some new people. I would hate to think you're lonely,' Gemma said.

Maddie pointedly turned to Greg, cutting Gemma from the conversation. 'Jade is nice. A single mum, which must be very hard. The father of her son isn't around, so she does it all herself. And Ben is a sweet kid, very quiet but calm.'

As she was saying this, Jemima was banging another spoon against the highchair table and gurgling, spit bubbles popping on her lips. Maddie smiled at her. Gemma scowled.

'Greg, babe, can you get her a book or soft toy or something? That noise is going right through my head.'

Greg scraped his chair back on the black slate floor with an ear-piercing squeal and started rooting in a box of toys in the corner of the room. Jemima was too far away from Maddie for her to reach out and play with her. Gemma had put her at a safe distance away on the other side of the table, but Maddie smiled and started making faces at Jemima anyway, who giggled and banged the spoon harder.

Greg sat down again and handed Jemima a book about lions, the cover bright with orange fluff like an untamed mane. He calmly swapped out the spoon.

'You're too nice for your own good sometimes, Mads. I'm sure she's great and all that, but don't let her take advantage of you, of your generosity, just because she has a kid,' Greg said.

Maddie stiffened. 'It's not like that. Yes, I think Jade has it quite hard, you know? And I'm happy to help her, but we also have a good laugh when we're together. The other night for instance. Nothing fancy, just a few glasses of wine at hers watching Netflix.'

'I'm glad,' Greg said. 'Sounds like fun – bet I'd have been asleep in minutes though. These days I can't keep my eyes open for very long.' He chuckled.

'Yes, we are both too tired for anything these days. Once we have Jemima in bed, we're lucky if we have the energy to eat before going to bed for a bit of a cuddle – we *always* have time for that, don't we, darling? – and a few hours' sleep before she wakes up for her feed,' Gemma said.

'Well, you look rather energised on it all, Gemma,' Maddie said politely.

'I put it down to yoga every morning and my special green smoothie with antioxidants. I'll give you the recipe if you like. It will brighten your skin instantly, maybe help with some of those fine lines, and give you a new lease of life.'

'It also helps that I do the night bottles so that Gem can sleep,' Greg said. 'I don't mind. It's a lovely opportunity for a cuddle with my baby girl.' He reached out and ran his hand over Jemima's halo of curls and Maddie's heart squeezed.

'You're too good, Greg. Not many men would be so hands-on. You're an amazing father,' Maddie replied softly.

He smiled at her in return. 'Thank you. That means a lot.'

Gemma scraped her chair back, the noise cutting through the moment. 'Is everyone done? We still have Madeleine's lovely pudding to get through and I'm sure you won't want to be getting home too late. Besides, we have bath and story-time to do soon.'

'Oh, Mads, you should stay for that. You could do her story if you like?' Greg said.

Gemma looked like she might implode. It would be so easy to accept Greg's invitation and Maddie was sorely tempted, but she was feeling drained all of a sudden. She said instead, 'Thanks Greg, but I'll head off after pudding.'

'Well, let's top you up with another glass then, while Gem clears the table.' He refilled her glass before she could object.

'I have to drive home though.'

'Oh, nonsense. I'll get you an Uber home and you can pick up your car tomorrow. It's just around the corner.'

'Ok, why not? Gemma, let me help you with the plates and I'll warm up the pudding too. It needs a careful touch so that it doesn't dry out.'

Gemma clattered the plates together unnecessarily.

Maddie followed her impossibly toned arse into the kitchen.

'That was delicious, thank you, Gemma.'

Gemma nodded in acknowledgement as she scraped leftovers, of which there were a lot, into the bin.

Maddie started rinsing the plates in the sink, lowering her voice as she said, 'You know, I'd really like us to be friends if we can. Greg is still a part of my life and I'm not here to get in the way. You two have a family now and I respect that.'

Gemma turned to her, her smile glacial. 'Of course, I'd like that too. But I think it's healthy if we keep some boundaries in place, don't you? Less *confusing* for you. I tell you what,

I have your number. I'll send you that smoothie recipe and if you need any advice or need to talk to anyone, you can talk to me. We all need friends – life is too short, as you well know – but leave Greg alone. He's mine now.'

As the pudding plates were cleared away, Maddie excused herself and headed down the corridor to the bathroom. She'd had more prosecco than she normally would and was feeling unsteady on her feet. The loo was in a tiny room hidden under the stairs and she noticed that they'd repainted it from what was once a citrus yellow to yet another shade of grey. As she sat on the loo, she had the awkward situation of staring straight at a canvas of Greg and Gemma, smiling and gazing at the camera, as though looking straight at her with her pants around her ankles. She got inexplicable stage fright and had to concentrate really hard to pee.

As she walked back along the corridor, she could hear Gemma and Greg talking in low but tense voices. She hung back and strained to listen in.

'She's doing fine, Gem,' Greg was saying.

'Is she? Is she though, Greg? From where I'm standing, she still depends on you for everything. And you are more than happy to oblige. But we need you here. I need you here.'

'I can't just turn my back on her. None of this was her fault.'

'It *was* her fault! It certainly wasn't yours – you've proved that! She's unstable, Greg, you said so yourself. She looks like she hasn't eaten a proper meal in weeks and the way she fawns over Jemima, it's… well, it's unsettling and weird after everything she went through.'

'I want her in Jemima's life. I owe her that at least. Please. She needs friends and I'm the only one she's got. I can't abandon her now.'

Maddie felt cold. Listening to them, the way they were making her sound like damaged goods, a fragile ornament with a crack in it, ready to split open any second, made her fizz with anger. And yet a voice in her head was saying they were right, that it was her fault. Even so, Gemma needed taking down a peg or two. She didn't own Greg. Not yet anyway.

She was about to storm into the room when a little body came crawling into the corridor in front of her. Jemima giggled when she saw Maddie and shuffled forward at quite a pace to reach her. She sat up and reached out, and Maddie lifted her into her arms, all fizzing anger forgotten.

She breathed Jemima in again as she cuddled her, letting Jemima pull on her hair with tiny fists. Maddie wanted to leave with her, run away, grab a bag and board a plane. She could picture herself living in a little village by the sea, a tiny cottage with room just for her and Jemima, where no one could find them. Maybe they'd get a dog and they'd walk it on the beach, throwing a ball with one of those plastic thrower things, then they'd treat themselves to ice cream from a van, parked up by the beach regardless of the weather…

'There you are!'

Greg was standing in front of her. Maddie hadn't heard him approach. She'd been too caught up in her daydream.

'She came to find me, I think,' Maddie said quickly. Her pulse was racing.

'Told you she was quick on her feet these days. Can I get you a coffee or something?'

'No, thanks, I should be going. Leave you two to your evening routine.'

'Really? You're welcome to stay longer.'

'No, no, best I leave you to it.'

He didn't know that she had frightened herself with how real the picture in her head was. How touchable.

By the time the Uber dropped her off, her head was throbbing like a wound. She pushed closed the entrance door to the flats and leant against it for a moment, her eyes closed.

The door opposite her opened and a tiny old woman in a pale pink dressing gown emerged with empty milk bottles in her hands. Her grey hair was permed into tight curls, reminding Maddie of a stereotyped character from old TV comedies with her wrinkled hands and thick, round glasses. The woman pulled up short at the sight of Maddie blocking the way out.

'Oh, hello,' Maddie said with a smile. 'I'm Maddie Lowe. I've just moved in, over there.'

The woman eyed her suspiciously.

The low thud of music erupted from one of the flats upstairs and the woman tutted under her breath in response and stared at the ceiling.

'It's a bit loud, isn't it?' Maddie said.

'She's a nightmare, that one.'

'I can have a word if you like? Ask her to turn it down?'

'You'd do well to stay away from her. She's spiteful.'

She moved towards Maddie, who realised she was still leaning against the door. 'Sorry, let me get the door for you.' She pulled it open and the woman shuffled out in her slippers to deposit the empties just outside the door for the milkman. Maddie waited until she had shuffled back inside before closing the door again.

'Well, it was nice to meet you, Mrs…'

'Aitkens. Peggy Aitkens.' She turned away from Maddie, then said over her shoulder, 'You should be careful who you make friends with around here. There's some rough sorts in these flats.' Her eyes travelled upwards again.

Maddie frowned, decided that a spoonful of sugar might help. 'I'm just over the hall there, so if there's ever anything you need, please knock. I'm happy to help.'

The music upstairs intensified for a moment as a door opened, then slammed shut again, followed by footsteps on the stairs.

The old woman paled, her eyes darting to the stairs nervously, before she shuffled back into her flat. Maddie heard two locks turning and a chain being drawn.

She turned to see Jade rushing down the stairs, her coat on and her hair pulled into a rolled bun balanced on the top of her head like a doughnut. Her face was sporting quite a mask of make-up, complete with painted on caterpillar eyebrows and lipstick that went beyond her lip line. She looked very different to earlier.

'Oh, hey,' Jade said, pulling up short.

'Hi, how's things? Got friends over?'

'Er, no, that's just music... you know...' Jade shifted from foot to foot. 'I'm, er, just going to get milk. I thought I saw you go out earlier?'

'Ugh, yeah, lunch at my ex and his girlfriend's house.' Maddie sighed. 'I got through it.'

'Seriously? That's how you chose to spend your afternoon?'

'I know – but there was prosecco, so that's something. I'm just... tired, I guess, and a little drunk and annoyed.'

'Oh no.' Her eyes flicked to the door.

'Yeah, I mean, besides having to sit through a terribly overcooked lunch with soggy veg and lumpy gravy while my ex-husband fawned over his girlfriend and daughter, you'll never guess what she's just sent me.' As Maddie was climbing out of the Uber, a message alert had come through on her phone. It was a WhatsApp alert saying that Gemma Scott had added her to a group called *Greg's girls*. Maddie showed Jade her phone, ignoring the fact that Jade looked very keen to escape. 'Look at this. His girlfriend has just created a WhatsApp group for me and called it *Greg's girls* and I'm not even sure what to do with that.'

Jade looked at the phone screen. 'For fuck's sake, what a bitch! It's like she's rubbing your face in it.' She rolled her eyes. 'You know, we don't have to kill him. Maybe we can kill her instead.' She took a step towards the outside door.

Maddie laughed. 'I was thinking that same thing earlier and it's very tempting. Anyway, I need to have a bath and shift this headache. I drank too much prosecco and now have to go back tomorrow to fetch my car because I couldn't drive home.'

Jade took a step towards the door, then paused and said, 'I'll come with you to pick up your car tomorrow if you like? Sort of like moral support.'

It might be nice to have some back-up. If Jade met Gemma and saw what Maddie saw, then Maddie would feel justified in hating her as much as she did.

'Sure, that would be great, thanks. Say ten-ish? I'll come up and knock when I'm ready to go?'

'Great. Right, I'm off to the shop.'

'Oh, I just met Mrs Aitkens. She was complaining about the music. Could you maybe turn it down a bit for her?'

'God, she's a miserable cow, that one. A right nosy parker. See ya!'

She rushed out of the building and Maddie realised that she hadn't said if she would turn it down or not. Maybe she did have company over. That would explain the make-up and the fact that Ben wasn't with her. But then why hadn't she just said as much? Maddie felt a little put out that she hadn't been invited to join in with whatever was going on upstairs. Not that she would've said yes, but it would've been nice to be asked. Unless it was a date.

Inside her own flat, the music was a persistent, dull thud, mirroring what was going on in her head. Maddie tried to block it out as she ran a bath. As the bubbles and steam puffed up around her, she typed a message in her new WhatsApp group with Gemma:

Thanks so much for lunch today. It was delicious. Please send my thanks to Greg too.

Maddie x

The reply was almost immediate.

Lovely to have you. Enjoy putting your feet up for the evening. You're so lucky to have your own space. It's soooo chaotic here with little Jem. G x

Maddie still wasn't sure what to make of all of it. In person, Gemma treated her like an annoyance, a mosquito she couldn't squash. And yet now she was trying to stay in touch rather than pushing her away. Was it a case of better the devil you know? Keeping her enemies close? Or just a chance for Gemma to get the occasional jibe in to remind her to stay in her box?

All this analysis was making her head pulse and she didn't want to think about it anymore.

She undressed quickly, flinging her clothes on the bathroom floor, and lowered herself into the steaming bath. She held her breath and ducked under the water, letting it close over her face. She lay still, cushioned, floating, hearing her heartbeat in her ears as her lungs started to strain.

Maddie blinked into the morning light. The sleeping pill she had taken the night before to stop her brain from whirling had left her groggy and heavy. Dribble had dried on her chin and she could feel her hair sticking up because she had crawled straight into bed with it still wet from the bath.

One look in the mirror confirmed that she looked a sight. She took a long shower and wet her hair again, ready to style it into another Gemma-ready do. She refused to turn up to collect her car looking anything other than camera-ready.

Feeling more in control, she headed upstairs to knock on Jade's door. The sound echoed through the cold hallway, which smelled damp and organic today. A door opened, but it was the flat opposite Jade's. Luke's pale face, this time wearing thick glasses, poked out, his dark hair still sticking up in all directions.

'Hi, Luke,' Maddie said.

'Hey.' He stood for a moment, seemingly unsure whether he should come or go, one foot hovering over the threshold. 'Just on my way to check on Peggy downstairs.'

'Oh, yes, I met her yesterday.'

He nodded. 'Right, well, I'd better…' He nodded at the stairs, then hurried off.

Maddie shrugged and knocked on Jade's door again. Eventually it opened and Maddie caught a whiff of what smelled suspiciously like weed wafting through the door. Jade looked initially annoyed and Maddie realised she might have woken her up. She was dressed in a thick pink dressing gown.

'Oh, sorry, did I wake you?' Maddie said, stepping back.

Jade glared at her for a second, then recovered and said, 'No, I was up. Come in.' She shuffled away from the door in enormous sheepskin slippers and Maddie stepped inside. There was definitely a smell and haze of something in the air.

'Do you still want to come with me?'

'Come where?'

'To pick up my car?'

'Oh, shit, yeah.' Her eyes darted around.

'Are you… nearly ready?'

'Give me a minute.' She disappeared into her bedroom. Maddie looked around while she waited. The place was even messier than the other day. Dirty cups littered every surface and there were empty wine and beer bottles and glasses on the coffee table. Maddie sighed and started to gather up some of the dirty dishes.

She heard the rumble of a man's voice in the bedroom with Jade, before the door opened and a huge mountain of a man with coffee skin and bulging muscles walked into the kitchen, pulling a T-shirt over his head.

'Hey,' he said.

'Hey,' she replied. He reached around her to turn on the kettle. He smelled musky and heady, almost overpowering. She stepped away and blushed as he made coffee. 'Want one?' he said with a grin of startlingly white teeth.

She felt like giggling coyly. 'No, thank you.' She tucked her hair behind her ears self-consciously and started wiping down the counters to give herself something to do other than stare at the masculinity parading in front of her.

Jade returned, now dressed in skinny jeans and a T-shirt with little holes in it where the button on her jeans had snagged. She stopped dead at the sight of Maddie in the kitchen with a dishcloth in her hand. Her male friend was stirring his coffee, the spoon clattering against the mug.

'What are you doing?' she said to Maddie.

'Just wanted to help while I was waiting for you.'

'I can do it myself.'

'I know, but sometimes it's nice to have someone else help too. I thought maybe you'd had a big night.'

The man leant against the counter and sipped at his coffee, watching their exchange like he was at a tennis match.

Jade glared at Maddie, who coughed and said, 'It can't be easy being a single mum, doing it all yourself. I'm here to help if I can, you know.'

The man frowned and went to speak, but Jade cut him off with a withering glare. 'Don't you have somewhere to be?'

He tutted, muttered something under his breath and left the room.

Jade turned on Maddie. 'A proper little Samaritan, aren't you?' Her words were clipped.

Maddie wasn't quite sure what was going on. The air in the room was frigid and Jade was standing with clenched fists, as though holding herself back from swinging for Maddie. All because she had washed some mugs and offered her help. 'I'm sorry, I'll go.' Maddie folded the cloth and put it down on the counter.

Behind her she heard Jade exhale slowly. 'No, sorry. You're right, it's not easy. I'm not very good at accepting help. And I am a bit hungover this morning. Deon and me – we drank too much, smoked a bit too, you know.' Her face had softened again, the tension and anger melting away.

'It's fine. I'm sorry if I offended you.'

Jade shrugged.

'I'm off,' Deon thundered from around the corner.

The front door slammed loudly and Maddie heard heavy footsteps pound down the stairs. 'Sorry, didn't mean to chase him off. Is he your boyfriend?'

'Deon? He's just... you know... friends with benefits. He's a lot of fun.' She grinned lasciviously.

Maddie nodded with a knowing smile. 'Ben isn't here then?'

Jade looked away. 'Yeah... no... um, we should go. Where are my boots?'

She dragged a pair of worn-down Uggs from where they were poking out from under the couch and pulled them on over socks that had pictures of llamas on them. One of her bra straps was dangling from her sleeve and her hair was loose around her shoulders. It hung down her back like a sheet, making her look younger. Her face was free of the make-up of last night and Maddie wanted to tell her how pretty she was without it all, that she didn't need it. But instead Maddie said nothing, worrying that Jade would take offence. Then Jade was rolling her hair into a bun and tying it in place with a hairband, and the illusion vanished.

'Right, I'm ready. Let's go,' Jade said. She chucked her phone and keys into a slouchy bag and headed for the door.

'So Ben is getting to see lots of his dad then?' Maddie asked as she followed her out.

'Yeah,' was all Jade said.

They started walking down the street, the air damp on their faces as a fine drizzle fell. Not enough to warrant an umbrella, but enough for Maddie to know her hair would be frizzy by the time she reached the house. Now she was wishing she'd also tied hers up, even though she knew her ears stuck out when her hair was pulled back.

Jade was quiet as they walked, her usual chatter stilled and her mouth gurning as she chewed on the inside of her cheek. Maddie hoped she wasn't still upset at her for cleaning the kitchen. It seemed a petty thing if she was, but some people were funny about stuff like that, as though you were pointing out their failures rather than taking it for what it was – an act of kindness.

'Is everything ok? You're quiet today.'

Jade watched a woman cross the road next to them. The woman was pushing a buggy with a very tiny sleeping baby inside. 'It's nothing. Just a headache. The hangover, like I said.'

There was silence again, then Jade flicked her eyes at Maddie and said, 'That woman... in the park. What was that about?'

Maddie was thrown for a moment. She'd forgotten about that, what with going to Greg's yesterday and seeing Jemima. 'Oh, er, nothing, a misunderstanding some time ago.'

'But she said I should keep Ben away from you. That's a bit weird, don't you think?'

Maddie stopped and turned to Jade, panic illuminating her wide eyes. 'Look, I'm not dangerous or anything, if that's what you think. She got the wrong end of the stick. I just – please don't keep Ben from me. I really like spending time with him, with both of you...' She trailed off, realising how manic and rambling she sounded.

Jade tilted her head to the side, then shrugged. Maddie wasn't sure what that meant.

They carried on walking. Maddie's pulse tapped in her throat. What if Jade stopped her seeing Ben because of what that woman had said?

'I think Ben's dad is going to try and go for custody soon,' Jade said.

'Oh. That's not good.'

'I can't compete with him. I don't have a proper job or anything. I'm on benefits. He would win easily.'

'You don't know that. They usually award these things to the mother and you've been much more of a parent to Ben so far.'

Jade looked at the pavement as she walked, her voice mumbling. 'They don't always – and money talks. I think I need to start putting a different plan in place. You and I need to sort this before it gets to the courts.' Jade reached out, stopping Maddie in her tracks, her fingers pincers on her forearm. A man walking behind them in a crumpled suit had to veer off sharply to avoid walking into them. 'You're my friend, right? You'll help me?'

'Sure, whatever I can do!' At that point, Maddie would move heaven and earth for Jade if it meant she would let her carry on seeing Ben. 'What are you thinking – character references, that kind of thing?'

Jade's eyes were alight now. 'We're going to help each other. We both have a tricky situation that needs fixing. I just need to figure out the details. How we're going to do it.'

Maddie frowned. 'I don't—' Jade's phone buzzed and she reached into her bag to check the message. She typed a quick reply before putting the phone away again. When she looked back at Maddie, her expression was neutral again, like someone had flicked a switch.

'How far is this place?'

'Not much further. Just a couple of streets down here on the left.' They were walking into the more expensive side of Teddington, with its big houses behind high gates, neatly tiled pathways and white wooden shutters.

'Must be nice to live in a house like this,' Jade said, envy dripping from the words.

Maddie looked around, unimpressed. She'd been there,

done it and it hadn't made her happy. 'They're just houses. A big house won't make you happy.'

'I'd like to try and see. Can hardly swing a cat in our flats.'

'Yeah, but houses like these need someone to clean them, don't forget.'

She looked offended again and Maddie wanted to kick herself. 'What are you trying to say? And don't tell me you cleaned your own house? I bet you didn't. You got someone in to do it for you while you sipped at an Earl Grey in your posh conservatory,' she sneered.

Maddie felt chastised, mostly because she wasn't far wrong.

Looking at the houses they were passing now, Maddie realised how all this must look to Jade, how extravagant. She wasn't proud of it, but she also knew she probably wouldn't have it any other way if it was all hers again. It's easy to be selfish when you have everything you could ever want. It's also easy to want more and not appreciate what you already have, like magpies chasing the next shiny new thing. Maddie only realised that when everything she had had was gone. None of it mattered or held any value in the end.

Jade scowled as they walked. Her feet dragged in the Uggs.

'You know, I will help you if I can,' Maddie said, partly to alleviate her own guilt and partly to bring the awkwardness to an end.

Jade stopped again and looked at her intensely. 'Will you, though? Because… I know we've only just met, but I really like you, Maddie.'

She looked so vulnerable to Maddie and she felt wretched for her, her struggles as a single mum, trying to fight against the system to keep her son, trying to keep it all together. Such different problems to her own. So Jade played music too loud and wore cheap clothes. So she liked a drink (and possibly a joint). Who was she harming?

'Me too. Honestly,' Maddie said and pulled her into a stiff hug. She could feel Jade pat her on the back in return.

Maddie coughed and pulled away. 'You know, I'm happy to take Ben any time you want. Maybe take him to the pool – I love swimming and he would probably love paddling around. If you trust me to, that is? I'll keep him safe, I swear.'

Jade thought about it. Maddie held her breath. 'Yeah, ok. Tomorrow. He can go with you tomorrow.'

Maddie was stunned at how quickly she'd agreed. 'Great! Tomorrow it is!' She wanted to hug her again, but smiled warmly at her instead. 'Come on, it's the next house down.'

Jade's eyes widened.

'Don't judge, ok? I've changed a lot since I lived here,' Maddie added hurriedly.

The large gates were open to the road and their feet crunched on the gravel as they approached the house. Maddie's Fiat was still parked where she had left it, but the other cars were gone and the house had an air of abandonment, like it was sleeping.

'Fuuuuck,' said Jade under her breath as she peered up at the house.

'I don't think Gemma is here. Her car is gone,' Maddie said, feeling surprisingly disappointed. She didn't realise how much she really wanted Jade to meet Gemma. Was it because she wanted a partner in crime, someone who would hate

Gemma as much as she did and therefore make her feel better about herself? Or was it to shock Greg and Gemma into realising how low Maddie had stooped to end up hanging out with the likes of Jade? No, that wasn't fair. Sometimes Maddie didn't like the thoughts that bounced around her head. She usually did a good job of keeping a lid on them, but lately all sorts of scandalous ideas kept clouding her brain.

'That's a shame. I wanted to see what she's like – and get an eyeful of that house. Don't suppose you still have your key, do you?' Jade said.

'I do, actually,' Maddie said without thinking.

'Great, show me around!'

'We can't just let ourselves in!'

'Why not?'

'Because I don't live here anymore! We can't snoop around someone else's house. It's illegal.'

'But it used to be your house. Your name is probably still on the mortgage. And you have a key, so we're not breaking in.'

'No, we shouldn't.'

'Yes, we should. We could mess with her a bit. Move some things around or something. A little bit of quiet revenge. Come on, it'll be funny!'

'But she would surely know it was me.'

'Trust me, if she thought you still had a key, she would've asked for it back by now.'

Jade was right. There was no way Gemma would let Maddie keep a key to her palace. And it would be cathartic to mess with her just a little bit.

'Ok, go on then. The spare keys are in my car. I'll get them.'

Maddie unlocked the car and rummaged in the glove compartment for the set of keys. As she went to put the key in the front door, she paused with a sudden attack of conscience. 'What if they've had an alarm fitted since I moved out?'

'Well, it'll go off and we'll leg it. We'll say it went off when we knocked on the door or something.'

'We should probably knock anyway, just in case.'

Jade giggled. 'She's probably watching us right now, wondering what the hell we're doing.'

Maddie knocked on the door, her heart thudding hard in her chest, adrenalin spitting into her veins over something she hadn't yet done. The perfume from the magnolia tree next to the front door was sickly sweet and cloying at the air, making it difficult for Maddie to breathe.

'She's not in,' Jade said impatiently, bouncing from foot to foot. 'Open the door.'

The key wavered in Maddie's hand with nerves. She felt like a criminal, albeit the most middle-class burglar anyone had ever seen with her white Superga trainers and lightning bolt jumper. Maddie looked over her shoulder, almost expecting the police to pull up, sirens blaring.

The key turned and she pushed the door open slowly. Jade shoved past her.

It felt different being there today compared to yesterday when she was invited. It felt deliciously wicked. Jade immediately started to pick things up, examining photo frames and opening the drawers in the console table in the front hallway, like she was looking for something, casing the joint.

'Wow, quite a place,' she said, her head swivelling.

'Yeah, it is,' Maddie said wistfully. She followed Jade as she headed into the lounge. 'We're not going to stay long though. I don't want her to catch us here. She could be back at any moment.'

'Yeah, ok, I'm just looking around.'

The lounge walls were now painted a dark, solemn green against the white woodwork, making it a dramatic but admittedly cosy room. It had been a warm honey colour when Maddie had lived there.

Maddie wanted to trash the place, throw the cushions around, leave marks on the paintwork and scratches in the wood, but instead she trailed behind Jade like a well-trained puppy.

Jade sat on the cream couch, then rubbed herself against the cushions, like she was leaving her scent on the cool leather. This place was off the charts – a dream house by anyone's standards. She looked over at Maddie, who seemed to be lost in a bit of a daze still in the doorway to the lounge, immobile.

'Hey, you ok?'

Maddie nodded. 'Yes, it's just strange being here like this.'

'Do something, it'll make you feel better.' She looked around her at the neat bookcases organised by colour and the alphabetised rows of CDs. Who the hell listened to CDs these days?

'I know, mix up the CDs a bit – that will mess with her mind,' Jade suggested.

Maddie looked at her for a moment, then went over to the CD shelf and pulled a Celine Dion CD out. 'This was

Greg's – he always had an eclectic musical taste,' Maddie said. The CD next to it was Deacon Blue. 'This one was mine.'

Jade sighed and pulled a random selection from the shelf, laid them out on the coffee table and opened them up. 'There, mix them up and put them back out of order. Let yourself go mad.'

Maddie woodenly started to put the wrong CD in each box. The more she did, the faster her fingers worked until Jade could hear her giggling madly.

'See! I told you you'd feel better.'

Jade jumped to her feet and headed through a double doorway into an enormous kitchen that could quite easily fit her entire flat in it.

The room was immaculate. No dishes out, everything packed away, shelves neat. Every countertop was bare and glistening. All mess contained behind a cupboard door. 'Does she do any cooking in here?' Jade said with a curled lip.

'She's not the best cook, so probably not,' Maddie said over her shoulder.

Jade spied a cardboard box by the bin in the utility room. 'There you go – she uses one of those meal delivery services. Spoiled cow,' Jade said. 'I use one of those delivery services too.' Maddie looked at Jade in surprise. 'It's called fish fingers from Iceland!' she added with a snort.

Maddie giggled. 'Gemma is vegan at the moment. It must be killing Greg, although she did serve beef yesterday. She didn't have any of it though. She just ate the potatoes and vegetables.'

'What a waste,' Jade said. Maddie was starting to freak

her out. She was all jumpy and anxious, like she thought Gemma would appear with a baseball bat or something. Jade found it amusing and was messing with Maddie as much as anything else.

She wandered out of the kitchen and headed for the cream-carpeted staircase. It was like something out of a movie, all sweeping and grand up the centre of the room. She padded up the stairs, the thick carpet swallowing her feet. Maddie followed behind her, twitching nervously. 'Maybe we should go. Gemma could be back any minute,' Maddie said behind her.

'Chill, would you?' Jade bit back. Now Maddie was starting to get on her nerves. She was following her like a puppy dog and Jade wished she'd leave her alone for a minute. Jade had seen a lovely silver necklace with a lightning bolt charm lying on the hallway console table downstairs, tossed there absent-mindedly. She could swipe that and the stuck-up cow that lived here probably wouldn't even notice. She probably had loads of them.

Jade went into the main bedroom and threw herself on the perfectly made bed, among the many throw pillows, her feet sinking into the fluffy blanket draped stylishly across the foot of the super king bed. 'Well, this is comfy.' But who the hell needed this many pillows on a bed, just to be tossed on the floor when you got into bed every night? A stupid concept.

Maddie was looking around what Jade assumed used to be her bedroom. Her face was blank, not showing any hurt, anger or anything at all.

'This looks so different now,' was all she said.

Jade wasn't surprised; she'd have found it weird if

Gemma hadn't redecorated, to be honest. It certainly wasn't Jade's taste, all these sterile shades of grey and white. There were photo frames everywhere, smiling faces and sparkling eyes, posing and preening for the unseen camera. Jade rolled around on the bed some more. Gemma had a small pile of novels on her bedside table, mostly romances from the looks of the covers. The top one had a bookmark sticking from halfway between the pages. She opened the book, removed the bookmark and slid it back in three quarters of the way through. Then she turned to the back and carefully tore the last few pages out, before folding them neatly into a square and putting them in her pocket.

She jumped up and started rummaging around Gemma's dressing table. There were lots of little bottles of perfume and jars of creams and potions, half of which Jade couldn't identify as they looked to all be in French. She picked up the nearest glass bottle and spritzed the perfume on her wrist. It smelled floral and strong, making her nose tickle unpleasantly. A lipstick case was standing to attention and Jade opened it, studied the pale hazelnut colour, then smeared it on her lips.

'This lipstick probably costs more than my entire make-up bag put together,' Jade said. 'And it's made to look like you aren't wearing any! Ridiculous!'

Maddie was at the bedside table, holding up a photo frame. It was a family shot of two adults and a baby. They looked happy. Maddie looked like she was going to be sick.

'Let's go. I don't want to be here anymore,' Maddie said.

But Jade was having a great time and didn't want to leave yet.

She sighed. 'Whatever,' she said petulantly. Jade looked around a last time, then had an idea. One last feat of rebellion. A statement, if you will. 'Wait, one more thing before we go,' she said to Maddie.

Jade headed into the ensuite bathroom at the back of the bedroom.

Maddie watched Jade head into the bathroom, but wasn't interested in what she was doing now. She just wanted to get out of here. Her initial flash of euphoria when she was mixing up the CDs had long gone and she was finding it difficult to breathe. Everywhere she went, she could smell Gemma's cloying perfume clinging to the curtains and carpets and bedclothes like a poisonous vapour. She left the main bedroom and wandered down the hall towards Jemima's room where she knew the air would be sweeter.

The room was beautifully decorated in pastel pinks with tulle curtains and stuffed toys everywhere. It had had many different faces over the years, this room. If she picked at the wallpaper on the far wall and peeled away the top layer, she knew exactly how many layers were hidden underneath. She sat on the tiny bed, breathing in the smells of baby powder and nappy cream. Her head hurt and she was exhausted. She curled up on the bed, snuggling into Jemima's pillow, wishing not for the first time that Jemima was hers, that she could snatch her up and run away. Tears rushed at her and she buried herself in the pillow.

Definitely time to go. She got to her feet unsteadily and swiped at her face.

Jade was just coming out of the ensuite bathroom when

Maddie went to find her. She was pulling up her jeans, fiddling with the zip as she walked.

'What are you doing?' Maddie asked.

'Just left them a little present in their now not so fragrant bathroom,' Jade said with a cunning grin.

'You pooped in their toilet?'

'Yip,' she said proudly and stalked from the room.

Maddie hurried after her, horrified, but she had to admit feeling a flare of shocked amusement. It was the idea of seeing Gemma's face when she discovered it. Of course, Greg would get the blame for not flushing, but still, it was kind of funny.

They both headed back downstairs to the front door, with Jade moving a picture frame out of place here and an ornament there as they went. She paused at the console table for a moment and shifted some things around as Maddie opened the front door.

'Come on, let's go,' Maddie said. Jade followed her out and closed the door with a slam.

Maddie unlocked her car and they climbed in, relief flooding over Maddie that her foray into criminality was now over. Just as she started the engine, a large shadow loomed over them and Gemma's Range Rover pulled up beside them. Maddie's breath hitched as she realised just how close they had come to getting caught.

'Oh my God, she's here,' Maddie said, her pulse racing.

'Fuck, that was close!' Jade said.

'Stay here.' Maddie got back out of the car and waved at Gemma as she came over. 'Hi, I just came to collect my car. I knocked but there was no answer.'

'Ok.' Gemma did not seem pleased to see her. She was

dressed in gym gear and held a rolled-up yoga mat in her arms. 'How are you?'

'Fine, fine.'

'You sure? You look a bit flushed.'

'My friend, Jade, had the heater on in the car,' Maddie gesticulated over her shoulder, 'and it was a bit hot for me. Anyway, I'll get out of your way.'

'You should watch that, Maddie. It could be the menopause. You're the right age for it,' Gemma replied. 'I'll WhatsApp you my smoothie recipe later. You should try it. It's great for women of your age – hot flushes can be quite debilitating. Or so I hear.'

Maddie's fists clenched at her sides.

'Thanks, I'll try it. Listen, can I come over and see Jemima sometime this week? Greg said it would be ok.' He hadn't, but she knew he would if she asked.

Gemma physically bristled in front of her. 'It's a busy week for us with her swimming lessons and art classes and things. I'll let you know.'

'Right, well, better get off.' Maddie waved at the back window of Gemma's car and Jemima waved back from her car seat.

Maddie got back in the car and started the engine. As she reversed down the driveway, Gemma was still standing in the same spot, staring after them. Jade wound down the window, leant out, flipped her middle finger at Gemma and cackled loudly.

Maddie shrieked, 'Jade!' She panicked and hit the accelerator too hard, making the wheels skid and squeal in the gravel as they pulled off. 'Oh my God! I can't believe you did that! And shat in her toilet!'

'Well, now that I've met her, I really can't understand why it's not her you would want to kill,' Jade said.

'Oh, don't get me wrong, Gemma is a giant pain in the bottom, but Greg is the one who cheated. Either one would deserve it, honestly.'

Then

'This time will be different. I can feel it,' Greg says to me as we leave the clinic.

I smile and try to join him in his optimism, but I'm struggling. With every miscarriage, a little part of me dies too. Greg is always so quick to hop back in the saddle so to speak, always ready to try again. Like the baby we just lost is that easy to replace.

He convinced me into trying IVF and the doctors are hopeful, considering that getting pregnant isn't the problem.

Staying pregnant is.

I'm tired and I want to go home, crawl into bed, turn my face to the wall and stay there until the baby is full term and ready to come out.

If there is a baby.

It's all I can think about. I try and get on with my day, doing everything required of me – shopping, cooking, cleaning. I have taken a step back from the business and have employed a PA for Greg so that I can take time out to concentrate on this project. I say I have employed one, but it is Greg who insisted. She seems nice, Gemma. Undeniably pretty and she has a lot to learn, makes some silly mistakes, but she's ambitious and she will keep Greg on his toes – and he needs that as he can be quite fickle and unfocused when it comes to the business. All grand ideas and schemes to make money, but not a practical bone in his body. That was my job – to tighten the purse strings, rein him in, burst his creative bubble when he was reaching too far towards the sun.

But my focus is now on a different expansion of Team Lowe. I found that I couldn't concentrate on work for very long, not really caring if someone hadn't paid their invoice for six weeks or whether the order was going out correctly. Greg suggested I take some time off, but instead of relaxing, I find myself trawling the internet looking at nursery ideas, baby names, anything related to a child I haven't had yet and feeling the weight of it all crushing my chest. The nursery has been redecorated after every failed pregnancy because I don't want my child to be haunted by the ghosts of siblings past. Greg just agrees to anything I suggest, despite the cost.

He's good that way.

I can feel tears pricking at my eyes as we climb into the car. I don't want to face another disappointment. But I can't not keep trying. The idea of the family we want consumes me.

I don't want to think about what will happen if I never achieve my dream – or the lengths I will go to make it happen.

I know I will do anything.

6

Maddie hung her house keys on a nail behind the door when they returned to her flat.

'That's a good idea, that is,' Jade says, pointing at the keys. 'I can never find mine.'

Maddie went into the kitchen to find wine, glasses and some crisps or something. The morning's excitement had left her starving. The wine was Jade's idea. 'Somewhere in the world it's five o'clock', she'd said and Maddie could do with steadying her nerves. She still felt twitchy and nervous, like ants were crawling on her skin. She expected her phone to ring at any moment, Gemma shouting at her, accusing her, or Greg telling her how disappointed he was.

Instead, it was Jade's phone that chirped, but Maddie still jumped. Jade was reading the text message and smiling. 'Ben is coming home, so there'll be plenty of time for you to take him swimming tomorrow if you still want to,' she said.

'That's great! You know, I'm happy to babysit any time if you need a night out with Deon or some time for yourself. You just have to ask.'

'Yeah, thanks.'

'You'll have to start thinking about schools soon, won't you? He'll be four before you know it.'

Jade paled. Perhaps she wasn't as tough as she made out as the idea seemed to upset her.

'You'll miss him when he's at school all day, I bet,' Maddie said softly. 'Still, it means you could get a job, which would work in your favour for the custody arrangement.'

'Yeah, I guess.' Maddie handed Jade a wineglass and Jade drank half in one gulp. 'I'm hungry,' she said. 'Let's get Chinese – you got any money? I'm so skint at the minute.'

'Yeah, sure,' Maddie said, the earlier nervous energy replaced by bubbling excitement at seeing Ben tomorrow.

Maddie watched as Jade poured herself another glass of sauvignon blanc. She offered the bottle to Maddie, but she waved it away. Her glass was still full, but Jade was knocking it back. She kept fiddling with a necklace at her throat, a delicate silver chain with a small lightning bolt hanging at the nape of her throat. It was very pretty, not something she would've thought was Jade's taste.

They'd had Chinese food delivered and the empty plastic containers littered the coffee table.

'That is quite a house you had,' Jade said. 'Your Greg does well, doesn't he?'

'He's not mine anymore.'

'Yeah, but I bet he could be if you wanted him. Sounds like he's still very much in the picture.'

'With Gemma having Jemima, that would never happen. He's devoted to Jemima and they're trying for another baby apparently.'

'Why didn't you have one yourself? Unexplained infertility, you said. What's that then?'

Maddie's stomach lurched, as it did every time someone asked why they didn't have a family.

She swallowed. 'We tried. I was pregnant a number of times, miscarried every time. Then we tried IVF, did the whole sex on demand thing, temperatures, ovulation charts, all of it. It became a bit like a business transaction. Greg and I were always so into each other, but after a while it was like my body was failing us and sex was just a means to an end.' She swigged on the wine. 'With every miscarriage, a part of me died too, until there was very little left. But we kept trying.'

'I'm sorry,' Jade said, unexpectedly putting a hand on Maddie's knee. It was hot and heavy, not the least bit comforting, but Maddie let her leave it there.

'It was shit. Harder for me than Greg. I think it's easier for men to move on from these things because it's not their body. Not that he wasn't understanding or didn't grieve because he did – but he had work, friends, a life away from it all, while being pregnant and having a child was my sole purpose and I was so single-minded about it that everything else became unimportant. I didn't see friends. I stopped talking to Greg. It was no wonder he turned to Gemma really.'

'Er, hang on! There's no excuse for him turning his back on you to shack up with that boobed bitch. If anything, he should have been more understanding and stuck by you!'

'I suppose everyone grieves in different ways though. I shut myself off. I was like a ghost and he was lonely. I don't blame him and I wish it could've been different, but it's selfish of me to expect him to put his dream of a family aside because I've got a faulty body.'

'Wow, you really are something, you know that?' Jade said with sudden venom and Maddie recoiled at her aggressive change of tone.

'Tell me what you really think,' Maddie said, diluting the criticism with more gulps of wine.

'I am, because you're making him out to be a saint! He should've stood by you, no matter what, not hopped into someone else's bed at the first sign of trouble. For better or worse and all that!'

'It wasn't the first sign, as you put it. This all went on for years.' Maddie was starting to get angry at Jade – for meddling, for telling her things she already knew but didn't want to hear. But she couldn't be angry at Greg, mostly because she didn't feel much other than sadness when she thought about her marriage. The whole experience of it was cloaked in a thin, grimy layer of disappointment like a lingering bitter aftertaste from a pill. There had been so much promise that it had left a gaping hole when it all collapsed in on itself. All of it had engulfed Maddie for so long that she felt hollow. It took a moment to fall apart, but a lifetime to pick yourself up from it.

'Let's talk about something else,' Maddie said. 'This is a really tough subject for me.' She drained her glass and refilled it straight away.

'No! You need to start standing up for yourself, fighting back! He shouldn't get away with it, Mads. They should both pay. Make them realise that we are not doormats for men to wipe their feet on.' Her voice was brittle.

Maddie knew she was right, but there wasn't much fight in her. She was trying to be more independent and taking baby steps away from Greg, but he kept drawing her in and a part of her still wanted him to.

'It's funny, I never thought I would end up getting divorced from Greg. When I married him, it was very much till death do us part.'

'You said it – till *death* do you part. We can make that happen. We can make them pay without putting ourselves in the frame.' Jade's eyes narrowed dangerously.

Maddie sighed. 'What are you on about?'

'You know what I'm talking about.' She leant forward and Maddie could feel spittle from her lips land on her face. 'We're going to get revenge on Greg and Mark. We agreed. You can't back out now.' Her face was a mask of bitterness.

'We didn't agree on anything.'

'We did! We talked about it! We said that I'd kill yours and you'd kill mine.'

Maddie laughed then.

'Oh God, Jade, I thought you were serious then! You really had me!'

But Jade wasn't laughing. 'I am serious. I need Mark out of the picture before he goes for custody and you need payback – or at least to get your hands on that house again.'

'Don't be silly.' But Jade's face was deadly serious. 'Seriously, this isn't funny anymore. It's twisted. Let's talk about something else.'

'No, I want to talk about this.' Jade got to her feet, the wine in her glass sloshing over the rim onto the carpet.

'Don't you dare back out now! I've already started making plans on how to get Greg out of the picture for you.'

'What?' Maddie's heart was thudding. Maybe she wasn't hearing her properly. Maybe she was drunk already.

Jade loomed over her, her jabbing finger pointing and sharp. 'You will not back out, Maddie! You have to help me. And one good turn deserves another. I don't care who goes first—'

'Woah! That's enough! I want you to leave.' Maddie was on her feet too, the two of them eye to eye.

Jade recoiled. 'What?'

'I said, get out. You've had too much to drink and this conversation is over. It's not funny anymore.'

Jade stared hard at Maddie with eyes like ball bearings. A cold sweat filmed Maddie's skin and for a second she thought Jade was going to lash out at her. She flinched as Jade lunged, but she was just reaching for her bag.

Jade stormed out, slamming the door hard behind her, making the keys on the nail swing like a pendulum.

Only then did Maddie exhale.

Maddie sat propped up in bed, sipping on tea and thinking about her conversation the night before with Jade. The morning sun was weak behind the curtains, but she felt safer in the gloom, less exposed. She couldn't believe Jade was anywhere near serious. She must've just had too much wine and got carried away. *We've all wanted to kill someone at some point when the anger and hurt took over.* It had been a funny day by all accounts, what with breaking into Gemma's house and everything.

She was worried Jade would've changed her mind about Maddie taking Ben for a swim. She'd been so angry and volatile yesterday. This thing with Mark was clearly stressing her out and she wasn't thinking rationally about it anymore. Maddie could sympathise – she'd had moments of irrationality herself over the years when desperation overwhelmed common sense. She needed to be patient with Jade, help her to see that she had options.

She sent her a text to see if her play date with Ben was still on, but got no reply.

She eventually got up and started doing some laundry, but was feeling restless and fidgety, so got dressed for a run. Something she hadn't done in a long time, but she had an urge to feel her feet pounding the pavement, her lungs bursting and her muscles stretching.

She managed half an hour before she realised that her fitness had nosedived. She let herself back into the building just as Mrs Aitkens shuffled from her house to check her post box in the entrance hall.

'Hi, Mrs Aitkens. How are you?' Maddie said, still out of breath.

Mrs Aitkens looked her up and down. 'Exercise will kill you,' she said and shuffled back indoors.

Maddie shook her head with a smile and pulled her key from the zip pocket on her running leggings. Then she noticed the white box sitting at the foot of her door like a present. It looked like a bakery box. She opened it and there was a huge cupcake inside. Red velvet, Maddie's favourite.

At first, she thought it was from Greg because he knew she loved red velvet cake. Then she saw the torn piece of paper inside with one word scribbled in biro:

Sorry.

She opened the door and carried the box inside, feeling conflicted. Should she go and knock on Jade's door? Talk it over with her and tell her she was the one who was sorry for telling her to leave so harshly? For not being patient and understanding what she was going through? She hated knowing someone was upset because of her. And Ben would be home. She needed to see him. She didn't want anything to jeopardise her chance at spending some time alone with him.

She decided to go upstairs before she showered. She took the stairs two at a time, her pulse still elevated from the run. She knocked loudly, but there was no answer.

Luke poked his head out of his door instead. 'She's not in,' he said unhelpfully.

'Right, ok.'

'You ok?'

'Yeah, just been for a run, need to shower.'

He nodded at her. 'Never been my thing, exercise, but each to their own.'

Maddie smiled and turned to head back downstairs.

'Hey, if you fancy a beer sometime… not a date or anything, just it'd be good to… talk.' He scratched his head, looking awkward. 'Well, if you fancy it, I'm here most of the time.' He nodded at her again and retreated back indoors.

Baffled at the offer, Maddie headed back downstairs.

After her shower, she made a strong cup of tea and sat at the table with the cupcake in front of her, her wet hair dripping down her back. She'd forgotten how hungry running could make her. Eating the breakfast of champions today though.

The cake was delicious, moist and soft and sweet with cocoa. *She can't have made this*, Maddie thought. There was no evidence in Jade's kitchen that she cooked anything other than heating up ready meals and shoving fish fingers under the grill.

The cake was finished in a few bites, then she went into the bedroom to dry her hair and get ready to pick Ben up for their swimming session, desperately hoping it would still be on. Jade still hadn't replied to her earlier text though. Should she send another one? Maybe if the swimming session with Ben was off, she could see if Gemma would let Jemima go with her instead.

Half an hour later and Maddie was in agony, all thoughts of swimming forgotten. Her stomach had clenched into an iron fist and waves of nausea were rippling through her, sending cold, sweaty shivers throughout her body. She crawled to the bathroom as her guts cramped. She wasn't sure which end it would come from, but it was inevitable.

Maybe it was the Chinese food yesterday. She'd had prawns while Jade had stuck to a chow mein. The prawns were clearly a big mistake.

She lay on the bathroom floor in between spells of either sitting on or leaning over the toilet, her arms wrapped around her belly and her hot forehead resting on the cold tiles. At one point she felt like she may have dozed off or passed out, she wasn't sure. She had no idea what time it was or how long she had been in the bathroom, but she didn't have the strength to get up.

137

Jade would surely be wondering where she was, why she hadn't called for Ben. Or was she still giving her the cold shoulder? But if she had texted, Maddie wouldn't know because her phone was in the other room. The thought forced her upright and she staggered into the kitchen for a glass of water, desperately searching for her phone, but it wasn't long before she was rushing back to the bathroom.

She was getting worried. She would need to take some nausea and diarrhoea medicine, but knew she didn't have any. There was plenty in her old bathroom cabinet in Greg's house though. But she couldn't call Greg or Gemma. Not this time. This was too humiliating. She didn't want either of them seeing her in this state on the bathroom floor.

So she was on her own.

Jade. She could call Jade. Maybe she would have something she could take or could go to the chemist for her.

Her phone was still in the other room. She managed to crawl her way to the lounge. It lay on the couch like a beacon. She summoned up the energy to send Jade a message through Snapchat.

Minutes later she heard a knock on the door. She was still in the lounge, curled up in a tight, cramping ball at the foot of the couch, a shivering mess with the stench of puke clinging to her.

She limped over to the door and opened it without checking who it was.

'Jesus H. Christ! Look at the state of it!' she heard Jade say, although she was now beyond the point of comprehension. 'Come on, let's get you into bed.'

She felt herself being dragged like a sack along the

corridor to her bedroom, plopped on the bed and the warm duvet flung over her. Then Jade tucked her in like a child, smoothed back her hair and said, 'I'll get you some water, then I need you to take these for your stomach.'

Maddie clenched her eyes shut as another cramp ripped through her. A hand propped her head up and said, 'Here, take these.' She opened her eyes to slits and accepted the small pills from Jade and the glass she was holding out.

Only after swallowing them did she say, 'What are they?'

'Just Imodium – don't worry, I'm not trying to poison you,' Jade said with a laugh.

Maddie managed to say, 'Thanks Jade, you're such a good mum,' before her eyes started getting very heavy. 'Wait,' she said, her eyes popping open again. 'Where's Ben?'

'Don't worry about him. He's fine. Just concentrate on you.'

'I don't think I should take him swimming.'

'You don't say! Another day is fine. Now sleep it off. I'll clean up the bathroom and you'll be right as rain in a bit.'

Something was ripping her apart. Someone had taken a scalpel and was slicing through her abdomen, pulling and tearing, probing and rummaging.

Her baby! They were stealing her baby!

She needed to wake up, shout out, tell them to stop! Her hands pushed out, fingers like claws, ready to scratch and cleave at them.

You can't have him! You can't have him! Archie!

Maddie sat upright, her T-shirt stuck to the cold sweat on her skin and her eyes wide and panicked.

The room was dark, the curtains drawn to the late afternoon light. She was alone.

Then she remembered the cramps, the sickness. Jade had been here. Had she left?

She lay back down, her breathing slowing. The tightness in her gut had loosened and it no longer felt like she was being ripped apart from the inside out. She swung her legs from the bed and took a few tentative steps on weakened legs. She peered into the bathroom. It was immaculately clean, any sign of her earlier illness washed away while the scent of citrus bleach lingered.

She kept a steadying hand on the wall as she headed along the corridor towards the lounge. 'Jade? Are you here?'

The only sign she had been was the box of Imodium on the kitchen counter next to a glass of water. Everything had been cleaned and tidied. Her breakfast dishes were washed and stacked next to the sink and the bakery box had been removed.

A wave of mortification flooded through Maddie. What must she have looked like when Jade arrived? She couldn't really remember what Jade had said or done. It was kind of her to clean up though and she wouldn't be standing here now if Jade hadn't brought her the medication.

She heard a key turn in the door and Jade walked in, carrying a plastic bag. 'Oh, great, you're up! How are you feeling?'

'Better, thanks – well, the cramps have stopped anyway.'

Maddie noticed the keys in her hand. 'Oh, I borrowed

your key from the nail behind the door so that you wouldn't have to get up.' Jade hung the key back where it belonged.

'Um, ok, thanks.'

Jade started unpacking the plastic bag in the kitchen. 'I borrowed some money from your purse to get some stuff for you – bananas, bread for toast, that kind of thing. It will help to settle your stomach. Sit, I'll make you some buttered toast – always works for me when I'm feeling gross.'

Maddie sat on command. She didn't have the energy to process the admission that Jade had helped herself to money from her purse as well as her front door key. 'Thanks so much for looking after me. You didn't have to go to all this trouble.'

'Oh, it's nothing – you'd do the same for me.'

'Where's Ben?'

'He's with a friend.'

A burnt smell filled the air and minutes later Maddie was presented with some charred toast, the butter melting into the black crumbs. 'Here, eat that. It might look burnt, but the charcoal will help settle your stomach.'

Maddie took a timid nibble of the corner. 'Thanks.'

'Go on, get it in ya,' Jade pushed.

Maddie took another bite, not exactly relishing the blackened taste, then put the toast down. 'You know, I think I'll go back to bed. I'm wiped out. But thank you so much for looking after me. I do appreciate it and I had no one else I could count on.'

'Oh, really, it's fine. I can hang out here if you like? In case you need me?'

'No, no, you get back to Ben. I'll be fine – I can text you if I need anything.'

'Ok, if you're sure.' Jade got to her feet. 'Let me know, yeah? And eat that toast!'

Maddie smiled and took another bite as evidence. As soon as the door closed behind Jade, Maddie took the plate of cremated bread into the kitchen and tossed the toast in the bin. She headed back to bed, but paused at the front door to slide the chain in place first.

Then

Everywhere I look I see children that are clearly being neglected. Overlooked, forgotten while their parents focus on work, their social lives, their phones.

Take the little boy over there by the swings, for instance. He has been running around with snot rimming the dummy in his mouth for about ten minutes, his mother oblivious to the germs he is sucking in with every tug on his dummy as she sits and natters away with her friend. She is as thin and shapeless as a French fry and she is guzzling what is probably a skinny frothy caramel something or other from a takeaway cup like it's a drug. Meanwhile, her little angel of a boy is swallowing snot, his head clearly full of a nasty cold. He should be at home, tucked in bed with her reading him stories or snuggling together watching a Disney film so that he can recover, not here, running around a cold and damp playground, sharing germs with the other toddlers like they're sweets from a packet.

Sometimes I am flabbergasted at how women like these have been given such a blessing as these beautiful little creatures when they clearly do not deserve it.

A little girl has tripped over her own feet not far from me

and she is crying. I can see her knee is grazed, the skin red raw and bleeding. I can't see the mother anywhere.

Another victim of neglect.

I get up and stride over to the girl. 'Hey there, Princess. Did you fall over? Have you hurt yourself?'

The little girl is sitting in the dirt, peering at her knee. Her big brown eyes are glassy with hurt and tiny pebbles of water have collected along the edges of her long eyelashes. She looks down at her bleeding knee, her lip trembling, and nods her head.

'Oh, don't you worry about that. We'll clean you up and then you'll be as right as rain. You know, a little scrape here and there is a sign that you've had a good day. You've done something unusual, extraordinary, dangerous even. Don't you think?'

The girl is peering at me like I'm an alien with two heads. She hasn't run away though, so she clearly hasn't had the *don't talk to strangers* conversation yet.

I lift her gently from the ground, brush the dirt from the back of her skirt and lead her over to the bench I have been sitting on. I look around again – still no mother has made herself known.

There is a café on the other side of the playground with a small bathroom where I could clean her knee and wipe her face.

'What's your name, Princess?'

'Mia,' she whispers with a hiccup.

'Where's your mummy?'

She shrugs. A tiny movement, but I'm sure I see it.

'Will you come with me to the café over there so that we

can clean up your knee? Maybe we can see if they have any cookies too? To make you feel better?'

She doesn't respond, but takes hold of my hand when I reach out to her. I look around as we walk away from the noise and bustle of the playground towards the café. Are there any women here who look like they might belong to this little angel? A childminder who has her hands full with a few children maybe? Or a working mother too busy answering emails to notice her daughter has hurt herself? There are a few women that could fit the bill, either staring at their phones or chatting to friends, another fawning over a tiny dog as it does a rather runny poo on the grass just beyond the fence that cordons off the play equipment from the rest of the park.

The girl is trotting next to me, still sniffing. Her pink shoes are freshly scuffed at the toe from when she fell. I push open the door of the café and walk straight past the tables, weave around the many pushchairs and beyond the queue of people waiting to pay for their beverages, heading instead to the bathrooms at the back of the room.

The bathroom is empty except for one cubicle with the door closed. The air smells chemical, like it has just been doused in bleach. Someone inside the cubicle is loudly praising a small child for not weeing in their pants for a change, saying in a sing-song voice that he's *such* a big boy now, that mummy is *incredibly proud* of him.

I pull a paper towel from the holder on the wall and wet it with some cold water.

'Now this may sting a little, Mia, but I know you'll be a

brave girl. But if you need to squeeze my hand, you can do that, ok?'

Mia stares at me, nods a little again. Her nose is still running and the beads of tears have stuck to her cheeks like dew drops.

I bend down and dab at her knee, but Mia stands still and straight, not moving a muscle.

'Wow, you are a brave girl, a warrior like Mulan, I think.' I clean away the mud and gravel stuck to the graze. 'Do you know Mulan, the Disney princess? I have the DVD at home.' Behind me, the door to the cubicle opens and a little boy in *Thomas the Tank Engine* wellies bursts out, bumping into me and almost knocking me over.

'Slowly, Cameron!' his mother says as she heaves her bulk around the toilet roll dispenser to emerge from the small cubicle. I can't help but think it must've been a tight squeeze in there for both of them. 'I'm so sorry, he's just so enthusiastic about *everything*,' she says with pride. 'Oh, you poor little thing. Did you fall?' she says to Mia. 'Oh well, Mummy will make it better. That's what mummies are for, after all,' she says delightfully.

I don't correct her. Instead, I say with a voice matching her in pride, 'She's being very brave, aren't you, Mia? She's a tough cookie, this one.'

The little boy is splashing more water on the floor than on his hands. The woman smiles at him in glee, then bundles him from the bathroom.

'There,' I say to Mia. 'That's all clean. Now, let's blow your nose and see if we can get you that cookie, shall we?'

I grab some toilet roll from the cubicle and hold it to her nose. 'Blow,' I say and she does so on command.

I wipe the tears away, then take hold of her hand again to lead her from the bathroom. Her hand is tiny and warm in mine. It feels right, like it moulds perfectly. The queue at the tills has lessened and there is now only one elderly woman in sensible walking shoes waiting for her polystyrene cup of tea. She smiles at us and I smile back, still holding tightly to Mia's hand.

'What would you like, Mia? Those chocolate chip cookies look yummy, don't they? And those ones over there have Smarties in them! Would you like that?'

She raises her hand and points to the Smarties cookie as the old lady moves away.

'What can I get you?' says the bespectacled woman behind the till.

'We'll have that cookie there, please,' I say and wink at Mia.

As I pay, I hear a commotion outside. Voices are raised and it sounds like a woman is shouting hysterically. I shrug at Mia and lead her from the café as she munches happily on the enormous cookie, the graze on her knee now forgotten.

A small group has gathered around the gate to the playground, all focused on a woman in tight jeans and a huge sweatshirt that swamps her small frame. It's the woman I saw picking up dog poo. I also recognise among the group the large woman from the bathroom, who is talking animatedly and then turns to point at the café. She freezes when she sees me. 'That's her!' she says loudly.

The entire group turns towards me, like a pack of lions, their faces feral.

'MIA!' the sweatshirt lady shouts and runs towards us.

'Mummy,' Mia says and breaks into the first smile

I've seen since I picked her up out of the dirt. It lights up her entire face like a spotlight and I think to myself how beautiful and pure she is. She breaks loose from my hand and toddles to meet her mum, the cookie still clasped in her hand.

I watch her go, my heart in freefall as our connection is broken, my hand immediately feeling empty.

The woman scoops her into her arms, hugging and kissing her, tears streaming from her eyes in an undignified display of emotion. I want to tell her to calm down, that she'll frighten Mia, but I am rooted to the spot, this openly demonstrative display paralysing me in its rawness. The love of a mother for her child.

I don't notice when the group of bystanders gathers around me en masse, blocking me from leaving. A pack of wild dogs, ready to tear me limb from limb.

But I can't tear my eyes away from Mia.

Greg paces around the windowless room, his stride shortened by the lack of space around the bare metal table.

'What the fuck were you thinking, Maddie? Were you even thinking?' His hair is sticking up where he has run his hands through it while waiting for the police to finish interviewing me.

I look at the bare grey walls, still confused at why I am even here, in a police station, being accused of trying to kidnap a child. Me. Of all people.

My throat is rubbed raw from trying to explain that I wasn't trying to *take* Mia. I was trying to help. I was looking after her. Her mother wasn't there.

The woman with the small dog was her mother, but had been distracted by the dog and its runny poo, worrying because she only had one poo bag left and the dog was especially active in the toilet department today.

But how was I supposed to know that? All I saw was a little girl with a sore knee in some distress. All I did was take her to the bathroom.

Apparently, the mother had panicked when she couldn't find Mia and the other mums had spent the whole time we were in the café calling her name and searching the vicinity for her.

'And you bought her a cookie? That just looked like you were trying to bribe her! What if she had some sort of intolerance or allergy? If the cookie had nuts in it or something? You can never know with kids these days – they all have an allergy to one thing or another. You of all people should be aware of that! Look at me! She could've ended up in hospital! Or worse!' He is shouting and I flinch at his words as they ricochet off my face.

'She also could've been fine. She *was* fine. All I did was clean her up, wipe her tears and buy her a cookie. That's not a crime,' I say quietly. I'm tired. I want to go home.

'It *is* a crime, Maddie! Walking off with someone else's child without telling them is tantamount to kidnap! They have a witness who heard you say you were taking her home to watch *Mulan*, for fuck's sake.'

He flings himself into the other chair in the room, suddenly deflated, looking like a man with the weight of the world on his shoulders. He starts to run his hands through his hair again, making even more of it stand on end. 'Jesus, Maddie. This is getting out of hand.'

'It was a misunderstanding, that's all. I was trying to do a good deed. She was alone and scared and hurt.'

'Maybe you need hel—'

The door to the room opens and the policewoman who has been grilling me for the last few hours walks in, but doesn't close the door behind her this time. 'You're free to go, Mrs Lowe. Mrs Marshall does not wish to press charges at this stage.'

'Thank you,' I say quietly. 'How's Mia?'

I can feel Greg's eyes burning into me.

The policewoman narrows her eyes and says, 'She's gone home now with her mother, *where she belongs*. Perhaps next time you see a child in distress, you should stay where you are and call for help rather than taking matters into your own hands.'

The drive home is awkward to say the least. Greg is still angry with me. He just can't seem to get his head around what I did. When I asked him what he would've done, he said he would've asked the other women if she belonged to them and if no one claimed her, he would've called 999. Like she was lost property, a misplaced purse rather than a vulnerable child.

But this is the problem with us these days. We are on different wavelengths. He has accepted that we may never have children. With each failed attempt, he seems to want it that bit less. He used to be as excited, as determined. Now it feels like he is just going through the motions for me.

Meanwhile, I just want it more. It is all I think about. Everywhere I look, I see cherub faces, can hear laughing and playing, smell baby shampoo and Sudocrem, like a drug I can't avoid. Everyone seems to be pregnant or pushing a pushchair, complaining about exhaustion and lack of sleep, wiping sick off their clothes – and I want all of it. All the messy, boring, tiring lot of it.

I suggested adoption to Greg the other day and he point blank refused to consider it, said he didn't want someone else's baby. If he couldn't have ours, he would rather go without.

How could he not even consider it?

Surely any child is better than none at all?

I can still feel the warmth of Mia's hand in mine, almost taste the salt of her tears on my tongue.

That can't be our future.

I won't let it.

7

Someone was knocking insistently on her door.

Maddie had been in bed for what felt like forever. She looked at the clock on her bedside table: 10.15 a.m. Yesterday's stomach bug was thankfully over, but she was weak and exhausted. She wanted sleep and lots of it, and she was determined to recover without any more help from anyone. Jade had been right the other day in telling her she was playing the victim too much. She was supposed to be getting back her independence and at the first sign of trouble, she'd had to call in reinforcements.

Pathetic.

So no more help from Jade. Or Greg. Time to stand on her own two feet.

Actually, she was beginning to enjoy living on her own. Her own little safe haven, she was no longer waking up in the middle of the night, listening in case every creak was a step in the hallway, an intruder coming towards her. No longer cooking huge amounts of food, forgetting that she was on her own. She'd even starting thinking about unpacking the remaining boxes in the spare room so that she could turn it into a home office, maybe start a small business bookkeeping from home, finally accepting the fact that she should step away from Greg's business permanently.

There was a jigsaw in that room that was begging to be started. Very rock and roll of her, but the idea of quiet evenings in front of rubbish telly with a jigsaw for company was comforting. She could imagine Jade's face if she saw her doing a jigsaw!

Then again, there were other boxes in that spare room that she didn't want to unpack, that were still too painful to open.

The knocking started up again, then Maddie's heart lurched as she thought she heard the sound of a key in the lock and a thud as the chain pulled tight, barring entry.

'Maddie? Maddie, are you in there? Are you ok?' Jade's voice was rattling and hoarse, her cigarette habit stripping her voice of its melody. 'I'm worried about you.'

Maddie wanted to weep. She just wanted to be left alone, but she figured she owed it to Jade to tell her she was feeling better, especially after she came to her rescue.

Maddie inched from her bed and threw her dressing gown on over the T-shirt and knickers she'd been sleeping in.

As she approached the door, she saw it was closed and that Jade was peering through the letterbox. Maddie glanced up and saw her key swinging from the nail where it was supposed to be. It must've been the snap of the letterbox she had heard.

She had a feeling that if she actually saw Jade, she would end up being persuaded to let her in.

'Maddie! Come on, I'm worried!'

'I'm fine, Jade,' Maddie called back. 'I'm just trying to sleep it off.'

'Let me in – I'll keep an eye on you.'

'I think I'd rather be on my own for a bit. I'm just going to sleep for the rest of today.' Maddie felt treacherous as she said it. She could already feel her resolve weakening the longer she talked.

'I don't mind, I just… I don't want to be upstairs on my own. Ben isn't there and it's a bit lonely.' Her voice was thin and needling.

Maddie scrunched up her face and took a step forward, then paused again.

No, Maddie. You can say no.

She clenched her hands into fists, her fingernails digging into her palms, before she spoke again. 'I'm sorry to hear that, but I'm really not up to company. I need to go back to bed. I'll call you when I'm back on my feet and see how you are, ok? Maybe we can go out for a bit – go for a walk or something. It might make us both feel better. Or I could come over and hang out with you and Ben tomorrow.'

She waited, her breath held, to see if Jade would carry on. For a few seconds there was nothing, then Jade said, 'Fine, whatever,' and the letterbox slammed shut.

Maddie exhaled, then headed back to bed. She pulled the covers up, but her nerves were jangling. She kept running the conversation over in her head, feeling more and more guilty about airing Jade.

It was done now though.

*

It was the smell that woke her this time.

At first she couldn't place it. She just had a sense that something was wrong, wafting over her in gentle waves and lapping at her throat. She sat up and rubbed her eyes, confused. Then, as she became more conscious, she realised why it was so familiar and yet so out of place.

Gas.

She looked at the clock. 10.10 p.m. She'd been asleep for almost twelve hours. Her head felt fuzzy, her tongue thick. She shrugged into her gown and went into the kitchen for a glass of water.

The smell wasn't obvious in the kitchen. She sniffed at the air near the oven to be sure and checked all of the gas rings in case she'd left one on by accident, but the smell had gone. Maybe it had been left over from a dream she was having.

She carried her glass of water back into the bedroom. The smell returned, stronger than before. Sniffing like a bloodhound, her nose led her to the air vent high up in the corner of the room. It was coming from there.

Maddie's breath caught. That vent led to Jade's flat above. Was the gas coming from there?

Was she just cooking something? Or was there a problem? A malfunction? What if she hadn't noticed and she was lying unconscious? If Ben was away with his dad, she would be alone and no one would find her until it was too late.

Maddie remembered how tiny Jade's voice was last night, how lonely she said she was. How irrational she had been acting. Maybe not being found was what she wanted.

Oh God, had she done something stupid?

Even worse, what if Ben was there and he couldn't wake Jade? He'd be frightened, confused.

The thought propelled Maddie into action. She slid her feet into her slippers, unchained the front door and took the stairs two at a time to the next floor, not caring that her dressing gown was flapping open.

'Jade! Jade! Open up!' She banged hard on the door, her hands in fists.

Luke stuck his head out of his flat. 'Everything ok?'

'She's not answering! I can smell gas! Do you have a key?'

'Er, no! Why would I? Should I call 999? I could try breaking the door in.' Maddie considered his thin frame and figured she'd have better luck than him.

Maddie banged harder on the door. 'Jade! Are you ok?'

She heard rustling and movement, then the door opened, but with the chain still engaged. Jade peered through the crack.

'What's going on?' she said.

'I can smell gas. It's coming through the vent in my bedroom. Are you ok?' Maddie's voice was high-pitched with stress.

'What are you on about?' Jade looked confused and Maddie realised she may have misread the situation, talked herself into a frenzy.

'Can you not smell it? Gas? Open the door, let me check.'

'No offence, Maddie, but it's not a good time right now.' Jade went to close the door on her.

She heard Luke exhale behind her and mutter, 'She seems fine, as ungrateful as ever,' before he headed back inside.

'Look, I'm sorry about earlier. I know you were feeling low and I should've been there for you. I was still feeling weak and exhausted, but that's no excuse. I should've let you in. But please! Don't do anything silly. We can find a solution. We'll work this out. Together.'

Jade's face seemed to fold in on itself. 'Do you mean that?'

'Of course I do! There is nothing so big that we can't fix it. I'm on your side. I want to see you and Ben happy, living your best lives. Come on, open up. Let's talk.'

Jade sighed heavily and closed the door. Maddie heard the chain being withdrawn and it opened again.

They sat on the couch, each wearing dressing gowns and slippers, and sipping at mugs of tea like two grannies in a care home.

The smell of gas had gone now. Maddie had found one of the burners on Jade's oven had been left on. Jade claimed not to have noticed, but the smell was unmistakeable once she was inside Jade's flat.

When Maddie questioned Jade, she denied everything, put it down to not concentrating when she had heated up some baked beans earlier. Funnily enough though, there were no pans or dirty plates in the sink. She could've already washed them, but from past evidence, Jade was not one for cleanliness. The pizza box stashed by the bin was more likely to have been her dinner.

Still, Maddie didn't press the matter. Jade was clearly in a vulnerable place and Maddie didn't want to push her.

Maddie put her mug down. 'Better?'

Jade shrugged. 'It's just hard, you know?' Her voice was low and trembling.

Maddie reached out for her hand. 'I know. Trust me, I've had some struggles of my own in the past and I've... been to some dark places. Sometimes it's hard to see past the mountain in the front of you, but there is light on the other side.'

'Did you swallow a self-help book or something?' Jade scoffed.

Maddie blushed. 'Sorry, it's just... I'm trying to help, that's all.'

'But you don't know what it's like, do you? You don't have kids.'

Maddie shrugged. 'No, but I know what it's like to want to control a situation and feeling helpless when it's taken out of your hands. I know what desperation feels like.' She swallowed. 'And I know what it feels like to not want to carry on.'

'What happened to you?'

'I don't think I can—'

'But it would help me to know. It would help me to feel understood if I knew what you had been through, not so alone.'

Maddie wasn't sure if she was capable of sharing her story.

Annoyance flashed over Jade's face. 'Ok, well, if you don't want to talk about it...' She stood up abruptly, took Maddie's half full cup from her hand and stalked into the kitchen. 'I just thought you wanted to help, that's all. I thought you were my friend.'

'I am, but it's not as simple as that. It's... really painful for me. One day I will tell you. But not today. I haven't got dressed for two days, I still feel awful and I don't think I have the resolve to tell that story right now.'

Jade nodded, but there was hurt painted in bold colours in her eyes. 'Fine.'

Maddie got up too. 'Listen, I meant what I said. I am on your side and I want to help. I know I tell you to talk to me, that it will help, and I should be listening to my own advice, but know that I am here if you do want to talk to me about how you're feeling. I don't want you to feel alone.'

'Thanks, I'm fine now. You can go. I know you're not feeling well.' Her lips were pulled into a straight line and her words were clipped.

Maddie watched her for a minute, but Jade had closed up.

'Ok, but why don't I take Ben out tomorrow? Give you a break?'

'He has his music class tomorrow morning at 10 a.m.'

'Ok, well, I could take him? I should be fine by then. What do you say?' There was a terse nod, but no eye contact.

'Great, I'll see you then.'

Maddie let herself out.

Jade watched Maddie go. That went well. A twist of the gas ring, a subtle waft with a gossip magazine towards the air vent and she had created the panic she wanted. She hadn't been entirely sure it would work, but it had been worth a try.

More than anything, she'd been curious to see how – or if – Maddie would react.

And boy, had she obliged! The look on Maddie's face when she thought Jade had tried to gas herself was priceless.

Interesting.

Jade had a sense that Maddie was slowly losing interest, that her initial urge to build a friendship was cooling as she became more comfortable with living on her own. She was talking about starting a business and all sorts. That would mean she would have less time for Jade – and that couldn't happen.

Jade felt like a spider on a web, inching towards her prey. She knew Maddie would be downstairs now, feeling terrible at freezing her out, wishing she had opened up and worrying that Jade would try something else. Another cry for help.

As if that was Jade's style. Maddie didn't know her well at all.

There was a lot at stake here, but all Maddie needed to see was what Jade wanted her to. On the other hand, Jade needed to know Maddie pretty well, most importantly if she was as innocent and trustworthy as she came across, but there was still so much Maddie was not revealing. It made Jade nervous, which was a feeling she was not familiar with. She liked to be in control, to know how things would pan out.

This was not comfortable territory for Jade.

Something had clearly gone on in the past that Maddie was holding onto tightly. Jade wanted to know what it was.

Maddie was tired.

Not only from the physical aftereffects of her recent bout

of food poisoning, but also from the night before. After leaving Jade's, she'd texted Greg and they had spent half an hour passing messages backwards and forwards – Maddie telling Greg about Jade and what was going on with her and Greg trying to convince Maddie to stay out of it, that it wasn't good for her state of mind to get too involved.

Maddie knew he had a point, but she couldn't just walk away from Jade – or rather, she couldn't walk away from Ben. She couldn't shake the feeling that Ben needed her, but she couldn't say why. Just that she had an overwhelming urge to take care of him and it was something she couldn't ignore. When she thought about having him all to herself today, her entire body fizzed.

She gathered up her handbag and shoved some mini boxes of raisins and a bag of breadsticks into her handbag and shrugged into her coat, enjoying the feeling of the smile riding her lips. As she grabbed her phone, it buzzed and vibrated in her hand. She expected it to be Greg again, following up on last night's texts, but it was a message from Gemma:

Lots of messages between you and Greg last night. What happened to standing on your own two feet?

Someone wasn't happy. Letting Maddie know she was aware of their messages, a little like she was pissing on a lamppost outside Maddie's door, marking her territory.

She shoved her phone back in her bag and headed out the door.

★

Although the sun was shining, Maddie felt some of her excitement wane as soon as she stepped outside with Ben in his pushchair. He'd flashed her a rare smile when she'd collected him from Jade, who had been almost embarrassed at the events of the night before and practically shoved Maddie and Ben out of the flat. As Maddie opened the door to the main building, two women stood back to let her past, then headed inside. Maddie hadn't seen them about before and assumed they were friends of Luke as they both headed upstairs, chattering away.

Interesting. He seemed so shy and awkward. Or were they friends of Jade's? Was that why she was so keen to get rid of her and Ben? Maddie felt like she had been shooed away, as though Jade hadn't wanted her friends to see Maddie for some reason.

Feeling irked at Jade's rejection, Maddie headed off down the street, but her mood dropped even further as a tickling feeling tripped over her, like she was being watched. She couldn't quite see around a parked van to determine whether it was Jade watching from her window or not. Maybe it was – checking to make sure they'd crossed the road safely. Maddie knew she would be doing the same thing, not wanting to let Ben out of her sight for a minute, worrying about him until he was returned to her safely. But that contradicted her bundling them out of the door. Maybe she was making sure they had definitely left the building then?

The feeling unnerved her and as she walked further down the street, it followed her, like a spectral breath on the back of her neck. She spun around quickly but there was no one behind her or following her. A car pulled out of the side street she had just passed and for a brief second Maddie thought it looked like Gemma's Range Rover. Then she dismissed that idea too – Gemma had just texted her, so she surely wasn't following her around in her car. And what reason would she have to do that anyway? There was nothing about Maddie that Gemma could ever find threatening, surely.

She shrugged it off, told herself she was just on edge because she was alone with Ben and carried on walking, but her pace quickened a little all the same.

The community hall was buzzing with noise and activity by the time she arrived. Little children ran in and around each other, climbing on chairs and crawling under the tables. It immediately made her feel better. However, Ben sat in his pushchair in the doorway with wide eyes as Maddie kneeled down to unclip his safety straps.

'There we go, Ben. Out you come.' She offered him her hand and he pulled on it to stand up. 'Let's get that coat off you.' The room was stifling, the central heating notched up too far, and Maddie could feel sweat trickle down her spine underneath her jumper. She unzipped his padded coat and pulled it from his arms.

He stood watching the children zoom around him, not ready to engage with them just yet. Maddie's heart ached. 'What would you like to play with?'

He looked at her, then pointed at a table in the corner where there was some paper and crayons.

'That looks like fun! Would you like me to come with you?'

He nodded and he led her by the hand to the table. He pulled out the miniature plastic chair and sat down very studiously before pulling a piece of paper towards himself and picking up a royal blue crayon.

Maddie stepped to the side and watched him as he pulled the colour across the paper with fervour, then set the blue aside in favour of a yellow crayon.

A little girl ran up, looked curiously at what he was doing and sat down on the chair opposite him. The crayon in Ben's hand stilled for a second, then he continued to draw a yellow circle on the blue background. Maddie thought it looked like he was drawing a sun.

A woman came to stand next to Maddie. 'Hi, I'm Chloe. That's my daughter, Polly.'

'Hi,' Maddie replied. 'I'm Maddie. I'm here with Ar—um,' she coughed, 'Ben.'

'He's a sweetie, isn't he? So quiet compared to the other boys here.'

'Yes, he's quite sensitive.'

'Jade not here this week then?'

'I wanted to bring him today, just wanted to spend some time with him.'

'That's so nice, getting to spend time with you. Jade can—' Whatever she was going to say was cut off by a loud female voice thundering over them, telling them to gather on the carpet as the session was about to begin. Chloe smiled and shrugged as her daughter grabbed her hand and dragged her away.

Maddie couched down next to Ben again and said, 'Shall we find a place to sit? The music is starting.'

He got to his feet and handed her the picture he had drawn. There was a blue sky and a yellow egg shape for a sun and what looked like two people holding hands. 'That's fantastic, Ben! Is that you and Mummy?'

He nodded.

'You are very good at drawing. She will love it.'

She sat on the carpet with crossed legs and Ben crawled up into her lap and leant against her. Maddie didn't want to move or breathe in case he pulled away. A glow spread through her.

The woman taking the session had a habit of bursting into song at every opportunity and Ben giggled, sang and clapped his hands along with the other children. He looked happy and relaxed, clearly enjoying every minute.

Afterwards, as she clipped him back into his pushchair, Chloe came over to say goodbye. 'Ben looks so happy today. He's usually much more withdrawn. I've never seen him join in like that. It clearly makes a difference having you here. I hope we'll see you again soon?'

Maddie smiled, feeling pride bubble through her, as Chloe waved and backed out of the door, riding the tidal wave of pushchairs.

Maddie didn't want to take Ben home just yet. She was having too much fun. If Jade really did have friends over, she wouldn't notice if they didn't come straight home. Instead of heading back the way they came, Maddie steered the pushchair in the opposite direction. She reached into her bag and turned her phone off as they walked along the street and she chattered away to him.

'I know,' she said as they walked. 'Let's go to the library. I used to love the library when I was little.'

Maddie loved everything about libraries. The smell, the

hushed atmosphere, the subtle buzz of activity. She peered around her at the rows and rows of shelves, the books lined up like soldiers, every one a different adventure with a million secrets ready to be discovered.

Ben seemed just as taken with the reverence of the place. He took it all in with wide eyes. Maddie suspected he'd never been in a library before. She left the pushchair at the side of the room and walked over to where a pile of children's picture books were laid out on a low table.

'Ok, let's see what we have here.' Maddie picked up a book called *The Dinosaur that Pooped Christmas* and showed the cover to Ben, who giggled at the dinosaur on the cover. 'Shall we read this one?'

Ben nodded enthusiastically and Maddie lowered herself onto a large green beanbag. Ben curled up in her lap once more. Maddie made the story come alive with different voices for the characters and when it was over, Ben jumped up to pick another book.

Three stories later and Ben was snuggling into Maddie, his eyes heavy as he yawned. Maddie felt her heart drop. She knew she had to take him back home – she'd already been out much longer than intended – but she didn't want this to end.

This was what she imagined it would be like. This was what being a mother meant – hugs and stories and crayon drawings. Jade was very lucky.

She wanted to spirit him away, pack everything into his pushchair and just keep walking. It reminded her of how she was feeling that day with Mia in the park – a sense of outrage that this little creature could be so much happier with her, that she could offer them so much more.

★

Jade took a shaky breath. Maddie and Ben had been gone for hours. She was starting to wonder if letting Maddie take him on her own had been a good idea after all.

At first it had been just a little niggle at the back of her brain, but as time ticked on and Maddie's phone kept going to voicemail, Jade had to admit she felt the first prickling of unease.

The image of the woman in the park came back to Jade then – her shaking finger and quivering voice.

You need to keep an eye on your son when she's around.

How could she have been so stupid? Just letting a relative stranger walk out of the door with him?

She'd been so focused on Stacey and Becca coming over to do her hair and nails before her date with Deon that she'd just wanted Ben and Maddie out of the way before the girls arrived.

Where the hell were they?

Reluctantly Maddie strapped Ben back in his pushchair, then on a whim, knelt down and told him to smile as she took a selfie on her phone. She knew she had been gone way too long, but her feet were struggling to find the way back home.

She took as slow a walk as she could, letting daydreams of another life flood her brain in which she lived near the sea with Ben, just the two of them, running on the beach, exploring rock pools, and eating fish and chips from the newspaper.

She felt like her heart was fracturing when she finally reached the entrance to the flats. She struggled up the stairs with the pushchair, trying not to wake Ben who had drifted off to sleep. She knocked on Jade's door.

Jade flung it open, looking annoyed and worried. 'I've been trying to phone you,' she said. 'I wondered where you two had got to.'

'Oh, sorry, my phone must be flat. I took him to the library after the music class and I didn't notice the time.'

'Ok, well, next time make sure your phone is charged.' Her voice was sharp-edged.

'Yes, sorry. We had a great time reading books and stuff though. I really enjoyed myself. Thank you for letting me do that.'

'God, you're so weird. I'd have been bored to death.'

'Not at all! I'd love to do it again.' She paused. 'Your hair looks nice.' It sounded accusatory. She shoved the pushchair through the doorway just as Ben started to stir. 'We're home,' Maddie said gently, running a hand over his head.

'Oh, yeah thanks, just trying something new while I had the time. Took a pair of scissors to it and the hairdryer. A bit of me-time, you know.' It looked like she'd done more than that. Her nails looked freshly manicured too.

Ben opened his eyes and his bottom lip started to quiver as he looked around him. 'He's probably still quite tired, sorry. Here, Archie drew you a picture,' Maddie said. She pulled the drawing from her bag and handed it to Jade.

'Archie? Who's Archie?'

Maddie paled. 'Sorry?' she replied.

'You said Archie.'

'Did I? Silly me.' She hugged her arms to herself and looked away.

Jade frowned, then looked at the picture, twisting it this way and that. 'What the hell is it supposed to be?'

'That's the sky,' Maddie said, pointing, 'and that's the sun, and that's you and Ben holding hands.'

Ben sat still, rubbing at his eyes and said, 'Mummy.'

'Yes, Ben, that's Mummy, isn't it?' Maddie responded.

'He's not going to be an artist when he's older, is he?'

'I think it's sweet.'

'Here, you can have it then,' Jade said and gave it back to her.

Maddie was annoyed at Jade's reaction, but let it go. She hovered, wondering if Jade would offer her a cup of tea, but nothing was forthcoming.

'Right, well, I'll leave you to it, but any time you want a break, you know where I am. Did you have a peaceful few hours?' Maddie tried to see behind her for evidence of having had people over, but Jade was blocking her view.

'Yeah, it's turning out to be an easy day for me – he's off to his dad's again later. Well, I think you've deserved a cup of tea and a sit-down. Wow, look at the time.' She made a play of looking at her watch. 'Almost snack time for you, big boy. Thanks, Mads. See you soon, yeah?' Maddie waved goodbye to Ben as Jade bustled her out of the door.

Once back in her own flat, Maddie airdropped the photo of herself and Ben to her laptop and printed it off. Then she stuck it to her fridge along with Ben's drawing, where she would see it every day.

Then

Positive.

There's that little, telling line.

But I've been here before.

No, think happy thoughts.

The pregnancy test is positive. This time it will stick.

I sit on the edge of the bath, marvelling at the little white stick in my hand. Greg had said one more try and then we were done.

That one more try had resulted in a miracle.

Slow down, Maddie.

I force myself to take a few steadying breaths. My stomach is gurgling with joy, flipping over and crashing in on itself as I let myself consider what this means. The gurgling is surprisingly close to nausea, but I'm enjoying it anyway.

We've been here before, Maddie.

Yes, we have. Countless miscarriages; countless disappointments. And I can name each and every one of them.

Ok, I must be only a couple of weeks pregnant, so I need to not move for the next while, just get us past the twelve-week mark and maybe we'll be ok. I put my hand on my stomach, but I can't feel anything. Nothing is different yet.

That's one of the hardest things. It never feels like there is something in there this early.

But you can always tell when it's coming out.

No, don't think about that. Positivity breeds positivity.

Deep breaths. Slow movements.

Greg. I need to tell him.

I step gingerly from the bathroom and grab my phone from where I'd flung it on the bed along with the empty test box and sheet of instructions. I certainly didn't need those. I'd done enough of these tests over the years to be able to write them myself. The money I'd spent on the tests alone didn't bear thinking about.

I dial Greg's number, but it goes straight to voicemail. I look at my watch. I was sure he said he was going to be in the office all day today. He should be there by now.

Frowning, I dial again. Still voicemail. I leave a message asking him to call me back urgently.

Now I'm fidgety. I was hoping to talk to him, share the news, hear the joy in his voice.

We're like strangers, he and I. We hardly talk. He works long hours and seems to find any excuse he can to get out of the house now. As far away from me as possible.

But then, I don't really ask too many questions about his day, his life. As far as I'm concerned, if he isn't in the house, then I don't have to feel the disappointment simmering from his pores, the pity when he looks at me, his frustration that I don't want to go out, have a drink, see our friends anymore. All the strange diets and health regimes while I try and find a fix for my broken body. Gluten-free; dairy-free; vegan. None of them have worked. I'm in the best shape of my life and it has made no difference.

He can't understand why I behave like I do – and I can't explain it to him.

All I can focus on is what I don't have in front of me. How many times has he said to me, 'Look at what we have, Maddie. Look at our lives. I love you. We have a beautiful home, a successful business. That should be enough.'

But it isn't. All the holidays and fancy restaurants can't fill the emptiness I have inside me, a chasm of longing.

I've tried explaining to him that I don't want to socialise with our friends anymore because I can't hear any more of their stories about family life, how brilliant little Annie is at dancing, how Connor is top goal scorer for the football team. Even the stuff they moan about – no lie-ins, constant whining, tantrums – sounds charming to me.

But worse than this is the fact that they don't tell us these stories anymore. They start, then they get that look on their faces, their eyes dart towards me and they stop, sometimes mid-sentence, before completely changing the subject to something inane, like the weather or the demise of British politics.

Greg says he hasn't noticed, but I know he has. He can't help but notice that the invitations to dinner parties have dried up. Thank goodness he has lots of work functions to attend, because he'd go stir-crazy stuck here with me every night.

I try his number again, but get the same response, so I head back to bed, still fully dressed, and lie with my legs propped up on a pile of pillows, a cup of jasmine tea at my elbow and daytime television on to distract me from letting my thoughts run wild with images of what our lives *could* be like if we had a little Evie or Casper or Lottie to keep us busy in nine months' time.

When my phone does ring an hour later, the television has not distracted me in the slightest and I have ended up making a new list on my phone of possible names, ones I haven't already used.

'Hello? Greg?'

'Hey, Mads. You ok?' His voice is flat.

'Yes. I'm good. Really good.'

'Oh?' His interest has been piqued.

'I'm pregnant... again.'

There is a pause. 'Ok...'

'Did you hear me?'

'Yes, I heard you.' He doesn't sound as thrilled as I thought he would. He sounds... tired.

'You're happy, aren't you?'

'Yes, of course. It's just... Well, we've been here before. I don't want to you to get your hopes up again.'

Suddenly I'm angry. Why shouldn't I get my hopes up? Why shouldn't I be excited? How dare he?

'Fuck you, Greg!'

'Excuse me?'

'How dare you!' I know I'm screaming at him, but I can't stop myself. 'Why can you not just be happy for me? For us? After everything we've gone through, you know how much this means to me. Is a little bit of excitement too much to ask?'

'I'm sorry, Mads, I just—'

'You know what, I'm not going to let your negativity ruin this for me.'

I hang up and fling myself back onto the pillows.

Breathe, Maddie. Stress is bad for the baby.

I focus on my inhalations and exhalations, letting my pulse slow again, then start searching up new ideas for the nursery on Pinterest.

8

The shoebox sat on the kitchen counter like a bomb.

Maddie sat on the bar stool, her hands resting flat on the countertop.

This flimsy cardboard box held what felt like a lifetime of pain, crushed dreams and broken splinters of promise. It had the ability to completely eviscerate her and yet she kept it.

However, spending time with Ben yesterday had fortified her enough to face this. She looked over at the photo on the fridge, Ben's smiling face, the sheer joy in her eyes.

She reached out slowly and lifted the lid of the box, setting it aside gingerly. The smell of lavender filled the air.

Inside, lying on a bed of scented, pale purple tissue paper, was what looked on the surface to be a pile of innocent pieces of paper. But each one could cut her like a scalpel.

The papers were tied together with a thin piece of silver ribbon, like love letters. And that's what they were.

Love letters from a mother to her children.

The ribbon had started out as quite a long piece, but as Maddie had added to the pile, so the ribbon had shortened until there was now only enough to tie one small knot at the top.

She untied that knot now with quivering fingers and forced herself to look.

A photo of every scan done for every one of her failed pregnancies – and for each child, a hand-drawn card with a name, date of conception and date of death, each one decorated according to the scheme they had picked for the nursery. One had zoo animals; another flowers; a third rainbows – all painstakingly hand-drawn and decorated while she was grieving yet another disappointment. The cards had been a kind of art therapy for her, cathartic in a way and an important part of her attempt at closure. There had been no way of knowing for some whether they were boys or girls, so she had gone with her instinct and by her reckoning, she had had more boys. But that didn't matter. All that mattered was that they were gone. And each one had taken a piece of her soul with them until she had felt like an empty husk, just a body carrying her around every day but drained of all feeling. Numb and hollow.

The only thing that seemed to raise her heartbeat now was the sound of a child laughing, the sight of a wide, innocent grin and the feeling of a tiny hand clasped in hers. That was why spending time with Jemima and Ben was so important. That was why she would do anything to spend time with them. It frightened her to think about the lengths she would go to to have even five more minutes in their company.

Perhaps that was what annoyed Gemma the most. On the surface, Maddie had assumed it was her relationship with Greg, but perhaps it was the threat of her being in Jemima's life, a woman who wanted to be there, to spend time with her, unlike Gemma who seemed to resent her daughter's reliance on her.

Maddie looked at each and every card, tracing the names with her fingers, remembering each and every one. At the very bottom of the pile, the drawing was an ink impression of a tiny hand and a tiny foot.

Archie.

The boy who breathed.

For a moment, she held Archie's card in her hands, feeling its smoothness against her fingertips, stroking her thumb over the ink impressions, not breathing.

After Archie, she was so far down in herself that for a while she couldn't see any light at all. Greg had learnt over the years how to reach down and drag her back up, but after Archie, even he couldn't reach her, his fingers barely grazing the heavy air between them. Even so, he never stopped trying.

Maybe it was time to let him go. She didn't need someone to reach for her anymore because she had survived.

Maybe it was her turn to reach out to someone new.

She put the card down and picked up her phone before sending a Snapchat to Jade.

Can we talk? M x

Then she got to her feet, poured herself a large glass of wine and waited.

Then

S omething is wrong.

  'Greg?' I call out.

He doesn't answer. He's in his study again. Muted conversations and hushed tones behind a closed door. I drag myself from the bed, but it is difficult to move at any speed now with my huge, distended stomach. For such a tiny thing, the weight of the baby is astonishing, pushing down on the floor of my stomach and pinching my sciatic nerve.

I had to stop driving weeks ago because I couldn't reach the pedals any longer and now walking is agony as the baby rests on my sciatic nerve, causing shooting pains down my leg.

But oh, how it's worth it.

I would take ten times more discomfort and pain if I had to.

I limp to the study and I'm about to knock when I hear his voice through the door. He's talking in a low voice, but he sounds agitated.

'No, you can't. She's nearly due and I won't let anything jeopardise this for her. For us. I'm sorry, I know it's not what you want to hear, but she has to come first now.'

There is a pause, then he mumbles something that sounds a little like, 'I miss you too.'

Perhaps it's his mother, threatening to come and visit. She lives in the Algarve with her second husband, a plumber called Gary with lambchop sideburns and a penchant for wearing T-shirts that say things like 'Cleverly Disguised as a Responsible Adult' and 'Fart Now Loading – Please Wait'. Greg dislikes him immensely; I can tolerate him in small doses. As far as grandparents go, they're not ideal but the only ones this little one will have.

I can feel the tugging again, deep and urgent inside my belly. 'Greg!' I burst in just as he is hanging up.

He takes one look at my face and says, 'What is it?' I register the fear and I'm pleased in a small, sadistic way. He's come back to me in the last few months and it's almost like we're the way we used to be. This pregnancy has brought us closer again and I like that he's worried. It means he's still here.

It hasn't been an easy pregnancy at all. Weekly scans at the hospital in London have meant lots of time off work. He has had to learn to cook while I have been mostly on bed rest. When he hasn't been at work, he's been at my beck and call, caring for me, meeting my every need, all without complaint. He's even been working from home more often, leaving the running of the office to his PA, Gemma. She has turned out to be a lifesaver in all this, a necessary cog in the business, keeping everything running smoothly in my complete absence. Surprising, considering her earlier incompetence. It's like she's trying to impress Greg. Maybe she's looking for a promotion. She's welcome to my job. I won't be needing it once the baby is born.

Throughout the last few months, despite the anxiety and nerves, Greg and I have laughed, joked, planned and experienced every moment of it together – at least once the pregnancy stretched past the twelve-week stage. Before that, it was like Greg was in denial, but looking back, I understand why he responded the way he did. Everyone handles things differently and for him, denial is the best policy. We've tried not to stress or worry and as the pregnancy progressed, we began to relax and enjoy it more.

'I think there's something wrong.'

'What? Are you in pain?'

'No, it's just... I don't know. It feels like something is tugging on me and my back is aching.'

'Maybe you were lying at a funny angle? There's still three weeks to go. It's probably nothing.'

I can feel tears building. 'I think we should go to the hospital.'

The rest of that day is a scattered collection of images in my head, like a kaleidoscope, at once moving into my brain, then hurtling away, as if I won't let myself fix on any one moment long enough for fear that I won't be able to come back from it.

There are flashes of doctors, eyes and frown lines above surgical masks. At one point Greg is looming over me, a surgical mask clamped over his mouth, but his eyes are recognisable as they peer into mine, tears dripping from his lashes.

There is pain, both physical and emotional, raw, open and searing, then retreating to a dull, throbbing ache.

Then a tiny baby is placed in my arms, all mottled and pink with the tiniest hands and feet I have ever seen. Out of all of it, this image is clear and crisp, as though I am looking down on myself. I can feel the weight of him, barely there, in my arms. I can smell the blood iron on his skin. I can taste the sweat on my lips. His hands are splayed and I expect them to flail at me in anger at being ejected from safety so brutally, but the hands are motionless.

There is not a sound in the room except for the beep of machines. Everyone is standing around me, watching, waiting like a held breath.

Then a sob escapes from Greg and I am dropped back into my body and I realise that while Greg and I are crying, the baby is not.

His tiny hands are still. His eyes are closed. His heart is not beating.

We named him Archie.

He was my last baby. The twelfth pregnancy.

He was the boy who breathed.

Just once.

Then no more.

9

Maddie felt raw. The scan photos and cards lay spread out in front of them on the kitchen counter. All twelve children, all named. Seven boys and five girls.

Every single one remembered and mourned.

'Fuck,' Jade said poetically.

She'd kept quiet while Maddie talked, getting up only to refill their wineglasses and then to open another bottle when they'd emptied the first.

She didn't ask questions or push for details. She just listened – and for that Maddie was grateful. Her face was unreadable. Maddie couldn't tell if Jade felt pity, sadness or anything at all. Maddie supposed not everyone would find this as heart-breaking as she had. Perhaps Jade would think it all a lucky escape, would wonder why Maddie had persevered for so long. She knew Jade struggled with Ben, after all.

Jade got to her feet, grabbed her cigarettes from her handbag and disappeared through the door to the garden.

Maddie put her head in her hands for a moment, feeling wrung out, her mouth cloying from the wine and words. This was the first time she had ever sat and detailed all of it, said the words out loud from start to finish. It made it all so much more tangible again. She hadn't even discussed it as plainly with Greg before – but then, he'd been there with her and it had seemed fruitless for her to talk to him so candidly about how she felt each and every time they lost another one.

And a loss was exactly what it was. Maddie had no idea where those tiny souls had gone or why they'd been taken. They were indeed lost to her, not even leaving behind a memory she could hold onto.

Just gone.

Therapists and counsellors had offered her advice in the past, saying things like it was God's way, that maybe He needed them for a higher purpose, that they were angels looking down on her, and she had wanted to rant that it wasn't fair. Why did He get to choose who He wanted? Why couldn't He let her just have one of them?

She took a breath and gathered together all of the scans and cards into a neat pile again before carefully tying them with the ribbon. She tucked them back into the tissue paper and replaced the lid. She rested her hand on the box for a moment, then went to find Jade.

The air outside was crisp, the evening having set in on them without them realising. Jade was standing with her back to the door, a cloud of smoke around her head as she pulled hard on the cigarette.

Maddie came to stand next to her and handed her her wine.

They stood in silence, staring out at the sky. It was a clear night, the moon full and open. Maddie thought she could just make out a face in it if she squinted.

'It sucks... what you've been through,' Jade said.

'Yeah, I guess it does,' Maddie replied.

Jade was quiet again and Maddie watched the end of her cigarette glow an angry orange as she took drag after drag, like a warning sign flashing on and off.

'I get it – why you haven't wanted to talk about it much.'

Maddie nodded, although she doubted if Jade noticed in the dark. Maddie drank her wine and folded her arms around herself.

'What happened afterwards? You know, after Archie?'

Maddie thought back to those long months afterwards, but it was like one eternal white canvas of nothingness in her mind. She couldn't remember actually being present for any given moment.

'I went to bed. Because I was so *tired* of it all, you know? I felt like every tiny shred of life and joy had been stripped from the bones of me. So I pulled the covers up over my head and stayed there. For a long time.' She paused, thinking back to that time, that emptiness. 'Greg came and went. But he had a focus, a distraction. He had the business to throw himself into – and he made a lot of money that year. Of course, I wasn't spending it on IVF treatments as quickly as he was making it, like in previous years, but he was also so much more single-minded. We never discussed it, but we both knew that Archie would be our last.' Her voice broke as she said his name. It still had a way of taking her breath away.

Maddie looked out at the moon again. 'I was operating on autopilot every day, doing very little, saying even less. And then one day, Greg had left the radio on in the kitchen when he left for work and I was making a cup of tea, not really listening to it, but it was an interview with an artist, who was talking about his depression and how one day he had an epiphany of sorts. He said that he had opened his bedroom curtains for the first time in a week and the sun had shone through the window and he realised that although there had been clouds there before, on that day the sky was back – and that actually the sky had never gone away in the first place. It was just that he couldn't see it.' She sipped on her wine, thinking back to that day. 'That made sense to me. How grief and depression are a little bit like that. Sometimes you can't see past the thing that is holding you down, stopping you from wanting to take your next breath, but that doesn't mean that thing will always be as suffocating or as big and powerful. You just have to hold on and wait it out in a way. He said that running had diminished his depression in his head, weakened it enough for him to push back at it. So I packed a bag and went to the swimming pool. It was the first time I'd left the house in weeks. But I had this *urge* to swim, to pull myself through the water, stretch myself out and feel weightless for a while, let myself float. After being hunched by the weight of my grief for so long, it felt liberating to reach out and pull myself forward. I started feeling like I was swimming away from the depression and then after a while I felt like I was actually swimming *towards* a future for myself.'

She wasn't sure if she was making any sense to Jade, but it made sense to her.

'So when did Gemma appear?'

'I don't know. I wasn't paying much attention. She had worked for us for years and, thinking back now, I think their affair began before I was pregnant with Archie.'

'What a dick.'

'Yes – and no. I wasn't there for a lot of our marriage. But finding out about Gemma being pregnant helped in a weird way. A baby – any baby – helped to fill the void. And Greg has been amazing at letting me spend time with Jemima, as have you with Ben.'

'How did you find out about them?'

Maddie pulled her cardigan tighter around her, the air like a cold breath on her face. She felt wrung out from her monologue – and a little embarrassed. As though she'd exposed herself and was waiting for her audience to laugh at her. Maddie had expected more empathy from her, but Jade just seemed to want gossip. 'Let's go inside. I'm cold.'

Jade followed her in, plopping herself on the couch and helping herself to more wine.

'Then you understand why I can't let Mark win, right?' Jade said, bringing the conversation back to herself again. 'I can't let him just waltz in and take Ben away from me.'

Maddie sighed. 'I get it, I do. I can understand how desperate you feel. But I also think it may not be as terrible as you think it will be. There may be joint custody or he may want you to have custody and him to have visitational rights or something. I think you and him should discuss it properly before it gets to court. Look at me and Jemima – she is not mine and I don't see her every day, much as I wish I could, but I feel whole when I'm with her and I will always be her Aunty Mads. Families come in all shapes and sizes.'

'But is that enough for you?'

Maddie thought about it, thought about the ache when she said goodbye, thought about how she almost hadn't brought Ben home earlier that day, how her feet had itched to keep walking and not look back.

'Most days it is,' she replied.

Jade sat forward and clutched onto Maddie's leg, her long talons digging into Maddie's thigh. 'Don't lie to yourself, Maddie. It's not enough for you and it's not enough for me.' Jade chewed on her lip. 'I can't afford the legal stuff, so he needs to be out of the picture altogether.'

'But maybe I could help with money? I could speak to Greg, see if we could come to some sort of arrangement for a loan or something if it would help you with the legal fees?'

Jade sat back against the cushions and looked at her closely. 'How much money?'

Maddie shrugged. 'I don't know. I'd have to talk to him about it.'

Jade looked thoughtful, then drained her glass again. 'Ok, but in the meantime we work to the original plan. If Mark is out of the picture, then I don't have anything to worry about. We can get them both out of the picture so that we are set for the future. Maybe we could even look at moving in together afterwards, the three of us – you, me and Ben. Imagine all of us living in that lovely big house of yours. You'd love that, wouldn't you? Seeing Ben every day?' Her eyes were manic discs, spinning and sparking, as she sat forward again. 'You must want to be free of Greg? A constant reminder of what you've lost. Him cheating on you after everything you've been through. That woman taunting you, parading her child in front of you. I saw your face that day when we broke in. You would love to be back there. For me, knowing that I am free of Mark, that I can live without worrying about it every day. That's what I want. And you need a clean break. Living your life vicariously through Greg's child with another woman is weird.'

Maddie could feel unease creeping up her throat. 'I don't know if I do want to be free of Greg. I've known him all my adult life, he's a part of me. And I quite like my life now, this place.'

'God, you're such a sap! Have some balls. Stand up for yourself! And stop lying to yourself.' Spittle flew from her lips. 'Where's your pride?'

Maddie could feel her own anger bubbling. 'What do you want from me? You keep saying you want me to help you, but it's only on your terms. It's so black and white to you. There is a solution and we will find it. You just have to slow down, take a breath and think rationally about it all.'

'But you've just offered his money! Are you saying you aren't going to ask him for me now?'

Maddie realised there was no talking to her tonight. She was drunk, contradictory and irrational, lurching from one thing to the next.

'That's not what I said. Look, let's talk about it when we're sober. I'm tired.'

'Oh right, so you want me to leave?'

'Well, I—'

'Fine, I know when I'm not wanted.' Jade heaved to her feet and stormed from the flat, slamming the door behind her.

Minutes later, loud music started blasting from the flat above, the bass vibrating through the floor.

Maddie sighed, thinking over what had just happened, trying to understand Jade, make sense of it all. Part of her brain was telling her that Jade had a point. What if the three of them could move into the big house that was built for a family? She and Greg weren't divorced yet. Half of that house was still hers.

She felt a flicker of joy as she thought about decorating the nursery one more time, but this time for a three-year-old boy with a serious smile and a love of cars. Maybe getting him one of those racing car beds.

No, she was letting her brain fog up again with daydreams, like that day with Mia. It was the wine talking.

She grabbed her phone to distract herself and found her fingers opening Facebook, looking at Greg's profile again. She opened a post from a few months ago – a photo of him and Gemma on her birthday, posing in London with the Thames behind them and the twinkling lights illuminating their happiness. Looking at them, all glowing and smug, she had a moment where she could imagine a life without them in it, without Gemma's shadow hanging over everything. Maybe Jade's crazy idea wasn't so crazy after all...

She zoomed into their faces, not sure what she was hoping to see. Then she noticed the necklace Gemma was wearing. It was a silver lightning bolt. She'd seen that somewhere before... recently...

Jade had been wearing it the other day.

Maddie sat back against the couch cushions, her mind reeling.

She must've taken it from the house. She'd stolen it.

Then

The parking lot at the swimming pool is surprisingly quiet today. Usually, at this time of the morning, I have to park in a side street and walk over the road because my session coincides with the old biddies doing aqua aerobics in a section of the large pool. I like watching them bounce and jiggle to eighties hits blasting in distorted melody as the instructor cajoles the bobbing swimming caps in front of her to mimic her high-energy moves. The ladies – and occasional man – are always smiling, pleased to see each other and having fun. They look out for each other too. If Joan hasn't been to a session for a while, they rally round and someone volunteers to check on her; when Sandra had her hip op, they clubbed together to send her flowers. They chat loudly in the changing rooms as they strip down to nothing, not afraid to bear their wrinkly bottoms and sagging boobs while discussing the Chelsea Flower Show and what the frost has done to their allotments.

This kind of community spirit is something I don't get to revel in much. I still feel hopelessly alone most days and can't remember the last time someone checked on my wellbeing. Greg says the right things – 'Are you ok? Can I do anything? How are you feeling today?' – but there's an absentmindedness about the questions, as though he's asking because he knows he should, but he's too busy with his own grief to hear the answers anymore.

In fact, it feels like that's all he says to me now.

Are you ok?

There's no point in answering truthfully, so I just nod.

When I get to the pool entrance, I realise why it is so quiet today. A sign posted to the door says a school has booked the entire pool for a swimming gala, so no adult sessions today, no aqua aerobics. Sandra, Joan and the rest will be disappointed.

I debate going up to the café and having a coffee and a bacon sandwich. The glorious smell of frying bacon wafting down from the mezzanine café must be torturous for the gym-goers after their hard work on the treadmill. My attempts at healthy, plant-based and gluten-free diets ended after Archie and I am fully committed to eating meat again – when I have an appetite.

Life is too short to deny yourself bacon.

Today, though, I'm not really in the mood for it. A swim usually helps me to reach a state of mind where I can get through the day. I don't often achieve much, but without it I achieve nothing. Today's disappointment is a setback and I have the overwhelming urge to go straight back home to bed. A voice in my head says I can do that if it's what I need, while another argues with it, tells me not to give in to the coaxing because that would be a step backwards and I need to think about going forwards.

I spend the whole drive home letting the two voices argue it out.

When I pull up in the driveway, Gemma's car is parked

up next to Greg's Porsche. I don't really want to see her – I was hoping Greg would've left for the office by now, but he was hanging around longer than usual this morning, faffing over nothing. Overwhelming exhaustion hits me as I contemplate having to pass niceties with her.

While she was friendly to me when she first joined the company, that has worn off and it's now written all over her face that she considers me to be a drain on the business. Someone who still gets paid, but contributes nothing. An unnecessary expense. That's a fair assertion, but Greg insists that I remain on the payroll, that the job will still be there for me when I decide I am ready to return to it. More than anything else though, it's the way she looks at me – like I am germ-riddled and she needs a facemask to be around me in case whatever I have is contagious. I sometimes catch her wrinkling her nose in disgust when she comes over and I'm sitting at the dining room table in sweatpants doing a jigsaw at 11 a.m. But I find the jigsaws as therapeutic as swimming, so she can do one, frankly.

Actually, I've started thinking that it would do me good to start getting involved at work again. I mentioned that to Greg over dinner last night. His reaction was muted and I think he is of the opinion that until he sees me sitting at my desk in the office, then he won't believe it.

That's ok though. I don't blame him.

I sit in my car in the driveway, the two voices in my head still debating, but now the sterner voice is saying that instead of swimming, maybe showing my face at work would distract me enough so that I don't crawl back into hibernation. Just an hour to see how it goes. I can always leave if it gets too much.

It is the sight of Gemma's car that convinces me in the end. The look on her face if I were to walk in. I bet she's taken over my lovely office with its big windows looking out over the local junior school. I used to like to throw open the windows and listen to the chaos and frivolity of breaktime. I bet she's been keeping them closed to the noise. She doesn't strike me as being child-tolerant. If I returned, she would have to gather up her stationery and move to a desk in the communal area, and the idea of humiliating her like that suddenly becomes irresistible.

I get out of the car with the firm intention of doing just that. I'll have a shower, get dressed into something a bit more socially acceptable than sweatpants and I'll go to work, just for an hour, just to see.

The house is quiet. I put my swimming bag by the front door and head towards the kitchen, expecting them to be sitting at the table, paperwork spread out in front of them along with mugs of coffee.

The room is empty. Maybe they're in Greg's small home office.

I start to make myself tea, delaying the inevitable now that I've decided on it. I hear Greg bustle into the room behind me.

'What happened to your swim?' he says.

I turn to face him, saying, 'The pool is booked for a gala.' My voice falters. There's something odd about him. I can't quite put my finger on it, but as he draws closer to me and pecks me on the cheek, the feeling intensifies. It's balanced on the edge of my tongue, teetering, niggling.

He is flustered, his cheeks reddened, and a bead of sweat stands out on his forehead.

Then I notice his shirt is on inside out.

'I see Gemma is here. Where is she?' I say.

His fly is down.

'Er, she's... in the bathroom.' He smiles manically and turns away from me.

Then the penny drops, loud in my head, and I almost laugh out loud.

I abandon the tea and walk past Greg, out of the kitchen. The downstairs toilet door is ajar. Greg's office door is open and the room is empty.

I walk up the stairs calmly, no need to hurry. I know what I will see when I reach the top and turn the corner.

Greg is prancing behind me, asking me if I want a biscuit, telling me to go back to the kitchen and he'll make my tea for me, anything to stop me from getting to the top of the stairs. I ignore him, can't really process what he is saying anyway.

I reach the top step and turn the corner without pause.

Gemma is in my bedroom, sitting on the corner of my bed. The bed I made this morning when I got out of it, which is now messy, the covers wrangled.

She is buttoning up her blouse, her feet bare and her long, usually sleek hair mussed like the sheets.

I look at her; she looks back. There is no sense of shame or guilt on her face; instead, it looks like victory.

I nod at her. I'm not sure why. Everything seems to have slowed down, the air thickening, until all I can see is this woman sitting on my unmade bed.

I turn around and walk from the room. Greg is poised on the top stair. His face has taken on the colour of ash. He can't meet my eyes. 'Mads...'

I walk past him, not giving him the opportunity to lie about this, to try and create a reasonable excuse for why his PA is in my bedroom, why I'm the one getting the wrong end of the stick, that it's not what it looks like.

I grab my bag from where I left it all of five minutes ago, get back in my car and drive.

I don't know where I'm going until I get there. I'm at the park, near to the children's play area and the café where I met Mia all that time ago. So much has happened since then. And yet nothing has changed.

Like a puppet, I go into the café, order a tea to go and a Smarties cookie and head over to the park bench on which I sat that day. I watch the children play, the mothers talking and laughing, the dogs chasing and panting. I can hear my phone ringing in my bag, but I ignore it.

I just sit and drink my tea, not thinking, not feeling. I want to rage, scream, throw something, but I can't, so I sit and watch.

When my tea is finished, I throw the cup in the bin and walk back to the car park and beyond. I keep walking until I reach the main road. I don't look at anything around me. All I can see inside my head is Greg's face as he stands at the top of the stairs, the guilt and admission like a neon sign flashing in his eyes, those eyes that couldn't meet mine. I think of all those years together, all that hurt, disappointment, sorrow, and I step off the pavement into the road.

I can hear the squeal of brakes and feel a sense of my body not being in control of itself anymore. Then I feel nothing at all.

10

The cup scalded her fingers as she passed it to Greg.

'Thanks for coming,' Maddie said with a quiet smile.

'No worries. It's nice to see you.' Greg put the mug down on a coaster on the coffee table. 'Listen, er, Gemma doesn't know I'm here, so...'

'Oh, right, that's ok. I won't say anything.' But inside she felt smug – and curious. Why hadn't he told Gemma that Maddie had asked him over for coffee? Was this how Greg and Gemma had started? Seemingly innocent chats over beverages that had developed into more than words? She hadn't answered Jade's question last night about how she had found out about Greg's affair, but that was because she was ashamed of herself for how she had reacted.

Looking back on it now, she frightened herself by realising that it could have ended very differently.

As it was, the road she stepped into was a twenty mile per hour zone, so the car that hit her was thankfully not going too fast. But if anyone asked her, she hadn't done it on purpose. It was just a lapse of concentration. She certainly hadn't done it because she had realised she had nothing left to live for.

The one thing that had dragged her through the darkest

times was the thought that she could always try again; then it was the thought that Greg was still by her side and she wasn't alone, despite feeling isolated. But once she had realised that he wasn't there either, well....

But she'd never admit that out loud.

It was a lapse in concentration. Nothing else.

'So what's up?' Greg sipped on the tea and reached for a biscuit, which he dunked into his mug. When he pulled it out, the end dangled soggily, threatening to dissolve before he scooped it into his mouth.

Maddie just held her mug in her hands, watching the steam rise, feeling shame warm her cheeks as she remembered the thoughts she'd entertained the night before.

'You remember I mentioned Jade, who lives upstairs?'

He nodded around a mouthful of biscuit.

'She's having some issues with an ex-partner and I said I would speak to you to see if you could help.'

He paused mid-dunk. 'Me? How could I help her? I don't even know her.'

'I know. It's just… Ok, let me explain. She has a son, Ben, who is three. Long story short, she was going out with the dad, he took a job on the oil rigs and dumped her by text. Then they briefly got back together, kind of a one-night stand, and she found out she was pregnant. He was away then, but she told him she was pregnant, sent him photos and stuff, and whenever he was off the rigs, he would come and see Ben, spend time with him. Now he's got a new job and wants a more permanent custody arrangement, but Jade can't afford a good lawyer. She's a single mum on benefits. He could win custody and she's terrified he will take Ben away from her.'

'Ok, so what can I do?'

'Well, I thought maybe you could help her by giving her a loan to pay for a good lawyer or something?' Maddie said in a low voice.

Greg was thoughtful for a moment, chewed quietly, then set his mug down.

'You hardly know her. Why are you so keen to help her?'

'No reason. I just... Ben is a really sweet kid.'

'I know, but if you ask me, the dad isn't doing anything wrong. In fact, he sounds like he's doing everything right. He wants to be involved in his son's life, even though it would be easier to walk away.'

'I know that, but I think for Ben, he should have both parents in his life if he can.'

'And what makes you think the father doesn't want that too?' Greg was watching her closely. 'Is there something else going on?'

'No, I just want to help, that's all.' She looked away. She didn't want to admit that she was worried what Jade might do if she lost custody. That she might take Ben away.

'What is she like? This Jade.'

'Um, complicated. Stressy. Quick temper. A typical exhausted mum, I think.'

He nodded. 'Look, Mads, you know I will always have your back, regardless of, you know, us... but I'm not sure about this. You hardly know her. How do you know she's not spinning you one just for money? How do we even know she can pay it back? What if she does a runner or something?'

'Then I will pay you back.'

'No offence, but how exactly? You're not working right now. You're still dependent on me for everything.'

'Hang on a minute. That's not fair. You know what I went through.'

'Yes, I know better than anyone and I'm sorry about that—'

'Besides, I've made a few decisions lately. I've decided to start my own business. Bookkeeping – I did it for our business and it's something I can do from home easily. I want to start living again, being more independent. This morning I sent out a few emails offering to do people's books.'

'That's great, but it won't happen overnight.'

'No, but it will happen.' She looked at his face, a face she knew so well. 'Sometimes I think you don't want me to sort myself out,' she said in a quiet voice.

'Why do you say that? Now *that's* not fair.'

'Because you can play the big hero if I am dependent on you. You like being the man on the white horse who gallops in and saves me time after time. It boosts your ego.'

'Maddie, don't be ridiculous.'

'I'm not. I'm being honest for a change. You've made sure you've stayed in charge of my life, even when you moved me out of my house. All those texts and inviting me to lunch, sending me flowers, just keeping me hanging on the end of the line, not quite letting me go completely.'

'You're being ridiculous and I'm not going to listen to you when you're like this.'

'And that too. Making me out to be unstable, on the edge all of the time. I bet you and Gemma love sitting and talking about how fragile I am. I heard you the other day at lunch!

Well, not anymore. I think it's time I stood on my own two feet.'

'You won't last five minutes before you run out of money, Mads. Be realistic.'

She got to her feet. 'I think we should get a divorce.'

He looked up at her, frowning. 'Is that really what you want?'

'Yes, it is. Gemma will be thrilled.'

He stood too, but it was sadness reflecting back in his eyes. 'You know I never wanted to hurt you, don't you? That this was never my intention. I still love you, Maddie, and I always will. I wish things could've been very different for us. You would've made an amazing mother. I see how you are with Jemima, so natural and caring, and I think... well, you're more suited to it than Gemma, anyway. You have a natural softness for kids and I wish...' He looked like he was about to start weeping. 'I want you in our lives, in Jemima's life.'

Maddie approached him and put her arms around him tightly. She still fit in his embrace comfortably, like a jigsaw piece. His arms wrapped around her back and she leant into him, breathing in his familiar smell.

He pulled away a fraction and reached with one hand to push her fringe from her eyes. 'I just want you to be ok.'

'I'll be ok,' she said more convincingly than she felt.

He pulled her back into the hug, his hands tight on her back, holding her like he didn't want to let go.

The scrape of the key in the front door woke her and she sat bolt upright. It was still daylight outside, but not for much longer. She didn't know how long she had been asleep. She looked over to where Greg lay, still asleep himself, and she put her face in her hands.

'Maddie? You here?' Jade's raspy voice shouted down her hallway.

Maddie grabbed her jeans from the floor and her jumper from where it had been flung onto the chair. She emerged from the bedroom and almost collided with Jade as she made her way down the corridor.

'Oh, there you are. Were you sleeping?'

Maddie smoothed down her hair with her hands. 'Um, how did you get in?' She pushed past Jade and went into the kitchen, hoping she would follow. 'What are you doing here?'

Jade dangled a set of keys in front of Maddie's face. 'I got a copy made of your keys, just in case. You never know when they might come in handy.'

Maddie felt ice inch over her. Her eyes flicked to the keys hanging behind her door. 'When?'

'When you were ill. Listen, that's not important. I just… wanted to apologise for leaving so abruptly last night. I was hammered and stressed, took it out on you. You're right, we should be putting our heads together to work on a plan when we are sober and thinking straight.'

'That's ok. I understand.' Maddie wasn't quite focusing on what she was saying.

'So I was wondering if… you know, the money… have you spoken to Greg yet?'

'Not yet. Thinking about it, I'm not sure what Greg would say and I've got a bit of a headache, so if you don't mind…'

'Yes, but will you speak to him?'

'Maybe,' Maddie avoided her eyes.

'Oh, hello,' Jade said suddenly and Maddie turned to see Greg emerging from the bedroom, his hair on end and wearing just his jeans. He stopped abruptly and flushed a deep red.

'I didn't know there was someone here.'

'Clearly,' Jade smirked. 'Well, three's a crowd and all that. I'll leave you to it.' She moved to leave, then turned back to Greg and said, 'I'm Jade.'

'Greg, hi.'

'Greg, huh?' she said and threw another smirk at Maddie. 'We were just talking about you. Nice to meet you. By the way, your fly is down.'

She left, slamming the door behind her.

The silence was awkward. 'You could've warned me,' Greg said.

'She let herself in. I didn't invite her.'

'She has a key?'

'Apparently.' They stood uncomfortably, neither sure what to say next.

'Well, I should go,' Greg said.

'Tea before you do?'

'No, I, er... I told Gemma I was going to the gym. She'll wonder what I've been doing for so long.' He waved his mobile phone in the air. 'There's been a few missed calls.'

'Yeah, I bet there have,' Maddie replied and started to giggle.

'Mads, about what we...'

'Don't worry, I won't say anything. As far as I'm

concerned, that was a goodbye. I still think we should get a divorce. It goes no further than this room.'

'Oh, right. Ok, um, well....' He looked surprised, as thought that wasn't what he was expecting to hear from her. He recovered his composure and stepped towards her with his arms open.

'No more hugs – that's how it started in the first place,' Maddie said with a smile.

He laughed and said, 'I'll get the rest of my clothes from where you flung them, shall I?'

She hit him playfully on the arm, blushing, and watched him go back to the bedroom, a wide smile on her face.

She could hear him making a phone call, probably spinning Gemma a lie like those he had spun for her before. Something under the couch caught her eye. His keys must've fallen from his pocket and were glinting in the light. She grabbed them and followed him into the bedroom just as he was ending his call.

He looked flushed, embarrassed. 'Told her I'd been for a drink after the gym with a friend.'

'I don't want to know.' Something about how easily he had lied annoyed her and she turned to look out of the bedroom window. She could see his Porsche in the car park and next to it a large Range Rover that looked familiar.

'Where was Gemma when you called her?'

'At home, I think, why?'

Maddie shrugged. 'No reason.' She watched as the Range Rover reversed out of the parking space and pulled away at speed.

*

Maddie climbed the stairs nervously, not sure what she was going to say to Jade. Sleeping with Greg had been stupid, spontaneous and, as much as she flushed with embarrassment when she thought about it, her stomach clenching and churning, it had been thrilling. For a second she could understand the buzz of an affair, if it weren't for the hurt that went hand in hand with the excitement.

Because no matter how much she disliked Gemma, Maddie knew first-hand what that kind of betrayal felt like and she never thought she would be the kind of person to inflict that on anyone.

And she had no doubt that it was Gemma's Range Rover parked out front, watching, knowing where he was. She was now also convinced it had been Gemma watching her when she was with Ben.

Maddie knew that moment of madness with Greg was something that wouldn't be repeated, but it had felt right at the time – a farewell of sorts – and she didn't regret it.

Even so, Jade would be full of questions that Maddie didn't want to answer.

And then there was the question of the money she had offered. Greg had planted a seed of uncertainty in her mind. He had a point – Maddie didn't exactly trust or know Jade. Who's to say she wouldn't disappear once she got what she wanted? Jade had proved herself to be greedy, a magpie attracted to sparkly things and expensive objects. Was all of this ultimately just about money? Would she take Ben away anyway?

Maddie paused halfway up the stairs as she heard a door open above her. She half expected Jade to come barrelling down towards her and braced herself. Instead, the footsteps headed away from her.

She frowned and carried on up the stairs, treading lighter than she had before. As she emerged on the top floor, she noticed a pair of scruffy trainers heading up the other flight of stairs set deep into the corner. She followed quietly and reached a heavy door that scraped lightly as she pulled on the handle. A blast of cold air greeted her as she stepped out onto the roof of the building.

It was like a different world up here. She could see for miles – buses and cars streaming past, tiny people walking with purpose, lights flickering on and off. A whole miniature town laid out before her.

She turned in the direction of where she thought her old house would be and found herself looking at Luke sitting in a deckchair, sipping on a can of beer.

He seemed unfazed at her sudden appearance.

'Oh!' she said. 'Hi.'

'Hey,' he said with a nod. 'Sit, have a beer.' He indicated the spare deckchair next to him.

She paused, thought it would be impolite not to and lowered herself gingerly into the deckchair, which looked quite fragile at close range. It creaked and groaned alarmingly, but held.

He held a can out to her.

'Thanks.' She opened it and took a sip, feeling the bubbles shoot up her nose. She hated beer, but her inability to say no kicked in again.

She smiled at him and took another sip. 'I didn't know this was here.'

'I found it by accident. It's nice up here. Quiet.'

'Yeah, it is.' They fell into a surprisingly comfortable silence as they both gazed out at the fairy lights of the city laid out below them and listened to the distant thrum of traffic.

'So Jade tells me you work in computers or something?'

'Yeah, something like that. I have my own company doing programming and stuff.'

He clearly wasn't much of a talker.

Silence had always made her feel on edge. It seemed to say more to her than conversation did. 'I'm thinking of starting a business actually, as a bookkeeper,' she said, even though he hadn't asked what she did.

'Cool. Actually, I could do with someone helping me with my books. I'm rubbish at it. Would you be interested?'

'Sure, I can help. You'd be my first client,' she said with a smile.

'I like the sound of that.' He smiled back, his thin top lip almost disappearing into his teeth.

Maddie got up, the deckchair straining as she did, and walked to the edge of the rooftop. Directly below her was her garden.

'Careful, there's no rail,' Luke said from his chair.

'It's surprisingly high up.' The ground seemed to sway, so she took a step back.

'I don't think we're supposed to be up here, but it's not locked or anything and I like it,' he said. 'Sometimes it can get a bit… noisy down there.' He gestured with a nod to the stairs down to the flats.

Maddie thought about this, then said, 'What's Jade like? As a neighbour, I mean?'

He looked at her sharply, then looked away again. 'Alright, I suppose. Why?'

Maddie shrugged. 'She just mentioned you two might have... you know...'

He chugged from the can, then wiped his mouth on his sleeve. 'None of your business, really, is it?'

'No, I guess not.' She looked off into the imperfect darkness. 'It's just... I'm getting to be quite good friends with her and I just wondered, you know...' Wondered what exactly? If she was trustworthy? 'Anyway, the woman opposite me said something the other day that made me think, that's all.'

'Don't worry too much about the old girl. She's a sweet lady if you're on the right side of her.'

Maddie figured that was all he was going to say on the subject. She took another sip from the can and winced as the bitterness coated her throat.

'Yeah, we did have a one-night thing,' Luke said quietly.

Maddie waited for more. It was slow in coming, so she sat back down in the deckchair.

'I should've known better, like shitting on your doorstep.' *How romantic.*

'It was the night after she moved in, I think. She knocked on the door, wanted to know about the other people in the building. I let her in, we got drinking and...' It was his turn to shrug. 'It just happened. Not one of my proudest moments, but there you go. It is what it is.'

Maddie hovered, unsure if he was finished. He had a habit of taking long pauses between sentences, like he was considering his words carefully or taking in air. As expected, after a lengthy breath, he continued, 'It really only got messy when things got funny with the woman who lived in your flat before you.'

Maddie tilted her head. 'Oh?' She twisted to look at him and the deckchair swung to the right before correcting itself with a thump.

He sipped; he paused. She leant forward. The deckchair objected.

'Nice girl was Lucy. Scottish. Young – well, in her early twenties maybe. Worked at a local school – receptionist or something. Very friendly, especially with Peggy Aitkens. Was always in there, checking on her, doing her shopping, that kind of stuff. Peggy's a nosy old girl, but most of it is loneliness. Just wants someone to care, you know? And to talk to. Don't we all…'

Sip; pause. Maddie wanted to give him a nudge, tell him to get to the point.

'Then one day Lucy was gone.'

'Gone? What? Moved out?'

'Dunno, just gone. Didn't even say goodbye to Peggy. She was gutted about that. Still goes on about it when I see her.' He leant forward and looked over his shoulder, then dropped his voice and said, 'But the night before she left, I heard a helluva argument coming from Jade's flat. Shouting, things breaking, Lucy crying, Jade accusing her of all sorts.' He sat back again, nodding to himself.

'Accusing her of what?'

'I dunno, something to do with money, a deal they had. I thought maybe Jade had borrowed money and hadn't paid it back – or vice versa, although Jade never seems to have anything. Last I heard from Peggy, Lucy had sent her a Christmas card from Scotland, so it looks like she moved back home. Anyway, Jade was then all friendly to me again, trying to invite herself over all the time, wanting to know what I had heard, if Lucy had said anything. None of my business though, is it? Better off out of it all.'

Maddie felt a bit deflated. She had wanted more, but she wasn't exactly sure what.

'Well, thanks for telling me. I'd better get back downstairs. Thanks for the beer too.'

'Any time,' he said without looking at her. He was still gazing at the view, can in hand, occasionally raising it to his lips, the picture of relaxation.

She walked over to the heavy metal door, which still stood ajar, and heard him say behind her, 'You remind me a lot of Lucy – you seem nice. I'd be careful of Jade, though. She can get right nasty when she wants to be. Just saying. Peggy would appreciate you checking on her though. I think Jade gives her a hard time. Borderline bullying in my opinion.'

Maddie paused, waiting to see if there would be anything else forthcoming.

'And you don't have to go if you don't want to?' he added, gesticulating at the deckchair.

Maddie thought about it and then lowered herself back into the deckchair and picked up the beer again. Jade could wait.

An hour and two beers later, Maddie knocked on Jade's door, her knuckles slapping against the wood. Seconds later, the door opened on the chain.

'Oh, hello!' The glee was plainly evident in Jade's voice. She unhooked the chain and flung the door open wide.

'Hi.' Maddie felt the flush creep over her skin as she remembered why she was here in the first place.

'Well, well, well! You dark horse,' Jade said with a wide grin. 'Wouldn't have expected *that* from you.'

Maddie closed the door behind her and went to lean against the kitchen counter. It looked like every plate and cup in the kitchen had been used and discarded. Crumbs littered the countertop and cupboard doors stood open.

'I'll put the kettle on and you can tell me all about it,' she said, the grin feline. 'Or would you like something stronger?'

'Tea is fine, thanks. I've had a couple of beers already.'

The noise of the tap running gave Maddie a moment to wonder how she was going to explain herself – or even if she needed to. Instead, she said, 'Who's Lucy?'

Jade's hands stilled on the kettle. 'Why?'

'I was just sitting with Luke, chatting and having a drink, and he mentioned her, said I reminded him of her.'

Jade snapped off the tap just before the kettle overflowed. 'She lived downstairs before you. She was nice enough, but I didn't know her that well. Since when are you friends with Luke?' She looked almost jealous.

'Oh, we just got chatting. He's really nice, got a really good sense of humour once he starts talking. He's asked me to do some bookkeeping work for him.' Maddie had enjoyed herself in the end. Once he opened up, they had chatted easily, joking and laughing about all sorts. It reminded her a little of when she first met Greg, but in a gentler and more mature way without the trappings of adolescence. 'He's a really nice guy.'

'You've said that already.' Jade's voice was clipped. She loudly washed a couple of mugs. 'Luke was keen on her, I reckon. He was always talking to her, offering to do things for her, stuff like that. I think he fancied her, but she knocked him into the friend zone.' Jade paused, like she was letting her revelation about Luke sink in. 'Anyway, that's not important. Let's talk about what went on with you and Greg!'

'It was a one-off, that's all. Like a goodbye – well, that's what it felt like to me, anyway.'

'A goodbye? Why?'

'I don't know. I think I'm just ready to put it all behind me and move on. Get my life in order.'

'Woah, hang on, what happened to helping me out? Asking him for a loan? You did ask him after I left, didn't you?' Desperation hung like a vapour around her.

Maddie shifted her feet, tracked a crack in the floor tile with her toe. 'Well, I mentioned it, but he wasn't really… he said he couldn't right now, what with Jemima and the business is tight at the moment and they're trying for another baby…'

'Fuck's sake!' Jade launched her mug across the room. It skimmed past Maddie to shatter against the wall. The handle flew off and landed, spinning, on the counter. 'What the fuck am I going to do now?'

'Woah, calm down!' Maddie backed away towards the door.

Jade spun at her, her finger pointing like a sharp stick. 'You said he would help. It was your idea!'

'I know and I should've checked with him first before I said anything.' Maddie took another step away. 'But that doesn't mea—'

'You're all the same, aren't you?' she spat at Maddie,

advancing on her, her finger still pointing and jabbing in the narrowing space between them. 'All promises to help and great ideas, but when it comes down to it, none of you actually want to do anything to help me. Well, we had a deal and I *will* see it through. And if I help you, you *will* help me.'

Maddie stepped away from the vitriol on Jade's face until she was backed up against the couch. 'Jade, you're frightening me.'

'Frightening you? I should think I am. Don't forget, I know where they live. Your precious Greg and Jemima,' Jade spat.

'Is that some sort of threat?' Now the fear was burning into anger.

They glared at each other, the air swirling and toxic around them. Maddie took a step forward, closing the distance between them, challenging Jade.

All of a sudden, the anger and bluster seemed to deflate from Jade as quickly as it had flared up. She sunk to the tiles in a heap and began to cry into her hands, her shoulders shuddering dramatically.

'I just don't know what to do anymore,' she said around gasps of air.

Maddie paused, wanting to make sure there were real tears first and that this wasn't another show of drama, then sunk down next to her. 'It'll be ok. We'll figure it out. Shhhh… shhhh…' she said as she put her arm around Jade's quivering shoulders.

'I can't lose him, Maddie, I can't! He's all I've got.'

Maddie let her cry. After a while the sobs melted away and she sat, sniffing, on the kitchen floor. Maddie was about to suggest they get up when Jade started talking again. 'I never had a good relationship with my own mother,' she said in a quiet voice. 'She was a single mum, very young. She got pregnant when she was at school and left to have me. But she never really forgave me for ruining her life.'

'You didn't ruin her life.'

'That's not how she saw it. She used to leave me alone for days when I was little. She'd disappear with her new boyfriends and leave me to fend for myself. Then she'd come back either with a new boyfriend or a new drug habit.' She rubbed at her eyes like a child. 'Then one day I came home from school to a letter and a twenty-pound note. She'd gone – and never came back.'

Maddie clasped a hand over her mouth, aghast. 'She left you?'

'Yeah, but good riddance to her. I've been on my own ever since. And I've done alright, you know? But I can't lose Ben – he's all I have. He's my whole world.'

'That won't happen. We'll make sure of it,' Maddie said in a whisper as Jade began to cry again.

'You have to help me get rid of him, Maddie, otherwise I have no choice but to run away with Ben.'

Maddie swirled the wine in her glass and stared out at the black sky. The clouds were thick and ominous, the night inky and slick behind them. Her mind was just as overcast as she considered what had just happened.

She'd eventually calmed Jade down, got the ugly crying under control, made her a cup of sweet tea and tucked her up on the couch like a poorly child, with the remote control and a grab bag of crisps. If she was acting, she was very good. Her eyes were red and puffy, her nose still sniffly, when Maddie let herself out of the flat and returned to her own.

The episode had unnerved Maddie. Jade's demeanour had switched in a matter of seconds and Maddie was left wondering which side of Jade was to be believed. It worried her for Ben's sake – how unpredictable she could be and how fiery her temper. Did she think Jade would ever hurt Ben? Probably not. But Maddie also had to consider her background, the stories she had just told Maddie about her own mother and her all-encompassing desperation to hold onto Ben, to not lose him. Maddie understood that level of desperation all too well. That feeling of clinging onto something with the very edges of your fingernails and the fear as you feel your grip failing.

Where was Ben tonight anyway? She hadn't seen any sign of him in days. If his dad had been looking after him more, that would explain Jade's mood swings and emotional outbursts. She was probably missing Ben like mad.

She hoped that was the case anyway.

But if not, if Maddie was even slightly worried about Ben's safety, then should she take matters into her own hands?

Jade blew her nose loudly and looked at herself in the bathroom mirror. She hadn't expected to feel as emotional as she had done in the end. The disappointment that Maddie wasn't going to present her with a fat cheque had made her furious, then panicked, and she hadn't needed to pretend this time after all, not after she'd had an uncharacteristic premonition that maybe this scheme wouldn't work out after all. It had seemed a no-brainer when she first met Maddie, but now she wasn't so sure.

Maddie had more layers to her than Jade had initially expected. For a while, Jade had considered calling the whole thing off because Maddie was clearly a woman on the edge and Jade didn't need to attract that kind of attention to herself. But then she realised that her very instability could be the hook Jade was looking for.

Hence the sob story about her mother. It hadn't taken her long to realise that the anger was not helping. It had worked on that stupid bitch Lucy, with her bouncy blonde hair and Bambi eyes, but Maddie was proving a tougher nut to crack – or coerce as it was. Raw, emotional tales of hardship seemed to work better on Maddie.

She liked to have someone to save.

The story Jade had told Maddie was inspired. She wasn't even sure where it had come from – maybe something she'd seen on telly. Jade's mother was alive and well and living in Milton Keynes. Jade had seen her last week when she went over to celebrate her sister's birthday.

Lucy had apparently fled back to Scotland to escape Jade's fury, but was still sending Jade money every month because she was petrified that Jade would make good on her threat to post on social media the video she had managed to get of Lucy in bed with the headmaster of her school. Not just any video though; a filthy, disgusting, leaves a little bit of sick in your mouth kind of video. Lucy had moved back in with her parents because she couldn't afford the blackmail payments on her small salary if she was living in London.

Her leaving hadn't been planned, but when Lucy had said she was going, Jade had been thrilled. Still paying her, but not on Jade's doorstep begging for the footage anymore. Win, win.

But what Jade needed from Maddie wasn't as simple as just money. Financial gains would be a nice bonus, of course, but that wasn't the endgame. Not this time.

She splashed some water on her face and dried it with the towel lying on the bathroom floor, still damp from Jade's bath earlier.

Ben would be back tomorrow, so she should do some tidying up, at least wash the dishes and make sure she had some baked beans in the cupboard. That was all he wanted to eat when he was at her house. Baked beans and those little pots of Petit Filous yoghurt.

Anger was still simmering in her stomach like indigestion. Bloody Maddie. Jade needed to put the next phase into action now. There had been times in the last few days when Maddie had got a little too close to the truth. And now Maddie was getting friendly with Luke, who'd proved troublesome with Lucy too.

Not great.

Jade stared at herself for a moment longer, then turned away.

Maddie heard the knock and thought about ignoring it. It could only be Jade again and she wasn't up to any more melodrama for tonight. She had a banging headache and was already in her pyjamas, a pasta sauce bubbling on the stove and some downloaded episodes of *Vera* lined up and waiting.

It's funny all the things she used to think she would achieve if she ever lived alone. The evening classes she would do – pottery, maybe drawing – or sports she would try. She used to be quite good with a hockey stick at school and could probably still hold her own on a netball court. But when it came down to it, what she really enjoyed doing was cooking something simple, opening a nice bottle of wine for one or two glasses and snuggling under her duvet in front of a box set.

She would never meet someone new if she hid under her duvet every weekend, but then, she didn't think she was at the stage where she wanted to meet someone knew yet. Greg was still too raw a wound for her to consider anyone else. Besides, the thought of dating – all that effort to dress up, chat politely and agonise over whether he would call again – it just left her feeling tired. What she really wanted was to indulge in some self-care for a while. She deserved it.

Having said that, she'd really enjoyed spending time with Luke earlier. It had been relaxed, comfortable.

Even so, tonight called for self-care. Without the wine though – her head was thick already after the beer earlier – but she had a family-size bar of Dairy Milk in the fridge with her name on it.

The knock came again, then the letterbox clattered open and Jade's eyes peered through the door. Maddie had taken to keeping the chain on all the time now.

'Maddie?'

She would have to open the door. Jade could probably see her sitting on the couch.

She heaved to her feet, slid the chain back and opened the door. 'Hey, feeling better?'

Jade looked better, still a little red-rimmed around the eyes, but more sheepish now and less likely to erupt in either fury or tears, thankfully.

'I just wanted to say I'm sorry. I was being stupid.' She pushed past Maddie and strode into the lounge without being invited.

'Hey, no, it's fine. I know you're under pressure and it's all very stressful for you, so don't worry about it.'

'Hmmm, something smells good.' Her nose twitched like a rabbit as she looked towards the kitchen.

Not tonight, please. Maddie's heart rate inched up at the thought of having to come up with a plausible excuse to not invite her to stay.

'Oh, just reheating a pasta sauce. I can feel a migraine coming on though, so I might just go straight to bed instead.'

'Well, if you're not going to eat it, I'll have it. Rather than let it go to waste, you know…'

Maddie paused, looked at the pasta sauce and then back to Jade. Was she actually going to let Jade take her dinner off her? She was really looking forward to a large, steaming bowl of pasta.

'Well, no, it's not really going to waste. I'll just have it tomorrow.'

'Oh, right, sure,' Jade said, her eyes dropping to the floor along with her lip. 'Well, I just wanted to say sorry. I didn't mean to intrude.' She turned to go, her shoulders slumping.

'You're not intruding, really, and there is no need to apologise. I understand.'

Jade sneezed suddenly, loud and eruptive. 'Ugh, I'm struggling so much with hayfever at the moment.'

'Really? At this time of the year? How odd.'

'Yeah, I know! Must be the dust in this building or something, but I'm just so... you don't happen to have any antihistamines, do you? I'm all out and if I don't take something, I'll be sneezing all night.'

'Yeah, I have some in the bathroom. I'll go get them.'

Maddie hurried into the bathroom, wanting only to get Jade out as quickly as possible. She opened the cabinet, found the box and pulled an entire sleeve of pills out. That should keep her going for a while.

When she returned to the lounge, Jade was in the kitchen.

'I turned the sauce off. It was about to bubble over.'

Maddie frowned. The sauce had been on a low heat.

'Thanks. Here you go – take the whole sleeve.'

'Great, thanks.' She had her hands tucked into her baggy hoodie as usual and took the pills from her with her sleeve, like she had cold fingers. She pocketed the pills and turned to go.

'Great, um, thanks again,' she said with a smile and rushed out.

Maddie closed the door and leant against it, exhaled, then reached over and drew the chain again.

11

Maddie knocked on Peggy Aitkens' door gingerly. Luke's words from last night echoed in her head and she'd spent most of the night wondering if she knew Jade at all and how cautious she should be of her. What had Luke said? Borderline bullying? Maddie had seen her kicking on the door all those weeks ago and the way Peggy flinched whenever she saw Jade.

She needed to put some distance between herself and Jade perhaps. There were too many things that didn't quite fit right – the volatility; the manipulation; the spitefulness. She felt like she was being quietly bullied and manipulated, but was helpless to stop it. Not seeing her would mean not spending time with Ben though and that was like a physical pain when she thought about it.

She still had Jemima though. Greg had said she could be a part of her life.

'Who is it?' a voice said from behind the unopened door.

'It's Maddie – from across the hall? I just wanted to check on you, make you a cup of tea maybe?' There was no response. 'I have a Victoria sponge I need help eating too.'

The door opened on the chain and Peggy's cataract-cloudy eyes peered through the gap.

The door closed again and the chain slid back.

'Come in. Wipe your feet.'

Maddie closed the door behind her and followed Peggy into a cluttered and stiflingly warm lounge. A floral couch and two armchairs were arranged around a surprisingly up-to-date flat-screen television. Every surface was covered with china and crystal ornaments, each one sparkling and dust-free. The patio doors revealed a bright and colourful garden full of herbs, vegetables and rosebushes in a late stage of flowering.

Maddie held out the M&S Victoria sponge and said with a smile, 'I'll put the kettle on, shall I?'

She opened tidy cupboards in the kitchen and found a teapot and two china mugs, along with plates and cake forks. She stacked everything on a tray and carried it through to the coffee table in the lounge where Peggy sat in her slippers, looking out of the patio doors.

'You have a lovely garden, Mrs Aitkens,' Maddie said as she poured the tea.

'Thank you. Not too much milk for me – and call me Peggy. I'm not your teacher.'

They sipped quietly for a moment. 'Have you settled in alright then?' Peggy asked.

'Yes, thank you. Still have a few boxes to unpack, but I'm getting there. I would love a garden like that though – mine is just a patch of mud.'

'It takes time, especially if you're working.'

'Oh, I don't work. I've taken some time off – I've had some... personal issues.'

Peggy nodded sagely. 'Then gardening might help with that. It helps to keep my fingers busy. The devil makes work for idle hands.'

'That is true. I'm thinking of setting up my own business. I think it is time I got back into work.'

'That's what Luke upstairs does. Lovely man, he is.'

'Yes, I've met him. He seems really nice. I'm going to be doing some work for him, actually.'

'He's a good lad, keeps an eye out for me. Got a caring heart, that one.'

The conversation lulled as Maddie cut into the cake and handed a plate to Peggy.

'Do you have children, Peggy?'

'No, never had them.'

'Oh, I'm sorry. I don't either.'

'You should do something about that. It gets a bit lonely when you get to my age.'

Maddie smiled. 'I think my time for that has passed.'

'You never know what lies around the corner, my dear.'

A clock ticked comfortingly. Maddie looked around at the bookcases lining the far wall. 'I see you like to read?'

'A lot of those are my late husband's. I started reading them after he passed away – I wanted to know what had stolen him away from me for hours on end. They were like a string of mistresses. And now I've read them all, some of them twice. They're my love affair now.'

'Well, if you ever need me to pick up some books from the library for you – or even accompany you there – I'm happy to. I love the library. I took Ben there the other day. You know Ben from upstairs?'

'The little boy? He's a sweet little one, isn't he? I can't imagine why anyone would want to hurt them.' She tutted and shook her head before scooping up the crumbs on her plate with the flat of her finger. It was a strange thing to say and Maddie was a little lost for a response, but Peggy continued, 'You should be careful of that woman upstairs. I'm not one to gossip, but she's vicious, that one.'

'Does she give you a hard time, Peggy?'

Peggy looked uncomfortable. 'I don't want to speak ill of her behind her back.'

'You're not at all, but I'd rather know than not. The truth is I've been a bit concerned about her behaviour myself lately.'

'I called the council on her once – a while ago – because I could smell marijuana coming from her flat. They didn't find anything but she got a bit nasty after that. Started keeping me awake at night with her music, banging on the door in the early hours of the morning, that kind of thing. It stopped for a bit when Lucy and Luke moved in because they kept an eye out for me, but then Lucy moved away and every now and again, when I think it's all over, she'll do something just to remind me she's there. Luke is good at keeping her in check though.'

'Oh, I'm so sorry.'

'Oh, don't worry yourself, dear. If I can live through Hitler, I can put up with the likes of her.'

'But you shouldn't have to!'

'Aye, well, I just keep myself to myself.' She drained her teacup. 'The worst was when she smeared excrement all over my front door once. I don't have any proof it was her, but someone had taken a baby's nappy and rubbed it all over my door, the door handle, everywhere and then left the nappy on the mat.'

Maddie was horrified. How could anyone bully and torture a little old woman like that?

She needed to have a word with Jade. This was unacceptable.

As if reading her mind, Peggy said, 'I don't want you getting involved though, my dear. She's a nasty piece of work and you don't need the aggravation. She gets bored quickly anyway. Like any bully, she'll find someone else to pester if we ignore her. In fact, she's left me alone for a bit, so maybe she's already got bored with me.'

Maddie sat quietly, unease trickling through her.

She had a funny feeling that she was Jade's new plaything now.

12

Greg heard the doorbell ring. Jemima was perched on his hip, his hair stood up in tufts from where Jemima had been pulling it and he had *Little Mermaid* stickers all over his cheek. Gemma had gone to a Sunday morning yoga class. She was still annoyed about the other day and his lengthy 'gym' outing. She'd been treating him to the silent treatment ever since, so a bit of space from her iciness was welcome. If he thought about how much he had enjoyed being with Maddie that day, compared to Gemma's attitude last night throughout a frosty dinner before she stormed off to bed, he knew what he would prefer any day of the week. Maddie had made it clear it was a one-off, but he had to admit that didn't sit right with him.

Let's see though... who knows what could happen?

He loved these moments when it was just him and Jemima. Gemma had a way of making him feel completely inadequate, criticising him for the way he spoke to Jemima, not cutting up her grapes small enough, not putting the nappy cream on properly. Anything and everything could be like a red rag to the bull and then Gemma would be off on one, like she was the only person in the world who knew how to look after a baby.

But the truth was that Gemma wasn't all that good at it herself and he was secure in the knowledge that although he may get the logistics wrong, he was nailing the cuddles and playtime. In fact, he was nailing the fatherhood thing full stop.

He opened the door to a woman standing on his front step, who looked vaguely familiar. She was wearing baggy tracksuit bottoms and an oversized hoodie that was pulled up over her head, so he couldn't quite make out her face. Her eyes were covered by large sunglasses, out of place on such a cloudy day. He immediately went to close the door on her, saying, 'Nothing today, thanks' in case she was one of those convicts selling tea towels or a Jehovah's looking to discuss the end of the world while shoving a copy of *The Watchtower* in his hand.

'Greg Lowe? I have a delivery for you.'

He hesitated. 'Oh?'

Jemima gurgled in his arms, her tiny fists still clamped in his hair.

'Ah, such a lovely baby.' The woman leant into the doorway and stroked Jemima's cheek.

Greg stepped back one pace, so that the woman was just out of reach. 'Thanks.'

She shoved a small, white box at his stomach. Greg took hold of the box and looked back at the woman, but she was already walking away, her immaculately white trainers crunching across the gravel.

He frowned and closed the door. He gently lowered Jemima to the floor and she took off on all fours. Greg looked at the box in his hand. It was the kind of thing they put your cakes in at the bakery and, lifting the lid, that was exactly what was inside. A selection of four, small, delicious-looking patisserie cakes decorated with edible flowers and delicate icing. His mouth started to water just looking at them. He'd only had Gemma's green smoothie so far today.

Oh, but the diet. Gemma would be furious with him if he brought these out after dinner. Just that morning, she had made him weigh himself in front of her and had tutted when he had only lost a pound. He hadn't told her about the sneaky pint he'd had with Mike on his way home from work on Friday – or the bag of pork scratchings that he'd washed down with it.

He scooped Jemima up and tucked her into her highchair, where she continued to destroy the sticker book in front of her. The box had no message with it. It was just a plain white box.

Maybe Maddie had sent them. It certainly wouldn't have been Gemma and it was far too feminine a gift for it to have been one of his five-a-side mates. There was a bakery down the road. Maddie probably had them sent from there – but why?

Unless it was because of what he'd told her the other day. He thought back to lying next to her again, the sheets wrapped around their legs, her cheeks flushed. She'd looked like the Maddie of old, before the pregnancies and the stress and the heartbreak. She'd looked like the girl he had fallen in love with. He'd been making her laugh by telling her about his disastrous attempt to deep-fry tofu last week for their dinner. She had said she thought he was fine the way he was and he had joked about maybe sneaking off to eat cake in his lunch hour when the lettuce and fresh air diet he was on got too much.

She must've sent these as a joke, something just between them. It was the kind of thing she would do. He smiled, feeling his stomach lurch like a boy with a crush on the girl next door.

Greg turned on the coffee machine, popped a strong espresso pod in the top and brewed a coffee, then sat at the table next to Jemima with his box of cakes and his cup.

Nestled inside the box like a cuddle were two slices of what looked to be a rich chocolate cake and two slices of vanilla and peach cake. He thought about getting a fork from the drawer, then just reached in with his fingers and grabbed the vanilla cake first, took a large bite and let the moist, delicious sponge dissolve in his mouth. Jemima reached out to grab the cake, but he moved it from reach. He wasn't sure if cake and cream were good for babies. Peaches were though, weren't they? One of her five a day?

Her hand reached out again almost instantly and this time he put a bit of the cake in her grasp. She shovelled it into her mouth with delight and he laughed. 'I know! Cake is the dog's bollocks, isn't it? Don't let your mother know I said bollocks though – or that I gave you cake,' he said conspiratorially.

Before long, the slice was gone and Jemima was wearing cream from one ear to the other.

'It would be remiss of us not to taste the chocolate too, don't you think?'

He was sure Jemima nodded.

The chocolate was just as rich and decadent as he expected. The slice was gone in minutes, shared with Jemima to an extent, but mostly consumed by Greg.

For a second he considered eating the other two slices

in the box too, but then thought better of it and got up to find somewhere to stash the box where Gemma wouldn't find it. He could save them for later. She had another yoga class booked tomorrow evening and he knew exactly how he would spend the time while she was out.

As he got to his feet, his throat started to itch and he coughed a little, then a lot. Within seconds, it felt like a hand had reached up, shoved some razor blades down his throat and then begun to squeeze his neck so that he couldn't breathe past the blades slicing the inside of his oesophagus. The pain and asphyxia caused spots to bloom in his vision. The spots swam in and out as he gasped for breath and lurched into the kitchen to the tap, hoping that perhaps some water would dislodge whatever was obstructing his windpipe.

But he knew what it was and he knew water wouldn't help him now.

He hadn't had a reaction like this in decades. In fact, since he was at school. But now that it was happening, he recognised the signs of anaphylactic shock. There must've been nuts in one of the cakes. He hadn't tasted nuts though. And if Maddie had sent them, she knew how allergic he was and had always been so careful about it.

He stumbled out of the kitchen on weakening legs. He had a syringe of epinephrine in the bathroom cabinet upstairs, but he couldn't remember when he last checked it or if it was out of date. It would have to do though, because he was starting to feel light-headed and he could hear himself wheezing as his throat closed up and slowly cut off his air supply.

He stumbled and fell in the corridor and had to drag

himself up the stairs. His heart was racing, his eyes were streaming and he was properly terrified for the first time in his life. As he crawled up each Everest of a stair, his thoughts turned to Jemima, her beautiful little face and her delightful smile. The sound of her giggle and the way she opened her mouth and clamped her gums onto his cheek in her version of a kiss. Then he thought of Maddie, her face filling his brain. His eyes were streaming, but now with tears rather than from the exertion of trying to suck in air.

When Gemma opened the front door, the first thing she heard was Jemima screaming from the kitchen.

So much for calm and relaxation.

'Greg?'

She threw her yoga mat down in annoyance. She'd only been gone a couple of hours and it sounded like all hell had broken loose. And she was thinking it wouldn't hurt to go for a green tea with Emilia after their class; Greg could cope for a bit longer. In fact, lately she'd been thinking that Greg could cope much better than her altogether. He was so much calmer than her, so affectionate with Jemima. Gemma had to admit it annoyed her that he had adapted to fatherhood so easily. Greg and Jemima were like a little compact unit and she felt like the outsider most of the time.

Well, clearly something had gone wrong today.

She stomped into the kitchen and found Jemima in her highchair, tears streaming down her cheeks and leaving track lines in what looked like cream on her face. Gemma unclipped her from the chair and lifted her at arm's length. She really didn't want to get that white stuff on herself.

'Greg? Where the hell are you?' she shouted.

There was no answer. Grabbing a wet wipe from the pack on the table, she wiped Jemima's face and gave her a brief cuddle before noticing the cake box on the table. That explained the cream then.

'Greg! Where did these cakes come from?' No wonder he hadn't lost much weight this week.

Now she was really annoyed. Jemima was still screaming into her ear. All she could think to do to get her to stop was to grab a bit of the chocolate cake left in the box and hand it to her. Jemima stopped screaming, her little body heaving in sorrow as she sucked on the chunk of cake.

Thankful the screaming had stopped, Gemma headed into the hallway to see if Greg was in the loo. Either he was hiding because he knew he had been caught in the act or he was on the phone in his office. Either way, she'd be having a word. Her mind switched to a few days ago, seeing his car at Maddie's, knowing he had lied to her. Was this what it had felt like for Maddie all those years ago?

Gemma didn't like it, not one bit. She would've happily killed him last night, sitting across from her at dinner like the cat who had got the cream, all while she was trying to figure out what was really going on between him and Maddie.

His office door was open, but he wasn't inside. Looking up the stairs, she noticed a brown sock on the landing. There was a foot in the sock. Gemma slowly climbed the stairs, a frown wrinkling her brow. The foot was attached to a leg, which was attached to Greg, who was lying on the carpet. What she could see of his face was blotchy, his lips were blue and his eyes stared at nothing.

It took her a second to comprehend what she was seeing. Why was he lying there like that and why were his trousers wet around the crotch?

Her next thought was, *Be careful what you wish for.*

Then she started to scream.

Maddie sat at her laptop, trying to work her way through the logistics of creating a website to distract herself from her conversation with Peggy. But the website was proving more complicated than she thought. So much for the adverts telling her how quick and easy it would be.

Maybe she should call Greg and ask him for help.

No. She could call Luke though.

She moved the text box to the other side of the screen and began to fiddle with the fonts. Which one looked more professional? And would anyone notice?

Luke would probably know best. If she couldn't figure it out soon, she might go and knock on his door. Maybe take a bottle of wine. She had started working on his books earlier and it was really good to engage her brain again. It would also give her a chance to talk to him about Jade and Peggy too before she confronted Jade about it. Best to have an impartial point of view before accusing someone. And she just liked spending time with him... the idea made her smile.

Her phone vibrated on the table next to her.

A Snapchat alert. That meant a message from Jade. Her stomach sank.

As well as watching YouTube videos on how to create a website, Maddie had been reading up on the latest social media tools too. She needed to know what was going on in the world if she was to start a business. She would need Twitter, LinkedIn and all those things. After years of ignoring it all when her mind was occupied with other things, she realised she needed to bring herself up to date now.

She opened Snapchat and pulled the message to the side without clicking on it – a trick she had learnt that meant she could read the message without Jade knowing she had seen it. It was a way of buying her time and she figured it could be useful, especially since Jade was in the habit of texting her repeatedly if she read her message but didn't reply immediately.

The message read:

I've done my part. Now it's over to you. You can thank me by repaying the favour.

Maddie frowned and read it again, then closed the app. What did she mean? What had she done?

She chewed on the end of her pen, mulling it over. It must be something to do with Ben. Maybe she'd taken Maddie's advice and found a lawyer or something.

Maddie pushed it from her mind and got up to make more tea. She'd add it to the list of things to talk to her about later.

13

Her phone was ringing, the insistent chime pulling at her, dragging her from sleep.

Maddie squinted into the semi-darkness. The television had gone into standby mode and a message scrolled across the screen. *No connection.* Moving in green letters across the charcoal grey background.

The phone stopped ringing, then immediately started up again as a voicemail came through.

Maddie sat up slowly and wiped the dribble from her mouth. She was on the couch under her duvet. She must've fallen asleep in front of the television. She had no idea what time it was.

The ringing stopped again, but Maddie knew it would just start up again until she listened to the voicemail. She had to figure out how to change that setting. She looked over to the clock on the kitchen wall, but couldn't make out the time. Her eyes were still blurry with sleep.

Nobody called her at night.

That was the thought that eventually got her to her feet.

She dragged herself towards the kitchen where her phone was charging. It was 23h15, so she hadn't been asleep that long. But it had felt like hours. She unplugged her phone and listened to the voicemail.

It was Gemma, but her voice sounded weird, all tight and raspy, like she had a sore throat. She was saying something about Greg, that he had been taken to hospital.

Her heart seemed to stop beating for an instant, then lurched into overdrive. She called Gemma back, both desperate to hear what she had to say while also wanting to put the phone down and crawl back under the duvet.

If Gemma was calling her, then it was serious. She thought about Gemma's car driving away the other day.

The phone rang for what felt like an eternity, then went to voicemail. She left a rambling message and disconnected the call.

She pulled herself up onto the kitchen counter, letting her legs dangle and sway, her hands tucked under her thighs, waiting for Gemma to call back.

It was mere minutes before her phone rang again. 'Hello? Gemma?'

The voice at the end of the line didn't sound like the Gemma she knew. 'Maddie, hi. I thought you should know. It's Greg. He's...'

Then she started to weep. Not ugly crying like Jade yesterday in massive, melodramatic gulps and wails, but a solitary keening sound that cut straight through Maddie.

'Gemma, what is it?'

'He's dead, Maddie. He's dead.'

Maddie felt the phone drop from her hand. It bounced on the countertop, landing face-up. The caller ID photo attached to Gemma's contact taunted her. It was a photo of

Gemma and Greg when she was pregnant, all bulging bellies and wide smiles.

She picked up the phone again, both to talk to Gemma and to not have to look at the photo again. 'What happened? He was fine the other day.'

'He ate some cake and the doctor thinks it had nuts in it.'

'But he's so careful with that.' But was he? Maddie had been the careful one. She was the one who had made sure his epinephrine was in date, checked the ingredients on food labels, alerted waiters in restaurants. Then her mind made a leap she wasn't expecting. Had Gemma done this? Because she had found out about them? No, she couldn't have, surely. Maybe she only meant to frighten him, but hadn't appreciated how fatal his allergy was.

'It's all because I put him on a diet,' Gemma was saying around her tears. 'If I had just left him alone, he wouldn't have bought the cakes.'

'No, you can't blame yourself, Gemma. He is – was – a grown man. He knew he was allergic.'

'What am I going to do without him?' Her breath was coming in gulps now, like she was having a panic attack.

'Gemma, you'll be ok. Just breathe. It's the shock. Where are you? Shall I come over? Where's Jemima?'

At the mention of her daughter's name, Gemma seemed to pull herself together a little. 'She's fine, she's with my mother. We've just got back from the hospital. I just thought you should know.'

'Please call me if I can help with anything.'

'I will, thank you, Maddie. Goodbye.'

The line cut dead.

Maddie sat, staring at the phone in her hand but not seeing it.

Greg.

Gone.

How much more could she be expected to take?

Jade swigged from the can, her eyes on the television but not seeing. Maddie had aired her.

How dare she? Anger fizzed and roiled in her stomach with the beer, acidic and bitter. She drained the can and opened another.

Maybe she should go down there, confront her.

But Maddie had started putting the chain on all the time, so she couldn't get in with the key. She was smarter than she looked.

Jade would have to bide her time. Maddie would come knocking soon enough.

Mere minutes later and Jade was smiling into the tin still clasped in her hand. Someone was knocking on the door.

She got up, adjusted the smugness from her face and opened the door a crack, keeping the chain on.

Maddie looked bereft. Her hair was tied into a messy ponytail, her eyes were streaming and there was a vivid red line on her cheek, where a pillow was still indented on her face. 'Oh God, Jade, I've just had awful news. I can't be alone right now.'

Jade adopted a look of sympathy and opened the door wide for Maddie.

'Sit, I'll put the kettle on for you. It's the shock, I think. You'll be ok in a minute.'

'I feel like I'll never be ok again.' She blew her nose loudly in a tissue clamped in her fist.

Jade frowned into the sink as she filled the kettle. She had expected Maddie to be upset, but this seemed a bit over the top. 'You will. Give it a few days and the shock will wear off. It's for the best.'

Maddie looked up sharply.

'It was what we planned,' Jade said. She pulled a bottle of milk from the fridge, unscrewed the lid and sniffed it. On the turn, but it would do. Just to be sure, she took a swig from the bottle. It tasted fine.

Maddie launched from the couch. 'What do you mean, Jade?' Her voice was like a slap.

Jade looked over at her, the milk bottle still poised in her hand. 'You know what I mean.' She nonchalantly finished making the tea, left the milk on the counter to sour even further and brought the mugs over to where Maddie was standing stiff and upright.

Jade handed her a mug, but Maddie didn't take it from her. Jade shrugged and put it on the coffee table.

'What do you mean, Jade?' Maddie repeated.

Jade sighed dramatically and flopped onto the couch. 'I sorted it for you. Our deal? I did my bit. Now it's your turn.' She put her sock-clad feet up on the table.

Maddie sank down next to her, the colour completely drained from her face. 'What did you do?'

'I may or may not have delivered some cakes to his house today. And those cakes may or may not have been laced with sesame oil. Just a little, mind.' She smiled at Maddie wickedly. 'From your reaction, I'm guessing it worked. You're good, I'll give you that. But don't overwork it. You want people to believe you are bereft, but too much will make them suspicious.' She lifted her mug to her lips.

Maddie's hand shot out and slapped the mug of hot tea into Jade's lap. She shot to her feet, crying out in pain. 'What the fuck? That's hot!'

Then Maddie was on her, grappling at Jade's throat, throwing random slaps and punches, most of which were not connecting at all. Jade slapped back and flung her off. Maddie landed on her back on the floor, blood trickling from her nose.

Jade loomed over her. 'I'll give you that one, but you won't get another punch in, I promise you that.' Jade's eyes glinted with red-hot anger.

Maddie sat up slowly and wiped at the blood. 'You killed him,' she said.

'Yes – *but you didn't.*'

Maddie sat back on the edge of the couch, putting as much space between them as she could, and put her head in her hands.

Jade swore under her breath, then went to grab a tea towel from the kitchen to mop up the spilled tea. When she was done, Maddie was still sitting, unmoving, her head still clasped in her hands.

'The deal was that I would get rid of Greg for you and you would get rid of Mark for me. I've lived up to my side of the deal; now it's your turn. I haven't quite figured out the logistics yet, but I will. Greg was easy. As soon as you mentioned his nut allergy, I knew how I would do it. And there is no trace back to you at this stage. It looks like an accident – him just being stupid and not checking the ingredients.'

'I thought you were kidding.' Maddie's voice was barely above a whisper.

'Why would I?'

Maddie's head shot up. 'Because people kid about these things. You know, they say, *I could strangle him* all the time, but they don't mean it! I never wanted him dead!'

Her face was a mask of disbelief and horror.

'Is that true, though? Really? If that's what you have to tell yourself, then go ahead,' Jade said and shrugged. 'Regardless, it's done now and you have to help me to even the score.'

'I don't have to do anything for you. I was not involved. This is all on you. I'll just go to the police, tell them what you've done. There'll be evidence.' Maddie rushed towards the front door with the look of someone who was trying not to throw up.

'Oh, but that's where you're wrong,' Jade said loudly, stopping Maddie in her tracks. 'You see, I built in a bit of a security blanket if you will. It's funny, but for a rich fella, he really should invest in one of those doorbells with a camera. You know, so you can see who's at the door? He just opened it, quite happily. Jemima is very cute, by the way.'

Maddie's face morphed from disbelief into horror.

Jade continued. 'No one saw me arriving. No one saw me leave. But if the police ever look into it, the bakery box has your fingerprints on it and I have a receipt for the cakes that were bought with your debit card.'

'But... how?'

'I used the box from your red velvet cupcake. You know, the one laced with laxatives? Wow, that little joke escalated quickly. I hadn't realised I'd put that much in, but you were a mess that day.' She made fake retching noises and laughed. 'Your fingerprints are all over that box. You know me, I always tuck my hands in my sleeves. That's the thing with long hoodies, they're very useful. And your debit card? You can have that back now. It's on the counter over there. You really should be more careful about leaving your purse lying around. Anyone could walk in to, oh, I don't know, maybe borrow some antihistamines and then take off with your card. No need for PIN numbers these days.'

Jade really did think Maddie was going to throw up. She had gone from a translucent white to sickly green in seconds.

'So if you ever go to the police or even suggest it wasn't an accident to anyone, I'll have you.' Jade smiled sweetly, her teeth showing like a rabid animal, enjoying the game she was playing. 'All it will take is one little call to the police suggesting they fingerprint the box. Now, maybe you should go and lie down. You look a little pale. Let me know when you're ready to discuss our little arrangement again though.'

Maddie burst into her flat and did in fact rush straight to the bathroom to throw up. When it was over, she sat and hugged the toilet, gasping and panting, feeling her chest ache.

Maybe she was having a heart attack.

Maybe that wouldn't be such a bad thing.

She couldn't take in what Jade had told her. How had they got to this? She thought back to all the conversations they had had, the times Jade had talked about their apparent 'deal'. She was so sure Jade had been joking... wasn't she?

The more she thought about it, the more she started to question herself. All those weird outbursts when she had felt uncomfortable with Jade's words, her demeanour. She had ignored it, brushed it away as if it was nothing, good manners dictating that she politely ignore what was right in front of her. But what about all those thoughts she'd been having herself? Running away with Jemima? Wishing ill on Gemma? Was this karma?

She pushed away from the toilet, flushed it and stood staring at herself in the mirror above the sink. She was waxen, her skin slick with oily sweat. She looked away.

She needed to think, to figure out what to do, but all her mind kept thinking about was whether he had suffered. Had he been scared? Of course he had. Oh God, had Jemima been with him at the time? Maddie could feel panic clutching at her chest again.

She lurched into the kitchen to the corner cupboard where she kept the few bottles of booze she owned. There was an unopened bottle of whiskey in the back of the cupboard. She'd bought it in case Greg wanted a drink when he came over. She usually hated the stuff, but it seemed fitting that this was what she latched onto now, cracking open the seal and pouring three fingers into a glass. She necked it, feeling the heat of it jolt her. She poured another more sensible measure and sat down heavily on the kitchen floor, the bottle between her legs.

Time to think.

What did Jade want? Mark out of the picture so that she had Ben to herself.

Which means she would be expecting Maddie to return the favour, maybe by killing Mark somehow.

There was no way she could do that.

Maybe she could talk to Mark, get him to drop the custody battle altogether. But then she'd have to explain why she was there, wouldn't she? Jade hadn't actually told her how to find Mark yet, but she wouldn't be happy with Maddie just giving him a stern talking to, would she? Not after what Jade had just done.

But what about Ben? The idea that Jemima would grow up without knowing Greg made Maddie go cold. She couldn't do that to Ben too. He was such a quiet, sensitive boy. This could only hurt him.

Her brain swirled and dived in and out of thoughts, intertwined with memories of Greg, the other night when he'd been here, the last time she had seen him.

She took another swig of the whiskey, wincing as it went down. She needed to pull herself together and figure this out, find out whether the police were suspicious, whether Gemma was suspicious. Because if they dug too deeply, Maddie could be in real trouble. Who would believe her if she said she had thought it was just a joke? Then there was that conversation she'd had with Greg only days ago. Incriminating to say the least.

She needed to talk to Gemma, find out what actually happened. And to think she'd suspected Gemma at first.

She also needed to start building some evidence on Jade. Just in case.

What had Jade called it? A security blanket?

Her heart dropped through the floor of her stomach again. That was why Jade had insisted on them using Snapchat for their messages. It was because the messages vanished once they were read. Maddie hadn't screenshotted any of Jade's messages, but she knew for a fact Jade had screenshotted hers. She thought it was just because she wanted to keep track of their conversation, but it was all evidence against her.

What had she said in those messages? Had she joked back about killing Greg? Made some flippant remark that would be incriminating if taken out of context?

Oh God, could this get any worse?

She needed air and space.

She drained the glass, grabbed the bottle and fled the flat, heading up the stairs, past Jade's door to the roof.

It was empty tonight. No Luke in a deckchair; no cans of beer. Just the town laid out below her, the lights twinkling innocently.

She desperately wanted to knock on Luke's door, but also didn't want to drag him into this.

No, she was on her own.

She stepped right up to the edge, her toes hanging in mid-air, and leant forward slightly, feeling a brief sense of weightlessness. The bottle dangled from her hand, heavy at her side. She unscrewed the cap and brought it up to her mouth, now used to the spicy bitterness of the alcohol. It was indeed helping to dull the pain in her chest. She swayed a little in the cold night air, goosebumps standing up on her bare arms.

Look at those people below me, casually going about their business. They haven't incited a murder today, have they? They aren't being framed for something they haven't done.

They aren't scared and alone.

She started to weep again, but silently this time, the tears huge glass marbles rolling down her cheeks. She pitched forward again, this time further, felt her heels lift slightly from the roof.

What would it feel like, she wondered, if she just leant all the way forward? Was it high enough to die from here?

Would anyone care? Who was left to care? Only Greg would've missed her. Her mother was dead, her father hadn't tried to speak to her in decades, she had no friends and no husband anymore.

A fat tear fell onto her top lip, salty with grief. She tipped forward some more, feeling buoyed by the breeze.

But if she did fall, if she decided to end it all now, would that be seen as an admission of guilt? Or would the police just put it down to her being the distraught ex-wife? Sorry, distraught *wife* since they were still married. That would be suspicious too, wouldn't it? Oh God, his life insurance! Had he changed any of it?

She was getting dizzy thinking about it again. She swayed and this time one of her feet left the ground completely. Her heart froze and she flung herself back from the edge, twisting her ankle painfully in the process.

She panted into the night air, then limped over to Luke's deckchairs and dropped into one, this time oblivious to the groans of protest from the wood and fabric beneath her.

She tried to steady her breathing with another swig of whiskey, then set the bottle at her feet and sat all the way back in the chair, staring up at the night sky and letting her mind work through the thoughts ricocheting around her skull.

'You ok?' a voice said behind her. Luke lowered himself into the other chair.

'Yes... no...' she replied.

'One of those nights, huh?'

'You could say that.'

They sat in silence for a bit and Maddie felt like it helped, just a little.

'Have you ever looked out into the night and wondered why we bother with it all?' she said quietly. 'Why we carry on putting one foot in front of the other when everything is ultimately out of our control?'

He heard him shift in the chair next to her. 'We do it for the people around us, I guess.'

'What if you have no one?'

'Everybody has someone.'

They sat in silence again. Maddie bit on her lip to stop herself from breaking into great heaves and gasps again.

Eventually, Luke said, 'For what it's worth, I'm really pleased we met.'

Jade was pleased with how that had gone.

Ok, so Maddie was visibly shocked, perhaps a bit more than Jade had anticipated, but all things considered, the air was now clear and Maddie knew exactly where she stood.

She had to laugh out loud when she thought about Maddie saying she had thought Jade had been joking.

What a load of bullshit.

Maddie had known from the start that she had been serious. But Jade had to give her a Noddy badge for playing around with that excuse. She'd be good if the police ever did get in touch.

Not that Jade cared much either way. She was convinced she was in the clear. Everything pointed to Maddie and, as long as she played things cool, Maddie would be too terrified to grass on her.

And if Greg had left her anything in his will, then maybe Maddie would be inclined to pass something on to Jade for all her hard work. Once the dust had settled, of course.

Now to fix this problem with Mark. Basically, all she had to do was point Maddie in his direction, wind her up and let her go. If Maddie messed it up, she was just a bit of collateral damage. No big deal.

Besides, Jade had put all the hard work into coming up with the plan for Greg. It was Maddie's turn now. Ok, so a bit easier in that Greg was local and had that very handy nut allergy, therefore handing Jade a wiped clean murder weapon, thank you very much. But still, Maddie could put in some work now. The less Jade knew about it, the better.

But it needed to be done soon. Christmas was just around the corner and that would prove a tricky time in terms of the logistics concerning Ben. It was also Halloween soon. Mark would start making demands for trick or treating, wanting to see Ben for Christmas shopping, trips to see Santa Claus, all that shit.

Time to amp up the pressure on Miss Goody Two Shoes downstairs.

14

The only signs of her distressing, sleepless night were the purple rings under Maddie's eyes, but her expert touch with a make-up brush meant she looked fresher than she probably should for a grieving widow.

And that was indeed what she was.

She hadn't pushed Greg to get the divorce sorted when she found out about the affair. She didn't know why; maybe because she had hoped that he would change his mind, even after Jemima was born. Perhaps deep down she had some twisted notion that he would come to his senses, grab Jemima and come running back to her.

It was thoughts like these that had kept her up all night, blaming herself, then absolving herself of all blame and pointing the finger firmly at Jade, then switching back to herself again. She'd tossed and turned as often as her mind had flipped and weaved, leaving her exhausted, drained and aching when she'd finally dragged herself upright that morning. The whiskey lingered on her cotton-wool tongue and in her brain, which felt like a hammer was chipping away at her skull.

When she had woken up this morning from what little sleep she had managed, for a second everything was like it had been. Then it had hit her, a body blow. He was gone. The realisation had stayed with her, followed her around as got dressed slowly and carefully, ticking away at the base of her throat like a muscle spasm.

She walked over to Greg's – Gemma's – house through the grey, drizzle-soaked streets.

It was about 9 a.m. Mothers with pushchairs pushed past her at high speed, leaving behind them clouds of expensive perfume as they rushed toddlers to swimming classes and music sessions and playgroups. Others walked slowly, catching up on text messages and Instagram, now that their kids had been safely deposited inside the school gates.

Maddie didn't see any of them. She kept her hands in her pockets, her eyes averted, as her boots slapped the puddles.

The gates to the house were open and Maddie stopped abruptly, her breath hitching when she saw his car in the driveway. She swayed on her feet, then crunched over the gravel to the front door.

She hesitated with her hand over the doorbell, trembling slightly, then pressed the buzzer.

Seconds later the door inched open.

A woman with a helmet of grey, no-nonsense hair stood in the doorway.

'Can I help you?' Her voice had an unmistakable Surrey clip to it.

'Um, hi, I was wondering if Gemma was in? I wanted to speak to her, pay my condolences...' Her voice trailed off as she fought back tears – mostly of shame and revulsion, but to the bodyguard on the door it would look like shock and grief.

'And you are?'

'I'm Maddie, Greg's... er...'

'Oh.' The look of distaste that passed over her face indicated that Maddie's reputation certainly preceded her.

'You must be Gemma's mother? Nice to meet you. I wish it could've been under different circumstances. How is she holding up?'

Maddie's unerringly good manners thawed the gatekeeper somewhat and the door inched open a little more. 'Ok, all things considered. Come in out of the rain. I'll see if she is up to seeing you.'

She closed the door behind Maddie and turned to go up the stairs, then said, 'You can wait in the kitchen – and please don't upset her.'

Maddie did as she was told.

Her eyes frantically scanned the kitchen as she perched on a bar stool at the enormous granite-topped island. The kitchen looked as immaculate as ever. No sign of fingerprinted bakery boxes or deadly cakes. She wasn't sure what she had been expecting. The chalk outline of a body on the floor?

She had the sudden bizarre urge to giggle and actually clamped a hand over her mouth in case a titter sneaked out.

Maybe she was still drunk from the whiskey last night. She and Luke had finished the bottle in almost absolute silence and she had only vague recollections of dragging herself out of the deckchair and back down the stairs to her flat, his hand on the flat of her back, steering her carefully to her door. He'd left her then and she'd crawled under the duvet on the couch and stayed there, not even bothering to go to bed.

Someone had placed a large vase of lilies on the edge

of the island, the flowers still new and tightly closed like pursed lips. Maddie hated lilies. Didn't everyone? The vase was dangerously close to the edge and Maddie had to trap her hand under her thigh to stop herself from reaching out and knocking the vase onto the tiled floor.

What the hell was the matter with her?

She heard footsteps behind her and swivelled in the stool to see Gemma striding into the room, wearing a long black dress and sporting a pair of enormous dark sunglasses, looking all the while like a footballer's grief-stricken wife.

Maddie got to her feet and approached Gemma with her arms outstretched.

Gemma hesitated, then stepped into the hug without actually touching her.

'Oh, Gemma, I don't know what to say. I'm shocked, distraught.'

'There isn't much to say. Jemima is without a father and I am now a widow.' She sounded livid, her voice trembling in fury.

Gemma flopped rather gracefully onto a bar stool and cupped her forehead in her hand like a damsel in distress.

'Is there anything I can do? I can help with Jemima maybe?'

Gemma's head shot up and her eyes glared. 'There's no need. My mother is staying with us.'

'Ok, well, let me know if I can help in any way.'

There was a terse silence, broken only by long-suffering sighs from Gemma. Maddie couldn't help thinking she was perversely enjoying playing the role of the widowed beauty.

'So have the police said anything?'

Gemma glared at her again. 'Why would the police be

interested? It was an accident. He ate cake with nuts in it and had a fatal allergic reaction. I was at yoga—' her voice cracked and a small sob escaped her lip-glossed mouth '—so I didn't get to him in time to save him. I called the ambulance straight away and when they arrived apparently he had a faint pulse, but by the time he got to the hospital, it was too late. I found him at the top of the stairs. They think he was trying to get to the bathroom for his injection.'

'Where was little Jemima?' Maddie had to know. It was slowly eating her up inside, thinking that Greg had died in front of Jemima.

'He had put her safely in her highchair, but she was screaming by the time I got home. I'm sure she knew something was wrong.'

'Poor lamb, how awful for her – and you, of course.' But that made Maddie feel better. The grip on her throat loosened a little. 'Well, if you would like me to help with any of the... er... arrangements, please let me know. I knew him quite well,' she said with a small, sad smile.

'I think I knew him well too, Maddie.'

'Oh, yes, no, I wasn't insinuating... I just want to help, that's all.'

Gemma dabbed at her perfectly made-up eyes. 'Well, I don't know when the body will be released yet.'

'But if it was an accident, then they should be able to release the body soon? If the police don't need it?'

'I don't know how these things work. I have never been widowed before.' Her voice had risen an octave. Her mother's face appeared in the doorway and it was painfully clear to Maddie that she had been in the hallway listening the whole time.

'Everything ok in here? You're not getting too upset, are you, Gem-Gem?'

Gemma got to her feet. 'No, not at all, Maddie was just leaving.'

Maddie stood up and went to give Gemma another hug, then awkwardly thought better of it and instead said, 'Call me if you need anything. Anything at all.'

Maddie walked from the room, past the narrowed gaze of Gemma's mother, but stopped when she heard a gurgle from the lounge. This time, instead of doing what she was told, she followed the noise and found Jemima sitting in a playpen, blowing bubbles from her mouth as she played with some building blocks.

'Hi there, baby girl!' Maddie said with delight and felt her heart squeeze in a good way this time. 'How are you doing?'

Jemima smiled and held her chubby arms out for Maddie to pick her up. Maddie complied immediately, ignoring the feeling of poison-dipped daggers being tossed into her back by Gemma's mother. Jemima nuzzled into Maddie's shoulder and rubbed at her eyes.

'You tired, Princess?' Maddie rocked backwards and forwards, crooning in her ear. She breathed in her sweet vanilla scent, feeling her warmth flooding through her.

'It's time for her nap.' Gemma's frigid voice poured cold water on the moment.

Maddie breathed in one more time. 'Of course, sorry.' She turned and handed a cooing Jemima to her grandmother, who whisked her out of sight.

Maddie walked from the room towards the front door. She turned, not sure what else to say, then left with a simple, 'Bye, Gemma.'

The heavy, wooden front door closed with a decisive thud behind her and she stood for a moment, letting the light drizzle fall onto her face. She found she could breathe a little easier now, knowing that Jemima was ok and that the police were not involved as yet.

She needed to keep it that way though. Because all hell could well break loose when Greg's will was finally read.

Three Days Ago

'Maddie, there's something I need to talk to you about.'

They were lying in her bed, the sheets crumpled between them, the air thick and musty. Maddie was about to drift off, but was pulled wide awake by his words.

Was he about to say what she thought he was?

'Oh?' She sat up a little. He reached out and smoothed a stray lock of hair from her face. She could feel it catch in the corner of her mouth as he moved it aside and she licked her lips.

'I've been thinking a lot lately. About us.'

Maddie's heart rate was already heightened, but it crept up another notch as he spoke.

'I mean, obviously this—' he indicated the two of them with his free hand (his other hand was pinned beneath her and she wondered briefly if he had pins and needles and needed to move it yet) '—wasn't planned at all.' He added quickly, 'And it was wonderful. I don't regret it at all.'

'Me neither. At all.' She smiled sheepishly.

'Good. Of course, you know we can't say anything to anyone… I mean Jemima… I can't lose her.'

'No, no, I know that.'

He was quiet for a moment.

'But it can't happen again, Greg. We're... We've had our time. I think I need to be my own person now. I've started working again – for the guy upstairs, Luke. He's really nice and funny and... anyway, I'm doing his books for him and I think it could become a really good little business for me. He has some other contacts and stuff.'

'Oh, right,' he said and she noticed the flatness of his voice. What exactly had he expected? 'I'm glad,' he said quietly.

After another moment, he said, 'Do you ever wish we could go back to the beginning?'

'What do you mean?'

'To the beginning of us. Maybe do it differently?'

She wasn't sure what to reply.

He rushed on. 'There is so much I regret, particularly the way I treated you. It was all just so... overwhelmingly sad and I handled it like an immature kid instead of a man. I wasn't really there for you during all the miscarriages and then with Gemma...' The sigh that followed his words was weighted with remorse.

'For what it's worth, I don't think there is a right or wrong way of dealing with it all.' Her voice was considered and gentle. 'You just have to go with what you have to do to survive – and that was Gemma for you. It was cutting myself off, isolating myself for me. But I don't blame you for any of it.'

Now that she had articulated the words and they were out there, between them, like speckles of dust, she realised she honestly believed that. Two minutes ago, she was thinking he was going to suggest they get back together and now she was absolutely certain that that was not what she wanted. She wanted a clean slate, to forge her own path, to create a life of her own outside of the bubble of grief in which she'd been imprisoned for so long. The thought left her almost breathless with relief.

'And in answer to your question, no, I don't ever think of going back because I don't know if I would have done anything differently. I think no one would've been able to convince me to stop trying to get pregnant. There was no point at which I would've even considered it. Until Archie, of course.'

'I've been thinking about it all so much lately. Jemima, Gemma, you and me. Our weirdly dysfunctional family. I mean that is what we are, aren't we?'

Maddie chuckled. 'Yes, I suppose we are.'

He peered at her in the semi-darkness. 'What I've been thinking is... I rewrote my will last week, made sure there were provisions in it for Jemima and... I did something that you should know about.' He paused again and Maddie shifted impatiently on his arm, which now felt like it was digging into her side. 'What would you say to being Jemima's legal guardian? I mean if something happens to me and Gemma?'

This was not what Maddie was expecting.

'Um... well, what would Gemma think about that?'

'I don't think she would go for it, to be honest. But if it comes to it, she wouldn't know a thing about it.'

'Right. It's the kind of thing you should discuss with her though.' Typical of Greg, burying his head and hoping it would go away.

'I know, I will. But I wanted to tell you first. I know it's a big ask, given everything we've been through, but there's no one I trust more than you with Jemima. You are a natural mother. I know she'd be safe with you and that you would raise her like your own.'

Maddie felt a warm glow spread up from her toes, through her stomach and into her heart.

'I don't know what to say,' she replied.

'That's fine. Think it over. We've got time. I don't plan on dying any time soon.' He chuckled.

'No, I mean, I don't need to think it over. Yes, I'll do it.'

'Really? You're sure? I know it's unorthodox of me to ask my ex-wife—'

'Current wife, thank you very much.'

'Oh, yes, we really need to do something about that, don't we?'

It was Maddie's turn to chuckle. 'Yes, we do before Gemma finds out you're not actually divorced yet. She'll be wanting a big white wedding once she's lost the baby weight.'

Greg looked at her in mock horror. 'Meow, Mrs Lowe! Well, at least I'm not having another affair this time.'

Maddie giggled. 'Seriously though, I know me and you are over. I wish we weren't, but it is what it is and I'd like us to stay friends. I'd like to be a part of Jemima's life if I can and it would be an honour to be her legal guardian. Not that I'm wishing anything bad on you two, of course! But watch your back. That's all I'm saying.'

Greg guffawed. 'Ooh, so dangerous. I love it!' Then he kissed her again. 'In that case, Mrs Lowe, if this is the last time we are going to do this, let's do it properly...'

15

Maddie's phoned chirped, pulling her from a fitful sleep. She was lying on the couch under her duvet, the lounge curtains closed to the midday light, trying to block out everyone and everything.

It was another Snapchat from Jade.

She pulled the message slightly to the left and read:

Halloween. Mark loves it and with so many people around in masks and costumes, you can get right up to his door. Perfect opportunity.

Maddie let go and the message pinged back as though she hadn't read it.

The last week was a blur. At least she had thought it was a week, but then she also suspected she'd lost a few days in between, because it was apparently Halloween tomorrow.

That meant today was Wednesday and Greg had been dead for ten days. Where had that time gone? She'd stayed indoors, buried away, like the old days, feeling that numbness blanket her like bubble wrap, cushioning her, protecting her. She had had no concept of passing time.

Jade had been peppering her with Snapchat messages,

threats, notes under the door – anything to get her to respond, to get her to admit she had a plan. But Maddie had ignored it all, not let any of it pierce the thick outer skin of depression she had wrapped herself in.

This all felt familiar. She had come full circle. Just when she thought she could see a chink of light shining through the heavy clouds after the miscarriages and her separation from Greg, just when she thought she was getting back on her feet, enjoying the flashes of autonomy her new life afforded her, the clouds had gathered again, shutting out that faint ray of light and plunging her into darkness once more. She had gone into survival mode again, functioning on only a basic level while trying not to think too much, not to feel too much. Just like those darkest of days when the most inconsequential of daily tasks had felt like a feat of endurance.

But now Jade was demanding action, commanding Maddie to respond. She'd even told Maddie that she couldn't see Ben until it was done, using him as a bargaining chip. Over the last few days Maddie had let her mind poke around the edges of what Jade wanted her to do and the numbing quicksand of grief in which she was trapped meant she was less horrified by the idea of the task at hand now.

Maybe it was because she had nothing left to lose. Maybe it was because she had nothing left to care for.

Snapchat pinged again – this time a video. Maddie was intrigued enough to let it play. Jade standing outside Teddington police station. The camera panned down to her feet climbing the steps up to the main doors. Then Jade's voice saying, 'Don't ignore me, Maddie.'

Maddie sat up, a flare of panic making her heart tick

faster than it had in days. All along, Maddie had kept saying to herself that Jade wouldn't go through with her threats, but seeing her in the video was enough to pull Maddie back to the present.

She couldn't think straight. Even if she was of sound mind right now, how did she go about planning a murder? It was all so callous, ridiculous, unbelievable.

Jade seemed to think Halloween was an opportunity. She had a point – everyone disguising who they were, causing mischief, knocking on doors. But what would she say if she got Mark to open the door? Should she say anything? And what did she intend to do? Kill him? Did she need a weapon?

Was this how you did it? One step at a time when you're planning a murder, right?

How the hell had she got here?

Back in those days when she had first met Greg, she certainly never thought she'd reach 38 and be childless, widowed, unemployed and contemplating the murder of an innocent man.

It was funny how things worked out. But Maddie wasn't laughing.

Perhaps the best plan was not to plan at all. Let fate decide how this would play out. Just turn up on his doorstep and see. Or she could do nothing and let the police decide what her future held. There was a calm acceptance of that as an option. A prison cell wasn't an unwelcome idea at this stage. This was all her fault, after all. She had brought Jade into their lives. She had brought all of this on herself.

She deserved this for what had happened to Greg.

She was faulty, broken, defective.

Yes, she'd been here before. The dull, numbing stillness that followed another shock, another disappointment, another sadness. She could feel herself settling into autopilot, letting her mind take over the logistics while her heart scrambled to repair itself.

Except this time, she didn't think she would come back from it.

If she went into that cell, she'd never come back out. She thought of Luke suddenly, how genuine he was, quiet and kind. That had potential, if she wanted it to.

So was she really ready to lie down and surrender?

Or was there enough of the old Maddie left, the one who kept going, who never gave up, even when everyone told her she should? That Maddie could figure a way out of this. That Maddie could see herself getting Jade off her back and moving away, far from here with its memories and ghosts.

She took a deep breath, closed her eyes for a moment and thought about Greg. What would he tell her to do?

And that's when she knew.

If she was blamed for everything, then Jade would get away with Greg's murder and that wasn't right. Jade should be punished too. She should be left with an indelible scar, something to remind her of what she had done. Greg deserved that at least. A surge of determination coursed through her veins, melting some of the ice that had settled there.

She had to make sure the truth came out somehow.

First things first, she needed to get a screenshot of the messages Jade was sending without her knowing. But how? Jade could tell when her messages were read and saved. She threw off the duvet as an idea came to her. All the boxes left over from her move were still piled up in the spare bedroom and her old digital camera was in one of them. She could take a photo of the screen with an old-school camera rather than a screenshot. That would work.

She opened boxes and rummaged among the mementos of her life, pushing aside books, letters and photographs. She felt a flicker of worry that she wouldn't find the camera, that it would all be in vain and she would have to think of something else, the idea of which was exhausting and demoralising. Then her hand fell on the slim, cold, metal body of the camera. Miraculously there was just enough battery life left to turn it on.

Resuming her position under the duvet in the lounge, she opened the Snapchat message properly and took a photo of it with the camera before replying:

Fine. I'll do it tomorrow. Send me the address.

Jade read the message and smiled. She knew Maddie would come through. She didn't want to know the details though. She screenshotted the message and closed the app. When it was all over, she would need to delete Snapchat from her phone altogether. She needed to wipe out her involvement, like taking an eraser to the whole episode. She couldn't quite trust that Maddie wasn't going to double-cross her.

Knowing that this would all be over soon and that she could stop living this lie made her feel elated. And a little sad, truth be told. It had been a fun ride, but it was time to close it all down.

Tomorrow.

It would all end tomorrow.

Maddie's eyes were tight and dry, like every drop of moisture had been sucked from them, leaving behind two glassy marbles. She drank her tea at the kitchen table, not really tasting it but needing the familiar warmth after a sleepless night spent staring at the ceiling.

Whatever happened, if she could be in the clear when it was all over, that would be a bonus, but a large part of her didn't care. There was a strong possibility that things would not turn out well. Worst-case scenario would be that she was arrested not only for one murder, but implicated in Greg's death too. Her brain struggled to comprehend how she had got herself into such a mess, but she couldn't think about Greg for too long without feeling like she was hanging over a precipice, staring down into an abyss.

If she went to jail, so be it, but she should try as much as possible to take Jade down with her. Greg deserved that at least.

She looked at the address Jade had sent to her, opened the maps app on her phone and factored in the travel distance, memorised the route.

She set her phone back on the table and sat staring at the room in front of her. Her little flat didn't feel much like a haven anymore. More like a place that had been violated by something poisonous and she needed to escape from it, to get as far away from it as possible.

There was nothing here for her anymore. Greg was gone; Jade was keeping Ben from her as punishment; Jemima wasn't her daughter, no matter how much she wished she was; and Gemma would probably be happier if Maddie was miles away.

The way Maddie saw it, she had two options after today if she wasn't arrested: to just take herself up onto the roof, lean over and watch the ground rush towards her. Who would miss her? Or to get away from here. Far away. To that little cottage by the sea, somewhere remote, where she could start over, have her own space that belonged just to her, free of memories. Somewhere isolated and quiet.

She had a dog in her daydream. She'd always wanted one, but Greg was allergic. She could hear a memory in her head, her telling him as he read the ingredients on some soup she'd bought that one day his allergies would be the death of her and he had replied, 'No, Maddie, the death of *me*!' and they'd laughed.

How they'd laughed.

She could feel panic clawing up her skin, so she thought about the dog she would buy. Something medium-sized, but not too energetic. Something that needed short walks and bursts of fresh air to get her out of the house, but not endless hours of running in fields. Maybe a rescue dog that needed a bit of love, one that would curl up in her lap.

Jemima would probably love a dog. Not that she would be able to come and visit. If Maddie left, she would be doing it in order to completely disappear. Like the woman who lived here before.

Maddie had a sudden urge to see Jemima, give her one last cuddle, maybe whisper an apology into her ear.

As she left the flat, she almost collided with Luke as he bundled into the building.

'Oh, hey,' he said with a wide smile, his top lip disappearing into his teeth. 'I haven't seen you in ages.' Then he frowned. 'You ok?'

'Not really, I had some bad news a few days ago.'

'Oh, shit, sorry. Do you want to talk about it? I could put the kettle on. You shouldn't be alone. I wish you'd said sooner.'

She fought back another dose of tears and said, 'That's sweet, thanks, but I have something I have to do.' She turned away from him towards the main door, then turned back and said, 'You're really nice, Luke. I'm glad we met.' Then she rushed out before she could change her mind.

When Maddie walked up to the front door, she could hear Jemima screaming through the woodwork. An angry, indignant wail symptomatic of a toddler in full meltdown.

She paused with her finger over the doorbell, then rang it apologetically. She fully expected Gemma's mother to act as doorkeeper again, but it was the lady of the house herself who pulled open the door. But this was not the neat, immaculately styled woman Maddie had seen a little over a week ago.

The woman standing in the doorway was wearing sports leggings and a stained sweatshirt, with feet stuffed into chunky slippers. Her hair was pulled into a loose ponytail, but strands had escaped and hung limply around her drawn face. The bags under her haunted eyes were plum-coloured and she'd made none of her usual effort at masking them.

Maddie was momentarily speechless.

How the mighty have fallen.

'Hi, is now a bad time? I can come back,' she said.

Gemma looked like she was about to crumble. Her face collapsed in on itself and Maddie stepped forward to take hold of her as she swayed on her feet. Gemma grabbed onto her and pulled Maddie into the house.

'She won't stop crying! I don't know what to do!' Gemma wailed, almost as loud as the cries coming from inside the house.

'Hey, hey. Let me help. Come on.' Maddie guided Gemma through the hallway. 'Come and sit down in the kitchen and I'll put the kettle on.'

Gemma's slippers shuffled across the wooden floor as she allowed herself to be led to the breakfast bar. Maddie lowered her onto a bar stool. Jemima was flailing around on the rug in the corner of the room, her face pressed to the floor, toys scattered where she'd thrown them in her anger. She looked up at the sound of Maddie's voice and the wails diminished into sobs and gulps.

Maddie walked over to her and Jemima immediately put her arms out to her, her lip trembling and snot pouring from her tiny nose.

'There, there, angel, what's all this noise about?' Maddie crooned at her as she scooped her up. Jemima buried her face in Maddie's shoulder and let out another tiny sob.

'You see, she hates me!' Gemma wailed. 'She's stopped crying for you!'

'No, she doesn't. She just needs a nap or something. I'll see if I can settle her, then we'll talk, ok?'

Maddie carried Jemima up to her bedroom, snuggling her close. She lowered into the rocking chair in the bay window and started to sing quietly as Jemima's sniffs grew quieter and her thumb sought out her mouth. With her thumb tucked in, Jemima's eyes grew heavy in a Pavlovian response. It wasn't long before she was asleep in Maddie's arms, having exhausted herself with her tantrum.

Maddie sat for a little longer, enjoying the closeness, then gently lowered her into her bed and tucked her in.

As she came back down the stairs, she noticed that the photo frames that had littered every surface had gone. Either Maddie was right in her long-held suspicions that Gemma only brought them out when Maddie was coming over or she had removed them altogether in her grief.

Gemma was still sitting where Maddie had left her, slumped on the bar stool, her head in her hands, but the crying appeared to have petered out.

'She's asleep. I'll make some tea.'

'Why is it so easy for you? You don't even have kids and you know what to do.'

Maddie's teeth clenched. 'Sometimes they need someone who isn't their parent to step in, I guess.'

Maddie turned on the boiling water tap and the scalding water gurgled and spat into the mugs.

She reached into the fridge for Gemma's usual soya milk, but there was nothing in there but some wrinkly apples and a pizza box. It would seem that clean eating didn't go well with grief.

'Oh, no milk. Shall I go and get some quickly?'

Gemma's head snapped up. 'No, don't leave!'

'Ok, that's fine. We can have herbal tea.'

She poured the black tea down the sink and found a box of camomile tea in the cupboard.

Maddie sat next to Gemma and said nothing for a

moment, just watched her as she stared into her mug, her eyes glazed and unseeing. It was a look Maddie knew well.

Eventually Gemma repeated, 'Jemima hates me.'

Maddie reached out and rested her hand on Gemma's tiny, very cold hand that was clasped around her mug like a claw. 'No, she doesn't hate you at all.'

Gemma looked up with panicked eyes. 'She does! She knows Greg is gone. She had such a close connection with him, but there's nothing there between *us*. I've tried. I really have tried. I can't do this without him.'

'I'm sure you're doing just fine. This is an impossible situation for both of you.' Maddie tried not to think about Jade or her own role in all of this because if she started thinking about it now, she would probably break down and tell Gemma everything. The truth was sitting on the tip of her tongue like a grenade.

'She isn't sleeping, she isn't eating,' Gemma said. 'Everything I try she pushes away. She doesn't want me to hold her, but if I leave the room she cries even harder. Greg was so good with her. He knew exactly what she needed. I have never known what she wants.' She was silent for a moment, still staring into the mug but not drinking any of it. Then, her voice very low, she said, 'That's why I fill our time with so many activities or I leave her in the creche at the gym. I don't know how to spend time with her.' It was a bold admission and Maddie could feel the shame and regret pouring from her. Her voice dropped to a whisper. 'Sometimes I don't *want* to spend time with her.'

She looked wide-eyed at Maddie, daring her to admonish her for saying that. Maddie kept quiet.

'Greg loved being with her,' she continued. 'They could

just sit in a room and laugh together over silly things, doing absolutely nothing at all. I don't know how he did that.'

'All she needs is love, Gemma. She doesn't need entertaining all the time.'

'It's not as simple as that.' Her voice rose an octave. 'And how would you know anyway? How would you understand how difficult it is when your own daughter rejects you? When her face lights up when her dad walks in, so that you're left feeling like an intruder in their moment? Except he's not going to walk in ever again.' Her voice dropped again. 'Sometimes I don't feel anything for her at all. Other times all I feel is resentment. I left my job, ruined my body – and for what? A child who doesn't even like me. And now he's left me to fend for her all on my own.'

Maddie was horrified at the revelations dripping from Gemma's tongue. How could anyone resent their child? At that moment, Maddie hated her. At that particular moment, she was glad Gemma was in pain – and glad Greg wasn't here to hear these confessions.

Then she remembered that this was all her fault. If she hadn't brought Jade into their lives, Jemima would have her dad and Gemma would be living in blissful, selfish ignorance of her feelings towards her daughter, spending her days at the gym and drinking kale smoothies, passing time until her daughter was in school and she could get her life back.

'Sometimes the connection needs time and work. Sometimes there isn't an immediate bond, I guess. But something like this could be just what you need to bring you closer to her.'

'And sometimes people aren't cut out to be parents.

Maybe that's me. And now she has no one else.' She started to weep again.

Maddie wanted to tell her she was wrong, but her lips wouldn't form the words.

'You agree with me, don't you? Oh God, you think I'm a terrible mother!' Gemma wailed.

'I think you're right in that I can't possibly understand what you're going through, but I know you are grieving and heartbroken, angry at Greg and unable to see past that right now. But she's just a baby. She doesn't understand what's going on and is probably picking up on your distress.'

Gemma started to sob again. Maddie got to her feet and wrapped her arms around the heaving shoulders of the broken woman next to her.

They sat that way until Gemma had cried herself out. When she pulled back, Gemma was pale and trembling.

The words were out of Maddie's mouth before she had even fully formed the idea behind them. 'Listen, why don't I take Jemima for a few days? To give you a break? You can get some much-needed rest and recover a bit? It would probably do both you and Jemima good. Let you get some perspective.'

Maddie held her breath.

'You'd do that for me?' Gemma said in a whisper.

Maddie exhaled. 'Yes, of course. You and Jemima are still family, regardless of what has happened. I will always be here for you.'

Tears started to roll down Gemma's cheeks again. 'You're an amazing person, Maddie. You have every reason to hate me and yet you're being so lovely. I do need some time. I can't do this on my own, not right now, maybe not ever.'

'Don't be silly. First, you're not alone. You have me and you can always ask me for anything. Jemima is probably the closest thing I will ever have to a daughter. She is very special to me, so all you have to do is ask. Secondly, you'll feel differently in a few days when you've had some space to breathe. Look, let's pack up some of her things – a few clothes, some of her favourite toys or a couple of books and we'll make it into a holiday for her. And when you're ready, I'll bring her back home. Take as long as you need – a day, a week, a month even.'

Maddie strapped Jemima into the car seat in the back of Gemma's enormous Range Rover that had never seen a country lane or a muddy path. Gemma had insisted that Maddie take her car and Maddie hadn't argued too much. She packed the pushchair and bags into the boot and looked over to where Gemma stood like a ghost in the doorway of the house, chewing on her fingernails.

Jemima was gurgling happily now, her earlier ferocity forgotten. Maddie smiled at her as she slid the clasp into place.

'Do you want to give her a kiss goodbye?'

Gemma looked momentarily frightened by the idea. 'No, no, I don't want to set her off again. Go, it's fine.'

'Ok, well, I'll let you know how we're getting on and please call me if you need me. I'm only down the road.'

Gemma nodded, then shuffled back inside and closed the door.

Maddie climbed into the car and sat for a moment,

watching Jemima in the back seat through the mirror. She smiled, then started the car.

As she pulled up outside the flat, she saw Jade standing outside, a cigarette clasped between pursed lips. Maddie's good mood evaporated.

She climbed out and went around to the passenger door. She could feel Jade's eyes burning into her.

Then Jade was right behind her, the smell of nicotine giving her away.

'What's all this then?' Jade said.

'Jemima is coming to stay with me for a few days.'

'Clever. Giving yourself an alibi -- and a different car for the CCTV cameras.' Maddie ignored the admiration painted all over Jade's face.

'No, I'm giving her heartbroken mother a break. You know, the wife of the man you murdered?'

'Yeah, you're a saint. Convenient though, isn't it?'

'Whatever, Jade.' Maddie's voice was a growl. 'But whatever happens today, I want you to stay the hell away from me from now on.'

Jade's eyes narrowed to slits. 'Ben has been asking after you.'

Maddie paused. 'Jemima is my priority now,' she replied, ignoring the tightness in her chest.

'Oh, I see. It's like that, is it?'

'Where is he anyway?'

'Upstairs, naptime.'

'Then you'd better get back to him.'

Jade watched her closely. 'You'll let me know when it's done.'

Maddie nodded and turned away to open the car door. She felt more than heard Jade move away.

She exhaled.

What the hell was she thinking? She now had Jemima to factor into this whole mess. She scooped Jemima and her bags up and hurried inside. As she juggled with the bags and a weighty Jemima in her arms, her grip on her keys slipped and they clattered to the floor. Before she could stoop to pick them up, Peggy from across the hall appeared from nowhere, her hair wrapped in a headscarf knotted under her chin and her raincoat buttoned tight.

'Here, love, I'll get them. Ah, who's this then?' She smiled at Jemima.

'This is Jemima. I'm looking after her for a few days for a friend.'

'She's bonny, isn't she?'

'She's a bit unsettled at the moment, so I hope there isn't too much noise for you.'

Peggy slid the key in Maddie's front door for her. 'Oh, don't worry. That kind of noise can't be helped. They're just trying to tell you something in the only way they know how.'

Maddie smiled in relief. 'Yes, but two children in one building could get a bit noisy if they both start shouting at the same time.'

Peggy patted Maddie on the arm. 'There are no other children here today, dear, and I doubt this little angel could be anything other than delightful.'

Maddie frowned as Peggy waddled away. The bag weighed heavy on her shoulder, so she shoved the door open with her hip and dumped everything just inside the door.

'Right then, missy. We need to get your travel cot set up in my room, then I think a trip to the shop for some of your favourite food.'

Jemima giggled in response and Maddie felt elated, but the feeling evaporated just as quickly. What would she do with Jemima later? She had to go and see Mark. She had to finish this.

But maybe Jade was right. Jemima was the perfect cover. She could pick her up a Halloween costume at the shop and use that as her way to get Mark to open the door.

Just another friendly trick or treater.

16

Mark Bennett was a simple bloke. Easy to please, his mother would say. And yet his life was anything but. He worked with a nice group of lads. There was plenty of banter, a couple of pints after work on a Friday and some good-natured ribbing about the football on a Monday. Not quite the camaraderie of the rigs, but still a nice place to work. And when he was finished at the end of the day, all he wanted was to get home, have a hot bath and then collapse in front of the telly with a cold beer.

But pregnancy had turned his girlfriend Gloria into a nightmare, truth be told. Before she was pregnant, they'd been strong. They liked a laugh, she enjoyed a few drinks and hanging out with his mates, and she was really good at her job as a hairdresser, which also meant he got free haircuts on the weekend.

But since the pregnancy, she'd become a lot more high maintenance. She didn't want to go out anymore, was always tired and now that she was a few weeks off the baby coming, everything was an issue. It was like she was sitting at home just finding things to complain about.

It hadn't been like this with Jade. That had been the perfect pregnancy from his point of view. A text message to say she was pregnant and a few photos of her swollen belly. Another message to say she was in labour but not to worry as she had her friend with her. She'd even sent him a smiling photo of the two of them in the hospital, then followed it up with a photo of a tiny Ben after he was born.

No worry; no stress. Pregnancy from a distance meant he wasn't bossed around, snapped at, sent on late night shopping trips for weird snacks – all that stuff you hear about and think your girlfriend won't inflict on you. Turns out she will.

He had been thrilled to hear he had a son. When he finally got off the rigs, he arranged to meet Jade at her flat and there he was. A pink, squirming three-month-old, with intense eyes and a strong pair of lungs on him. Mark fell in love immediately.

He'd felt really heartsore leaving him that day and every other time since then. That was one of the reasons he'd left the rigs. He wanted to see more of Ben. He wanted to be there to teach him to kick a football and ride a bike, clichéd as it was.

And he'd had a few opportunities like that, especially when Ben was a baby. He would spend entire afternoons with them. They took him to the zoo once when he was about eighteen months old and it had been a brilliant day.

When he met Gloria, he had been upfront about Ben, told her that he wasn't with Jade. In fact, he'd never really been with Jade. She'd been a one-night stand in the beginning and then an unfortunate drunken mistake the night before he headed back to the rigs had resulted in Ben. Jade was just not his sort of girl. But Gloria was. She liked to dress up, make herself look pretty, banter with the boys, but also knew when to leave him to it.

Well, she used to anyway. Now it was all moaning, baggy tracksuit pants and not closing the door when she went to the loo.

It was her baby shower this weekend, so she'd gone to stay at her mother's house, which meant he had all weekend to do just what he wanted. He suspected it would mostly involve the couch, football on the telly and pizza. He could spritz some Febreze around the place before Gloria got back on Sunday night and she'd never know.

He'd actually sent Jade a message to ask if he could have Ben for the weekend, but she'd said no. She'd been doing that a lot lately.

Maybe it was a weird jealousy thing over Gloria. You could never tell with women.

The fact that it was Halloween hadn't escaped his notice. There were small kids everywhere, dressed in random costumes, trawling the streets, knocking on doors and asking strangers for sweets. Mark wondered if Ben was trick or treating, and his heart contracted as he thought about how it should be him taking Ben around. Not for the first time he wondered if Jade had a new partner and maybe that was why he was being frozen out of Ben's life.

A mate of his had told him recently to get some legal advice on it – he had rights after all. But Gloria was due soon and then he'd have two kids to worry about. Maybe when the new baby was born, he would do something about Ben.

Right now, he was happy to sit in front of the football. He had a bowl of sweets next to the door for trick or treaters if they knocked – he loved seeing the kids' faces when they were digging grubby hands into the bowl – but other than that, he wasn't planning on moving from this chair.

Maddie realised halfway along the motorway that she really should've thought this through a bit more. She looked into the rear-view mirror to see Jemima in her car seat, fast asleep again, dressed in a pumpkin onesie. That was all that was left in the supermarket.

She was about fifteen minutes away from Mark's house. Fifteen minutes in which to decide what she was going to say – or do.

She glanced over to her handbag on the passenger seat. She could just make out the handle of the large knife.

Maddie gripped the wheel tightly, conscious of the tiny person behind her. She had sent Gemma a message to tell her that she was taking Jemima trick or treating and had expected a message back telling her to watch how many sweets she ate, but she had received nothing back.

This was madness. What the hell was she doing? Maybe she should turn around, go home, pack up her stuff and disappear somewhere.

But she couldn't. Jade would talk to the police and then Maddie would always be running, looking over her shoulder. The more she thought about it, the more she wondered what Jade had had on the girl who lived in her flat before her. Lucy. There was definitely a story there. Jade didn't do anything for nothing.

Looking at Jemima now, Maddie realised she did have a reason to carry on, someone who needed her.

This had to end.
Today.

Mark wished he'd bought more sweets – and recorded the football. The cul-de-sac was teeming with kids, dressed in everything from ghosts and zombies to princesses and pirates. He was down to the dregs of the sweet bowl and had resorted to rationing the kids to one lollipop a piece. He would have to hunt in the cupboard for some biscuits or something soon – or stop answering the door. He'd thought about turning the lights off and pretending he wasn't home once the sweets did run out, but his delight as seeing all the kids dressed up swayed him from that idea.

He'd missed all the goals in the match and instead of avoiding the final score, he'd caught a glimpse of it and knew his team had lost. But it didn't matter. He was actually having fun.

The gaps between trick or treaters were drawing longer, so he might get some peace and quiet soon, maybe see if he could find the highlights of the game somewhere. He was sitting on the couch, counting the seconds between doorbell rings like a kid during a thunderstorm.

Yes, it was definitely slowing down. He opened another beer and put his feet up.

Maddie pulled the car up to the kerb in the cul-de-sac. There were one or two vampires and Buzz Lightyears wandering the streets with hands clasped tightly by grown-ups, along with the occasional teenager still trying to eke out the benefits of free sweets despite being taller than most of the people opening their doors. Sunset had turned the lights down and shadows were lengthening along the pavements and gardens.

Jemima stirred as the car stopped and rubbed her eyes.

Maddie sat for a moment watching number 11. It was a small, semi-detached house, with a neatly paved front garden and a dark red door. Artificial light from a television flickered in the front window. Someone was home.

What if he wasn't alone? She hadn't thought about that. She hadn't thought about any of it. She'd have to take the risk.

She looked over at the cheap, plastic Shrek mask sitting on the passenger seat next to her handbag.

She felt numb, her mind struggling to process what she was about to do, so she tried not to think at all.

She grabbed her bag and the mask, before slipping from the car.

Jemima was still yawning and sleepy, but smiled as Maddie reached in to unclasp her seat restraints. Maddie felt her chest clench. 'Hello, little pumpkin. Shall we go and do some trick or treating?'

She lifted her into her arms and straightened up the pumpkin suit. Taking a deep breath, she slipped on the Shrek mask. Jemima giggled and reached out to pull on the big, green ears.

Maddie locked the car and looked around. A few houses down, a group of witches and wizards were chatting as they headed off down the street. Maddie watched them go, then stepped towards number 11.

The doorbell sounded like a siren, loud and intrusive, announcing her presence to the entire street.

For a second, she hoped no one would answer. Her pulse was racing and she felt ridiculous and weirdly sinister behind the mask.

A shadow fell over the frosted glass of the door and it was pulled open.

A tall, slim man with a receding hairline stood in front of them, an awkward smile on his face. Maddie searched his face for some sign that he was the man she was looking for, maybe a resemblance to Ben, but there was nothing.

'Oh, now that is a fabulous pumpkin!' he said, then added, 'I'm embarrassed to say I have run out of sweets, but I found some boxes of raisins in the cupboard – will that do?'

'Oh, er, perfect. Much better for her anyway,' Maddie replied.

He held out a small box and Jemima took them happily. 'Brilliant, well, better luck next door I think. They seem to be quite popular with the kids.' He winked at Jemima and went to close the door.

'Er, Mark, isn't it?' Maddie said a little too loudly.

He paused and turned back. 'Yeah, do I know you? Or are you in disguise?' He chuckled at himself.

'I ... I know your son, Ben.'

His face froze. 'Oh, you do? Is he ok?'

'Yes, yes, he's fine. I just... can I come in for a minute?'

He was looking at her curiously. 'Um, sure, I guess?'

He stepped aside to let her past.

They were standing in a tidy hallway. A pair of men's trainers lay under a console table on which stood a lightbox saying, 'Love is all you need' alongside a large fern. A bowl held keys, loose change and a few business cards. Everything looked like it had a place.

'Come through,' he said and she followed him into a small lounge. This room was equally as tidy and decorated in soft pink and silver tones. It was all very feminine, apart from the football scores trawling across the television as commentators got excited about penalties and goals. He lifted a remote control from the couch and muted the sound.

'You can take the mask off now,' he said.

'Oh!' Maddie had forgotten she was wearing it. She lowered Jemima to the carpet and snatched the mask from her face.

They sat looking at each other for a moment, then he said, 'So how do you know Ben?'

'Well, I... I live...' She was stammering and stuttering, not sure what to say, how much to give away. She started again. 'I know Jade and I've spent some time with Ben, play dates, that kind of thing.'

Mark smiled. 'He's a sweet kid, isn't he? Is this your daughter?'

'This is Jemima.' Jemima sat at Maddie's feet, playing with the laces on her shoes.

'Cute costume. So what's this about? I must say, this is all a bit weird.'

'Sorry, I know. I just wanted to talk to you about Jade. She's really struggling with this whole thing.'

'What whole thing? Does she need more money? Is Ben ok?' He sat forward with concern. 'I asked if I could have him this weekend, but she was having none of it.'

'She's just really worried about the custody situation.'

He looked at Maddie blankly. 'You've lost me. What custody situation?'

It was Maddie's turn to be confused. 'You're filing for custody – of Ben. She's worried she'll lose him.'

Mark frowned. 'I'm not filing for custody. I think you've got the wrong end of the stick. What was your name again?'

Maddie avoided the question. 'But she said you're filing for custody because your girlfriend is pregnant and you're getting married?'

'Look, love, I don't know what she's told you, but first off, I'm not filing for custody and second, I'm not engaged. Yes, Gloria is pregnant, but that's got nothing to do with Jade.' He sounded like he was getting annoyed. Maddie pulled her handbag closer to her, could feel the wooden handle of the knife through the zip. 'That woman loves to mess with people. Actually, maybe I *should* be filing for custody. It's not like I get to see much of Ben at the minute as it is!'

'What do you mean? You've seen him loads. She's the one who has to look after him on her own all the time, a single mum, struggling to make ends meet. It's not easy for her.'

'Back up a bit, honey. I haven't seen Ben in over six months. I send her money every month without fail, but she always has a reason why I can't see him. She never lets him sleep here overnight either. It's like she doesn't trust me or something.' He raked a hand through his thin hair. 'I love my son and, sure, I could've pushed harder to see him, but with Gloria pregnant and work, it's sometimes hard to find the time to get over to see him, you know? That's why letting him come for a weekend would be great, but she blocks me every time. I went over there a few weeks back, but Ben wasn't even there. He was at a play date or something and Jade sent me packing.'

Maddie's brain was swirling. 'I don't understand. She said she needed a lawyer and that you were threatening to take him away. She said you had him all the time at the minute, that he was sleeping over. The other day she said was worried that Ben would start calling your girlfriend "Mum".'

'Well, she's been lying to you.'

Maddie felt sick to her stomach. What was going on? 'I'm sorry, I shouldn't have come here.' She lurched to her feet.

'Wait, you can tell her something from me. Tell her she's given me a great idea and that I *will* be going for custody. I don't know what game she's playing, but she can't keep my son from me.'

This was not going well. If he did that, then everything would unravel. She looked at Jemima and knew she couldn't risk ending up in a jail cell, not now, not when she had a chance at being a part of Jemima's life after all.

She reached for her handbag.

Behind Mark on a coffee table stood a framed photo. Maddie stepped closer to it, her bag clasped tightly to her chest. In the photo Mark was playing with a younger Ben, who was sitting on his back and riding Mark like a horse, his face lit up in delight. In the background you could just make out Jade sitting on her couch, watching them carefully with a strange smirk on her face.

'That's Ben,' she said to distract him.

'Yes,' he said, turning towards the photo.

Maddie reached into her bag and her hand fell on the handle of the knife.

'That was one of the last times I saw him. I spent the afternoon with him. He really is a great kid. I love him to bits and I miss the very bones of him. I just want to teach him how to ride a bike and play football and stuff, you know? The little things.' He shrugged with shoulders that looked weighed down.

Maddie felt like she had stopped breathing altogether.

'I can't. I'm so sorry. I think I've made things worse for you.' Maddie pulled her hand from the bag, then reached down with one arm to scoop up Jemima and fled from the room. As she passed through the doorway, the strap of her bag snagged on the door handle and it was yanked from her shoulder. The bag swung from the handle like a macabre tableau, the blade of the knife now sticking up and glinting in the light as the bag swayed like a pendulum.

Mark looked at it in horror, then back at Maddie. He took a few steps away from her, but she mumbled another apology and reached for the knife. She felt the blade slice her palm, but didn't register the flare of pain as she stuffed the knife deep into the bag, then unhooked the strap and fled from the house.

She unlocked the car and clipped Jemima back in her seat. Jemima was still clutching the box of raisins as Maddie closed the car door. Mark was standing in the doorway of his house, looking bemused, a phone clutched to his ear.

Maddie climbed into the car and started the engine, her mind whirling and tumbling. She needed to get back and speak to Jade before the police turned up. She looked down at her palm where blood was dripping from between her fingers as she clutched at the steering wheel. She wiped it on her shirt, but the blood reappeared instantly along with a sharp stinging that helped to bring some clarity to her vision. She grabbed a loose serviette from the pocket in the car door and wrapped it around her hand before she sped off.

17

Jade stared at her phone, willing it to ring. Surely Maddie had sorted it by now? It was 7 p.m. and she had heard nothing. She had hammered on Maddie's door about half an hour ago, but the only person it had stirred was nosy Peggy opposite, who had opened her door a crack, scowled at Jade, then closed it firmly again and slid the chain into place.

Jade poured another vodka and topped it up with the rest of the Coke in the bottle. Great, now she was out of mixer.

She knew Maddie had probably chickened out and was lying low. Jade needed to send her a reminder of what she had to lose.

She put the glass down on the kitchen counter and grabbed a pair of Marigolds from the cupboard under the sink.

Standing on a small set of children's steps, she reached into the very top corner cupboard and pulled out a plastic carrier bag. She stepped down and took a photo of the bakery receipt with her phone, then sent it to Maddie through Snapchat, the message simply saying, 'Tick tock.'

She watched for a moment to see if Maddie opened the message. It remained unread.

'Shit!'

Jade had the feeling something was wrong. Very wrong. Maybe Maddie had done it after all. Maybe she hadn't been in touch because Mark was lying dead in his front hallway. She smiled to herself, the idea refreshing her like an ice-cold draught on a sweltering summer's day.

She put the receipt back in its hiding place and stared out of the kitchen window. The occasional trick or treater was still pestering for sweets, but they were few and far between now, with most kids safely indoors eating sausages and chips. Out of the corner of her eye, she noticed a big 4x4 pull into a parking space outside. It was the same as the one Maddie was driving when she came home earlier.

She thought it a stroke of genius that Maddie had managed to convince her ex's girlfriend to lend her that car. There would be no signs of Maddie's own car on the CCTV cameras. The woman was actually quite adept at crime and Jade was secretly impressed.

She was back then.

Jade drained the vodka in three big gulps, then threw her Uggs on her feet and went to find her.

'Maddie! Open up!' She hammered on the door, but this time it was flung open almost straight away.

'SHHH!' Maddie said, pointing down the corridor. 'Follow me,' she whispered, grabbing her door keys from the hook and disappearing back up the stairs Jade had just come down. She didn't stop at Jade's door but kept going up the stairs to the roof.

The air up here was chill. The breeze brought with it the smell of car engines and fireworks that flashed in the distance, bright and metallic against the night as Halloween celebrations continued.

Maddie stood at the edge of the roof, looking down onto her own patch of garden. She was wearing a chunky cardigan and had her arms crossed tightly against her body. There was something clasped in her hand, which kept making a static noise, like a radio not tuned in properly. Jade stepped closer to her and could hear thin sounds of breathing and realised that it was a baby monitor.

'What's the monitor for?'

'Jemima is asleep downstairs,' Maddie said, her back still turned to Jade.

'Did you take her with you? Wow, that's sick – and a bit ballsy.' Jade came right up behind Maddie. 'So is it done?'

Maddie spun around and glared at her.

'Is it done?' Jade repeated.

Maddie took a step away from the edge towards Jade. She dropped her arms and the cardigan fell open to reveal a smear of blood on the T-shirt underneath.

'I went to see him.'

Jade stared at the blood.

Bloody hell, she'd actually done it.

Jade started to laugh.

'You actually did it!'

Maddie turned away again and looked out at the night laid out before her. Jade grabbed her arm and spun her around. 'Just tell me what the fuck happened.' Then she noticed the cloth wrapped tightly around Maddie's hand.

'Did he fight back or something? I hope you cleaned up, didn't leave any of your own blood at the scene.'

'Like you care whether I get caught or not.' Maddie snatched her arm away.

'So is he dead or what?'

Maddie's voice was low. 'I spoke to him.'

Jade's pulse quickened.

'I knocked on the door and spoke to him. He let us in and I asked him what he intended to do about Ben.'

'You weren't supposed to speak to him. What did he say?'

'He said there is no case, Jade. He said it's all lies. So are you going to tell me what's really going on?'

Jade looked like Maddie had slapped her. Panic, surprise and confusion rolled over her face all at once. Jade squinted, looked again at the blood smear, then beyond Maddie to the dark sky, like she needed a second to come up with a viable alibi.

Maddie waited.

Eventually, Jade said, 'He's lying to you.'

'Is he though? He says he hasn't seen Ben in over six months. But I've hardly seen Ben around much lately because you've been telling me he's been with his dad a lot. Someone isn't telling the truth, but I can't quite figure out who yet.'

'Come on, Maddie, you know me. What would I have to gain from lying about all of this?'

'Money, I guess, to pay for your make-believe legal fees? I almost walked straight into that one. Greg was right, wasn't he? This was all about fleecing me for money. You never actually wanted me in Ben's life.' Maddie's voice cracked.

'That hurts, Maddie, that you would think I was only after money from you. This wasn't about money.'

'Then I don't get it. Explain to me what Mark would have gained by lying to me tonight. And he's a very good actor if he did, because he was incredibly convincing. He showed me the last photo he had taken with Ben. It looked like it was taken months ago.' Maddie could feel tears building like a wave and she swallowed hard to keep them at bay. 'After what you did to Greg, what could you possibly have to gain from sending me to hurt Mark? What is so awful about that lovely man, who genuinely seems to care for his son, that you would want to wish harm on him? Was it that he didn't want you? That he thought it was just a drunken fling, but you wanted more? So you got yourself pregnant to trap him? But it didn't work out, did it? And to think I spent all those years desperately wanting to have a child, all those miscarriages and heartbreaks, while there are despicable women like you in the world who use pregnancy and children like weapons. You repulse me.'

The words fell like stones between them.

Jade stared at her, eyes like flints, then she took a step towards her so that Maddie could smell the vodka on her breath. 'You think you know all about me, don't you? You don't know anything. You never took the *time* to get to know me. You made your mind up about me the first time you saw me in the park with that needy little brat. You labelled me right then, someone that needed you to save me, a charity case, which is a bit rich coming from you. A woman who couldn't even make a clean break from her rich ex, who needed his charity to survive. You're the pathetic one here, not me.'

'How can you speak about Ben like that? He's your son!'

Jade started to laugh, the sound hollow and caustic in the diminished space between them.

'You still don't get it, do you?' she smirked.

Maddie went cold. 'Where is Ben anyway? Have you left him on his own? What if he wakes up and gets scared?' She went to step around Jade, but Jade grabbed her arm and shoved her back. Maddie's heels hovered in the open air over the lip of the roof and she tilted backwards a fraction, enough to make her heart leap at the realisation that she was teetering on the edge with Jade blocking her way.

'He's with his mother.'

Maddie mustn't have heard right. 'Sorry?'

'Ben is with his mother, no doubt tucked up safe and sound in his own bed after a fun night trick or treating. In fact, he'll probably have a belly ache from eating too many sweets, the greedy little shit that he is.'

Maddie grappled at the words. 'But…?'

'He's not my son, Maddie,' Jade enunciated clearly, as though Maddie was hard of hearing. She had a villainous smile on her lips.

'I don't understand.' Maddie tried to shuffle around her, but Jade spread her feet so that she was planted firmly in place, blocking Maddie's path to the door.

'Let me explain it to you then. I was never pregnant. Ben was never mine. I only told Mark I was pregnant because I needed the money. He has been sending me child support for years for a child that doesn't exist.' She laughed, loud and hollow. 'I know, it's brilliant, isn't it?'

Maddie was beyond horrified. She remembered the look on Mark's face as he spoke about Ben, how much genuine love and affection he had for a small boy he had only had snatches of a relationship with.

'But there are photos of them together. There are photos of you pregnant. I've seen photos.' The images in her head were like a broken teacup, shards of porcelain that she couldn't quite fit together and each one threatening to cut her.

'It's simple. I'm his childminder.'

And then it did all tumble into place.

Jade continued, 'My friend Shona was pregnant and I was there when she gave birth to Ben. I wasn't lying about being in the hospital, but he didn't come out of me. I took photos of Shona's belly and passed them off as me, just to reel him in, then I offered to babysit Ben when he was a baby. Shona went back to work quite soon after he was born and I offered to be his childminder. After that, it was easy to take pictures or arrange for Mark to come and visit when I was watching him. It was quite sweet how besotted he was with him. But when Ben got a bit older, Mark started asking to have him overnight and that's when I realised that this would all get a bit complicated the older Ben got. Then I met you.'

She jabbed at Maddie with a long, painted and pointy fingernail. 'You were besotted with Ben. You would've believed anything I told you. And that's when I saw my way out. When you suggested we kill each other's partners, it was like a lightbulb moment. Of course, then you got all nervous on me and tried to back out, pretended you had been joking. If you'd stuck to the plan, we would both be free by now.'

'Oh my God,' was all Maddie could say.

'I know, it was a cracking plan and I got some good money out of it too.'

'But what about Mark? He thinks he has a son!'

'Yeah, well, if you'd done your bit properly, he would never have found out, so that's on you.'

'No. NO.' This time Maddie stepped forward, forcing Jade back, her own finger jabbing at Jade's chest. 'It will be like a death for him! You gave him a child and you've taken it away! Do you have any idea what that feels like? What kind of excruciating pain that is?' She wanted to stab and stab at her until Jade's chest was an open, bleeding sore. Maybe then she would have an inkling of what the death of a child could do to someone. If Maddie had the knife with her now, she wouldn't think twice about plunging it up to the hilt in Jade's unfeeling, frozen heart.

'Oh please! If he loved Ben as much as you claim he does, he would've tried harder to see him! He has his new girlfriend, a baby on the way. He'll forget about Ben soon enough. It's me you should feel sorry for. He dumped me *by text*! Used me, then threw me away like rubbish. Then came back for more months later when he was drunk. I was just there for him to use. It serves him right.'

This time Maddie smiled. 'He's probably calling the police right now. And when they come knocking, I'll make sure they know all about your ridiculous scheme. You think I haven't saved any of our Snapchat messages, but I have. I've gone old school and taken digital photos on a

camera. It's all there ready for the police. Evidence of this
and of your involvement in Greg's death. The receipt for the
bakery that you just sent me; your fingerprints on my debit
card; even that necklace you stole from Gemma is evidence
you were in their house.'

Jade snarled at Maddie. 'You bitch! That is not how this
is going down!'

Maddie had a second to notice that Jade's hands
were splayed at her side. Then those hands darted up,
ready to shove at Maddie. Ready to shove her backwards.
In that split second, an image of Greg and Jemima flickered
through Maddie's brain and she flung herself to the side
just as Jade surged forward. Maddie hit the rooftop
hard on her right shoulder and cried out in pain, but the sound
was muffled by a scream of rage from Jade. Maddie looked
over her shoulder to see Jade leaning over the edge of the
roof, her arms pinwheeling like a slapstick comedian, before
she lost her fight with gravity and fell.

There was a sickening thud from below, mixed with the
sound of ceramic shattering.

Maddie got to her feet quickly, her mind scrambling to
stay in the moment. She grabbed the baby monitor that
had been flung from her hand as she landed, then surged
towards the door to the stairs. She took the stairs two at
a time, pulling her front door key from her pocket as she
did.

At the edge of her consciousness, she could feel her
shoulder throbbing painfully but she paid it no attention.
She unlocked her front door with shaking hands, almost
dropping the key as she struggled with it. A door opened

behind her and she spun around. Peggy stood in her doorway in her nightgown, her face unreadable.

'I heard shouting and a crash. Is everything ok?' Her eyes flicked to the blood on Maddie's shirt.

Maddie swallowed against the brick in her throat. 'Everything is fine, Peggy. Nothing to worry about. Must've been something upstairs. You get yourself back to bed.' Her voice was pitched too high. She tried to smile, but it sat more like a grimace on her stiff face.

Peggy tilted her head and said, 'I'm sure whatever has happened will sort itself out. What goes around, comes around.' Then she closed and locked her door.

Maddie flung herself inside. Resting against the door, she tried to get her breathing under control.

What had actually just happened?

Maddie's curtains to the garden were closed and she was scared to open them. She fully expected to see Jade pressed up against the French doors, a weapon of sorts in her hand, ready to come at Maddie, like in a horror movie when the monster never dies on the first go.

So instead of looking outside, she went to check on Jemima, who was sleeping the peaceful slumber of a toddler, her mouth open and her arms splayed.

Maddie backed out of the room and pulled the door to behind her.

She tiptoed back to the patio door, her heart in her mouth, making it hard to swallow.

She took a breath, then yanked open the curtains. At first she saw nothing and thought perhaps Jade had been fine after the fall, had limped away into the night.

Then the garden was illuminated with flashes of cerise pink, emerald green and citrus yellow as fireworks exploded in the night sky, and she saw the crumpled heap in the far corner of the garden, a pile of limbs draped at unnatural angles among the plant pots not yet filled with flowers and herbs.

18

Maddie sat with Jemima on her lap, the curtains in the lounge drawn to the still dark morning sky. It was 5.30 a.m. and Jemima was already a bundle of life and energy.

Maddie less so.

She had closed the curtains on last night's fireworks and debated taking a sleeping pill to try and stop her heart from racing. But then she worried that she wouldn't wake up if Jemima stirred in the night.

So instead, she had lain awake, listening to every sound, the creak of a floorboard or a tap on the window, worry gnawing at her and leaving her red raw. Her hand was still smarting where the knife had bitten into the flesh, but that was nothing compared to what was going on in her brain. It was a relief when Jemima had stirred and grizzled in the early hours. It gave Maddie something else to concentrate on other than the ghosts stumbling around her head.

She knew she had to open the curtains and confront what was out there at some point. But for now she was content to sit here and cuddle Jemima tightly to her, breathing in the very essence of her. They sat that way for a while, Jemima happily playing, climbing and exploring the new room around her while Maddie drank her in.

What would happen when Gemma wanted her back? Could she honestly bear to return her? What would she do afterwards? Move away like she had planned to that little cottage by the sea, even though that would mean being far away from Jemima?

No, that was not an option.

And was she comfortable with handing her back to Gemma, knowing what she did about how Gemma felt about Jemima? That wasn't right either.

Her eyes flicked to the curtains again. She had to know, had to see.

She put Jemima on the carpet and turned on the television, searching for a children's programme to distract her.

Then she approached the glass doors slowly, carefully, like a lion's den. Morning was just starting to break as she inched open the curtains, the light weak and pale.

And there she was, still lying amid the broken pots and dirt.

Maddie stared at her for a moment, taking it in, making sure, then she exhaled with relief. It was over.

She'd been expecting the police to turn up all night. She was sure Mark would've called them by now. But they hadn't, which meant she would have to call them. She'd tell them she had made a grizzly discovery upon opening her curtains this morning. That her dear friend had done something rash and desperate. Maddie hadn't heard her fall, what with all the fireworks going off.

After that, she thought she would make another call. Perhaps she should have a conversation with Gemma, let her know that she shouldn't feel bad about not being up to the task of looking after Jemima, that not everyone was born to be a good mother. Sometimes a good mother was one who knew when she was out of her depth. Jemima deserved better now that Greg was gone.

She deserved someone with a natural flair for parenting.

Someone who had spent most of her adult life yearning for it, dreaming about it, *preparing* herself for it.

She drew the curtains closed again and headed into the kitchen, humming to herself, and began to make a cup of tea, with one eye on Jemima and a smile on her lips.

Seven Months Later

The spray was salty against her skin as they walked along the coastal path. Maddie hoped it would warm up soon. Her coat wouldn't zip up over her swollen, pregnant belly for much longer. But the early glimpses of spring she'd noticed a few weeks ago had been mere teasers. The real thing had yet to make a proper appearance.

Beaker, her rescue dog, named after Greg's favourite character in *The Muppets*, darted in and around her legs and the wheels of the pushchair as they walked, occasionally barking in excitement, running ahead, then stopping and running back. Maddie smiled and breathed deeply, letting the sea air fill her lungs. In the distance, just around the next corner, her little cottage would come into view, with its tiny white fence and front garden full of wildflowers.

Jemima sat in the pushchair, talking away to herself and pointing to the seagulls that twirled and swooped above their heads. Maddie was in need of a cup of tea, so she walked a little faster, her sensible walking boots pounding against the pathway.

Back inside the cottage, she released Jemima from the pushchair, who ran off to the make-believe kitchen in the corner of the lounge, where she would spend the next hour making tea for her dolls and teddies. Beaker followed her and took his place at her feet, hoping that this time the food would be real and not the plastic bananas and hamburger he was used to Jemima serving him.

Maddie hung her coat up and went into the kitchen to fill the kettle. As she reached into the cupboard for a mug, she felt a sharp jab and roll in her distended stomach and reached out a hand to rub it gently, smiling as she did.

She knew it was a risk being so isolated this far into her pregnancy, but this time around she had absolute faith it would be ok. There was a calmness about this pregnancy, a sense of destiny. Who would've thought that she and Greg would finally have the child they had always wanted? She only wished he was here to get to know the little miracle when he or she was born.

But she did have the next best thing. She had Jemima.

She filled a mug with hot water and let her thoughts run over the days following Jade's death. In the end, she had told the police she thought Jade had been upset and worried about an impending court case for custody of her son, Ben. That maybe she had thought she had no way out other than to take her own life by throwing herself from the roof of the building. It was a cry for help that had fallen on deaf ears. Maddie had described how unstable Jade had been in the days before and how awful she felt at not realising the depths of her friend's pain. The tears of sorrow and grief that Maddie had cried had been for Greg, not Jade, but the police weren't to know that.

As she was closing the door to the police, Peggy had

opened her door and nodded across at Maddie in a strange, all-knowing way. Maddie had said nothing in return and they had each gone about their business without ever mentioning that night on the few times they saw each other after that.

Of course, the subsequent investigation uncovered Jade's fraud and the truth about Ben finally came to light. Mark had been in touch with the authorities to say he was worried after not having seen Ben for so long. He made no mention to them of a Halloween visit by a woman dressed like Shrek and carrying a small, squirming pumpkin.

But by the time the truth was out, Maddie had other things to focus on. News had reached her that while Jade had been unsuccessful in ending Maddie's life, Gemma had been successful at ending hers. All it had taken was a few too many sleeping pills and she had drifted off into oblivion to be with Greg. The inquest had ruled accidental death, a simple case of not monitoring the dosage in her grief-stricken state, helped by her mother's testimony that Jemima was Gemma's whole life and that she would never have abandoned her. Not intentionally.

When asked, Maddie had agreed with them.

No one needed to know about her last conversation with Gemma.

At least Gemma knew Jemima was safe before she died.

And when the legalities were formalised, it would seem Greg had indeed requested Maddie as legal guardian of Jemima.

So here they were now, this strange little convoluted family, in their seaside cottage. Maddie supposed it had all worked out well for her, but she didn't like to dwell on that. There had been too much heartbreak and agony, too much hurt and anguish.

Her eyes fell to the fridge where the photo of herself and Ben was still displayed. His drawing was there too, tucked in behind some of Jemima's celebrated pieces.

She still thought about Ben often, wondered how he was, hoped he was happy. She thought about Mark often too, who she hadn't seen again. She could only imagine how the news about Ben had affected him.

Her mobile buzzed as she pulled the teabag from the mug.

She read the text, feeling delight thrum through her.

On my way. I'll bring pizza – with pineapple and anchovies, right? L x

Luke had been a godsend in those weeks after everything had happened. He'd been a true friend, a shoulder to cry on. He wasn't much of a talker, but he turned out to be a good listener. As it came closer to Maddie selling up and moving on, they'd both been surprised to realise that their friendship had blossomed into something deeper. They were still taking things slowly. Maddie was enjoying her newfound independence too much to take too big a step too early with Luke, so he came to visit most weekends and was ready to drop everything closer to the time when the baby was due. He adored Jemima and was excited about the new baby – and Maddie wanted him in her life, in all of their lives.

She hadn't told him the truth about what happened that night on the roof or to Greg and Gemma – and she never would.

All those secrets and lies would be buried with her.

Acknowledgements

Families, in whatever shapes and sizes, are at the heart of this book. I finished writing the first draft of *The Pact* just before the world was forced to pause and everyone headed indoors. For many of my readers, that has meant being separated from their families at a time when they have really wanted to hold them close. For others, it has meant a chance to spend quality time together without the distractions of everyday life. My hope is that all of my readers remain safe and well, and that you have had a chance to reconnect with your families, whether remotely or in person.

My family is always at the heart of everything I do and write, and I wouldn't be able to do this without their support and faith in me, whether near or far.

I am also lucky to have the tremendous support of my lovely agent, Jo Bell, who is always bursting with energy and enthusiasm for whatever I write, and the publishing team at Aria Fiction, in particular my editor Hannah for her unwavering passion and dedication to creating brilliant books. My books wouldn't exist without the team behind me and I am truly grateful that they are there, propping me up and pushing me forward.

My friends are an endless source of encouragement, bottomless glasses of wine and much-needed laughs, not only those I have known for years, but also those I've met through the incredibly generous and open writing community. I know and am in awe of some very talented writing friends and it's good to know we have each other's backs.

Finally, as always, my eternal thanks and love go to Ted, Paige and Erin, who are my constants, my muses, my world.

About the Author

D AWN GOODWIN'S career has spanned PR, advertising and publishing. Now, she loves to write about the personalities hiding behind the masks, whether beautiful or ugly. Married, she lives in London with her two daughters and a British bulldog called Geoffrey.

Hello from Aria

We hope you enjoyed this book! If you did let us know, we'd love to hear from you.

We are Aria, a dynamic digital-first fiction imprint from award-winning independent publishers Head of Zeus. At heart, we're committed to publishing fantastic commercial fiction – from romance and sagas to crime, thrillers and historical fiction. Visit us online and discover a community of like-minded fiction fans!

We're also on the look out for tomorrow's superstar authors. So, if you're a budding writer looking for a publisher, we'd love to hear from you. You can submit your book online at ariafiction.com/ we-want-read-your-book

You can find us at:
Email: aria@headofzeus.com
Website: www.ariafiction.com
Submissions: www.ariafiction.com/ we-want-read-your-book

🖪 @ariafiction
🐦 @Aria_Fiction
📷 @ariafiction